## "HAVE YOU NEVER MET AN OTTER?" THE MAGICIAN ASKED ALICE, AMAZED AT HER IGNORANCE.

Alice pulled a face and shrugged. "Don't think so," she said. "Have I, Will?"

William shook his head and Mary, who was sitting on the side of the boat nearest to the creature, leaned forward and held out her hand to it.

"Lutra, my dear," the Magician said softly. "I want to show my friends Blackwater Sluice."

The otter turned his twinkling eyes and darted a look at the Magician. "Spare them nothing," the old man continued. "They are my good and constant friends. They must understand everything. . . .

As he finished speaking the otter turned, and with a plop, it disappeared from view down below the surface, right beside the boat.

"Oh, don't go!" Alice called, leaning over the edge of the boat, searching the dark below her. Then, almost before she had time to snatch a breath, the ice-cold of Goldenwater enveloped her and she felt herself being dragged, gasping, down into its twilight depths.

**The Magician's House Quartet**

The Steps up the Chimney
The Door in the Tree
The Tunnel Behind the Waterfall
The Bridge in the Clouds

Available from ARCHWAY Paperbacks

THE MAGICIAN'S HOUSE QUARTET

# THE
# TUNNEL BEHIND
## THE WATERFALL

## WILLIAM CORLETT

**AN ARCHWAY PAPERBACK**
Published by POCKET BOOKS
New York London Toronto Sydney Singapore

An Archway Paperback published by
POCKET BOOKS, a division of Simon & Schuster, Inc.
1230 Avenue of the Americas, New York, NY 10020

Copyright © 1991 by William Corlett

Originally published in Great Britain in 1991 by The Bodley Head Children's Books

ISBN: 0-7434-1003-3

First Archway Paperback printing August 2001

10  9  8  7  6  5  4  3  2

AN ARCHWAY PAPERBACK and colophon are registered trademarks of Simon & Schuster, Inc.

Cover art by Lisa Falkenstern

Printed in the U.S.A.

IL 5+

*For William*

# Contents

# 1

# Goldenwater

William pushed forward with his hands and, spreading his arms, glided through the tingling, ice-cold water. As he did so, the distant trees came a fraction closer, rising in a thin heat-haze above the lake. Sunlight sparkled all around him and a soft breeze wrinkled the surface of the water into a shimmering pattern, like silk.

"William!" he heard a distant voice calling. It was his youngest sister, Alice. Turning his head he could see her standing in the shallow water on the edge of the lake.

"Come on!" he yelled. "It's OK once you're in."

"It's freezing!" Alice complained.

William turned his head once more and, taking a gulp of air, dipped his face into the soft water. Then, with strong strokes, he struck out toward the center of the lake.

"Mary," Alice complained, watching William's

receding outline and the thin wake of foam made by his feet. "He's going miles out."

"He'll be all right. He's a strong swimmer," a dozy voice murmured behind her.

Mary lay stretched out on her back in the hot sunlight. As she spoke, the sounds of the summer day faded once more to the edge of her consciousness. The hot sun burned deep into her body, ironing out her muscles and flattening her against the dry turf. A bee buzzed close beside her. A few birds sang in the branches of the trees that she could just see through her half-opened eyes and, somewhere, a woodpecker was drumming against a trunk. Mary sighed contentedly, stretched her arms, put her hands behind her head and sank back into semisleep.

"Oh, honestly!" Alice murmured in a grumpy voice. "I might just as well be here on my own." Then she shouted, "You're so boring, Mary!" and, taking another tentative step away from the shore, she slipped on a submerged boulder and toppled over, falling into the icy water with a splash, followed by a shout.

"Oh! It's agony!" Alice gasped, struggling up and immediately toppling back in again, with another splash and a scream.

"Alice?" Mary called, sitting up and squinting into the sunlight. "What happened?"

"I fell in, didn't I?" Alice replied irritably.

"Are you hurt?"

"Not much." Then she shrugged and giggled. "Oh, well. I'm in now," she said and, lowering herself once more into the lake, she made a few nervous strokes with her hands, her teeth chattering and her head sticking straight up, because she hated getting water into her eyes.

"It's quite nice really," she gasped, calling to her sister. "Mary, come in. Please, Mary," her voice coaxed. "It's more fun swimming with other people."

"You're a little coward, Alice!" Mary murmured. "I'm not coming in just to make you feel safe. Besides, I don't want to get wet. I'd rather lie here in the sun."

Typical! Alice thought, then standing gingerly on another submerged rock, she stared down into the water that surrounded her.

"William!" she squealed. "Come and look! There are tiny fish all round my legs . . ."

But William was now some distance from her, with his head below the water, and he didn't hear her.

Alice crouched down, scooping water in the cupped palms of her hands and letting it trickle back into the lake.

"D'you think you can drink it?" she asked. But neither of the other two answered her. She sighed again and, shading her eyes with her hands, she looked slowly round at the view.

The lake was surrounded by forest, with only a

narrow band of pebbles and mossy ground between the water and the trees. The distant bank was covered by dark conifers, ranged in regimental ranks, which spread up the steep hillside and disappeared from view over the top of a long ridge. On the near side, behind Alice and where Mary now lay dozing among the remains of their picnic, the vegetation was lighter and leafier; broad oaks, birches, chestnuts and other woodland trees and bushes crowded down to the water's edge. Here the sunlight danced and glittered through the branches, casting shadows and making an ever-changing scene of light and shade. In contrast, the top of the lake was marked by a flat area of marshy ground, backed by a steep cliff, covered with bushes and young sapling trees. Among their branches a mountain stream could be glimpsed as it cascaded down from the heights in a series of falls. Distantly beyond this cliff, the peaks of higher mountains were just visible through the milky afternoon light. At the other end of the lake, the land rose gently toward a solitary stone which stood as high as a person, leaning sideways against a holly bush. Behind this stone the branches of a massive yew tree were just visible, marking the edge of the escarpment which formed one side of Golden Valley, where the children were staying with their Uncle Jack. It was in this yew that the children had discovered a secret room, now hidden by the thick branches of the tree, during the previous holidays.

"Let's go and see Meg," Alice said, wading back toward the shore and picking up her towel from the ground near the pile of clothes.

"You out already?" Mary murmured, her eyes closed. "I thought you said you were going swimming."

'I have swum,' her sister replied as, drying her back, she turned once more to watch William out on the lake. "He's nearly in the middle now." Then, a moment later, she let out such a shout of surprise that Mary sat bolt upright, very wide awake.

"Alice! What is it? What's happened?" she asked.

"It's William!" Alice cried. "He's disappeared."

Mary rose quickly to her feet, shading her eyes and scanning the lake. The flat, rippling surface lapped gently to her feet. There was no sign of William.

Mary started to run along the shore, shouting desperately.

"What happened? Did you see him struggle?"

"Oh, Mary! Where are you going?" Alice pleaded with her as she splashed out into the water. "He must be drowning. Come quickly."

"No! Alice! You can't go after him. You're not a strong enough swimmer," Mary yelled, changing direction and dashing down into the water in pursuit of her younger sister.

"But we've got to *do* something," Alice whimpered.

Just as Mary caught hold of her and started pulling her back toward the shore, the surface of the lake in front of them parted and William appeared from its depths, rising up out of the water like a dolphin at play. The girls both stared, open-mouthed with surprise and relief. As if in slow motion they saw drops of water falling away from his body, sparkling in the sunlight like shreds of gold.

"William!" Mary yelled angrily. "You scared us half to death!"

"Why?" he shouted, swimming toward them with strong strokes.

"We thought you'd drowned," Alice said.

"I just went underwater," William protested.

"A place where a human being doesn't naturally belong," a voice behind them said sternly.

The sound was so completely unexpected and seemed to come from somewhere near to the girls. They swung round in astonishment.

Stephen Tyler, the Magician, was sitting on the ground, under an oak tree, a short distance from where they were standing.

"Mr. Tyler!" Alice gasped.

The Magician stared at them silently. His thin red hair circled his head like a cloud and his eyes flashed gold in the sunlight. He was dressed in his long black coat and leaned forward, holding on to his silver cane with the twining dragons at the top. His other arm was supported in a sling made of rough material. He sat so still that he seemed more a part of the trunk of the tree than a separate being, but he glared at them so fiercely that they felt his presence almost more than they saw him.

"Is he really there?" Mary whispered.

"Speak up, child!" the Magician snapped and, as he did so, his body came into sharper focus—like the image through a pair of binoculars which becomes clearer as you adjust the lens. Slowly he rose to his feet, leaning heavily on his cane. "And you, boy," he called to William, who had reached shallower water and was wading toward the shore, "come to land at once!"

"You gave us such a shock," Mary said, taking a step toward him.

"I have been here for some time," the old man told her.

"Where?" Alice asked.

The Magician shrugged.

"Half here. I am finding the concentration is becoming more and more difficult. *Tempus fugit!* 'Time flies!'" Then he sighed and said irritably, "You're always popping backward and forward. Never here when I need you. Shall you be staying long, this time?"

"Ages and ages," Alice said excitedly. "It's the summer holidays."

"Then we must put them to good use."

William was drying himself vigorously with his

towel. Now that he was out of the water, he felt cold and was having difficulty stopping his teeth from chattering.

"So, my fish," the Magician said, looking at him, "you have been exploring Goldenwater. And what do you make of my lake?"

"Your lake?" Mary asked him, surprised.

"Of course," the Magician answered. "All this land belongs to Golden House. It is part of the estate."

"Well, it isn't in our time," William said, fixing his towel round his waist and struggling into his pants and shorts. "I remember Uncle Jack telling us when we first arrived here that he only owned two acres. I remember thinking that sounded quite a lot. Our house in London only has a back garden."

"Two acres?" Stephen Tyler exclaimed. "Two acres? What has he done with it all? He must get it back at once. Goldenwater is essential to my plan; as is Goldenspring and the twin view points. Two acres? How can one hope to balance the universe on the head of a pin?" Then he shrugged and nodded thoughtfully. "It might be possible," he said. "The universe is beyond comprehension and as such is open to infinite possibilities. But if Jack Green does not own Goldenwater, who does?"

"I don't," William replied.

"You remembered Uncle Jack's name!" Alice

exclaimed. "You don't usually remember things like that."

"Don't be impertinent, child!" the Magician snapped.

"But it's true. We're always having to remind you of that sort of thing. I bet you don't remember my name."

"I only remember important matters," the Magician told her, in a withering voice. Then he added, "Your name is Minimus."

"No, it isn't!" Alice said, indignantly. "It's Alice."

"Well, you're Minimus to me," the Magician retorted, and he walked slowly away from them along the shore, tapping pebbles with his cane. "At least we know the next step now," he said, thoughtfully. "You must find out about this land ownership—and get it back."

"Is it so important?" William asked. "It sounds rather boring to me."

"What would you rather be doing?" the old man inquired, not sounding too stern.

"Going in animals!" Alice exclaimed.

"Flying!" William cried.

"And you, girl," the Magician said, turning to Mary, "what do you hope for?"

Mary shrugged and blushed.

"She's in love with Uncle Jack's builder," Alice told the old man in a confidential voice.

"I beg your pardon?" the Magician asked, mystified.

"I am not, Alice," Mary whispered furiously. She could feel more and more blood rushing to her cheeks until they were burning.

"He's called Dan," Alice said, "and she worships him."

"My Mary," the old man said, gently, putting his good arm lightly round her shoulders. "Don't be in such a hurry. *Tempus fugit.*"

"What has happened to your other arm?" Mary asked, desperate to change the subject.

"I had a nasty encounter with a wild dog," Stephen Tyler replied.

"D'you mean at the badger meet? When we were last here? When you had to fight that foul Fang?" Alice said breathlessly.

"Ah, I had forgotten you were there then," the old man said.

"But that was ages ago," William protested.

"It still has not healed."

"Have you had some penicillin?" Mary asked.

"What is this stuff?"

"After your time, I'm afraid." William sighed. "Don't ask it'll be so difficult to explain."

"But you must try."

"Well, it's . . . medicine. I think it comes from mold—or something like that. It kills germs."

"From mold?" Stephen Tyler pondered the thought. "Fascinating! We use much the same technique. Cobwebs are very effective."

"Cobwebs?" William repeated doubtfully.

"I must go. I have to conserve my strength. This period is going to be intensely productive. Oh, a word of warning. Morden, my assistant, is very close to time-traveling. Be on your guard!"

"How would we know him?" Mary asked.

"How would you know Morden?" the old man snapped, as though it was an absurd question. "Why by his aura, of course. Morden is the dark to my light. Wherever there is evil—look for Morden!"

"What's an aura?" Mary asked.

"No time now," the Magician answered, raising his hand to silence them. "I must away." And he walked back toward the trees, saying, "Find out about that land!"

"But—where will we see you?" Alice called.

"I'll be about," the old man replied, without turning his head, and he disappeared from their sight into his own time from the middle of a patch of sunlight.

# 2

# Meg Lewis Gets a Letter

As the children walked back to the house, the afternoon was gradually fading into evening. Although it was still very warm, the sun had lost its fierce intensity and smoldered through the trees behind them, as it slipped slowly out of sight into the west.

They entered the walled kitchen garden through the back gate and strolled down one of the paths between the rows of fruit trees with the sadly neglected beds beyond. As they passed the dovecote at the center of the garden, Spot came bounding toward them from under a clump of tall mint, in which shade he had dozed the afternoon away.

"Where've you been?" he barked, his tail wagging as he jumped up at Alice, licking her face.

"We looked for you everywhere," Alice protested, squatting down and fighting off his enthusiastic tongue. "Stop it, Spot! You're soaking me!"

"Serves you right for leaving me behind," the dog told her.

"You could have found us," Mary protested. "You could have followed our scent."

"What? All the way up the side of the valley?" Spot said, grinning. "Too hot for that!"

"Honestly, Spot. You'll get fat, you're so lazy!" Alice told him, rubbing his tummy. "Besides, you could have come swimming. That'd have made you cool again."

"Come on," the dog said, rolling over and jumping to his feet. "There's something going on. Meg's here!" And, barking and jumping, he led the way toward the yard gate.

The kitchen was cool after the heat outside and was filled with the smell of newly baked bread. Meg Lewis was seated at the table with Phoebe and Jack, and Stephanie was asleep in her cot, beside the range. In front of Phoebe was a teapot and a sponge cake, from which a large wedge had been removed. As the children entered, the three grown-ups looked toward them.

"Oh, good! Cake!" Alice exclaimed, dropping her wet costume and towel on the floor and hurrying to her seat at the table. "Can I have a piece, Phoebe? I'm starving! Swimming always makes me hungry!"

"Swimming, Alice? You only did three strokes!" Mary said. "Hello, Meg!" she added, giving the old lady a warm smile.

"Hello, dear!" Meg responded, her voice sounding sad.

"Get yourselves cups and plates," Phoebe told them, rising and putting more boiling water into the teapot from the kettle which sat permanently on top of the range. "Mary, cut some slices of cake, will you? And you may as well make them big slices. Supper will be late tonight."

"Oh, why?" Alice wailed. "I'm starving, Phoebe."

"I can't help it. You'll have to wait. Jack's going into town with Meg," Phoebe told her.

"You hardly ever go to town, Meg," William said, in a surprised voice as he sank his teeth into the slab of cake, which Mary had just cut for him.

"No dear," Meg replied miserably. "Well, I don't very often get letters, either."

As she spoke the children all noticed the letter lying open on the table in front of Jack. It looked official, on headed notepaper and covered in typing.

"What's it about, Uncle Jack?" William said with his mouth still full of cake.

"You must ask Meg that," Jack replied. "She may not want to discuss it with you."

"Of course I do. You're my closest friends— after the badgers— and my badgers owe you their lives. Go on, dear, you can read it if you want to."

William picked up the letter and stared at it.

"Read it out loud, Will," Mary said nervously.

She had an awful feeling that whatever it was, it wasn't going to be good news.

" 'Dear Miss Lewis,' " William began. " 'I am instructed by my clients, Playco' . . . Playco?" William exclaimed. "What a funny name!"

"Yes, dear," Meg said, "but I doubt that they're funny people. Go on reading, dear."

" 'I am instructed by my clients, Playco UK,' " William continued, ' that the land adjacent to your smallholding is about to be developed, subject to planning consent, and would ask you to call at my offices at the soonest possible opportunity to discuss certain matters which would seem to be of mutual benefit to both yourself and to the directors of Playco UK. If you would like to contact my secretary to arrange a meeting, I will look forward to seeing you then. Yours sincerely, Martin Marsh, solicitor.' "

William lowered the letter and looked at the silent faces round the table.

"What does it mean?" Alice asked, in a whisper. "What does 'developed' mean?"

"Buildings, dear. It means buildings," Meg replied in a shocked voice.

"At Goldenwater?" Alice cried, horrified that the beautiful peaceful place that they had so recently left should be changed in any way. "What sort of buildings?"

Jack shrugged. "We don't know," he said. "We know no more than you do."

"But any buildings at Goldenwater would be horrible . . ." Phoebe said. "I mean . . . who could possibly think of building up there? They can't mean houses. It's miles from anywhere."

"People do extraordinary things, dear, if there's money in it for them," Meg said quietly.

"Who owns the land, Meg?" Jack asked.

As he did so, William gasped and looked quickly at Alice and Mary.

"What's the matter, William?" Phoebe asked.

"Nothing," William mumbled, "it's just that . . . well, we were told to find that out, just this afternoon."

"Told to? By whom?" Phoebe asked, looking at him suspiciously.

"What I mean is . . . we were wondering who owned it . . . that's all," William said, lowering his eyes, avoiding her questioning gaze.

"When old Miss Crawden died," Meg said, "the estate went to Sir Henry Crawden, her nephew."

"Yes, that's right. It was through Sir Henry's solicitor that our sale was negotiated," Jack said.

"A real Sir?" Alice asked. It sounded very impressive.

"He is now," Meg answered quietly. "He was plain Henry Crawden when I knew him."

"You knew him, Meg?" Mary said.

"Oh, yes, dear. I knew Henry Crawden. But that was years ago. In another lifetime."

"Are you really saying that all the land round

here used to belong to Golden House?" Phoebe asked in amazement. "Including Goldenwater? And the yew tree with the secret house?"

"Yes, dear. That's how my grandad was able to stay at Four Fields when he was turned out of this house. Otherwise there'd have been nowhere for them to go. They were penniless, you see. The house went to pay off the debts, but they got no money for it."

"Who owns the land on the other side of your fields, Meg?" Jack asked.

"The Jenkinses did, originally. They owned both sides, but they sold it to the Forestry Commission, dear. Short of cash. That was some time ago. I was worried at first. Government people owning the land . . . But they leave me to myself, look after the woodland pretty well and of course, as luck would have it, they've left the broadleaf trees, and not replaced them with those miserable firs, as they did the other side of the water. All in all, it's been quite satisfactory, really."

"So what land is being referred to in this letter then?" Jack asked her.

"Between my fields and Goldenwater, dear. The whole area round the lake is still supposed to be owned by the Crawdens. Acres of land, from Goldenspring in the west all along the side of the bridle path, round the Standing Stone and spreading as far as the yew tree and the edge of Golden Valley. Or that's what's always been said."

She frowned for a moment, then shook her head, as if dismissing a thought. "There are always rumors, you know. And anyway, it's never mattered who owned the land. It's not suitable for farming. It may look pretty, but farmers see land in terms of productivity, not beauty."

"What about the valley?" William asked.

"Well, dear, I couldn't say. I'd have thought the steeps up behind the house here still belonged to you."

"I don't think so," Jack said, shaking his head. "My deeds only show me owning two acres here round the house, in the valley bottom."

"Strange, dear," Meg murmured. "It wasn't always so."

"You should check, Jack," Phoebe said.

"I will, don't worry. It'd make a huge difference if the valley sides belonged to us. Not that I think anyone could build anything on them; they're too steep . . . but, even so . . ."

"You can never be sure of anything, dear," Meg said glumly.

"Just let me get this right," Jack continued, thoughtfully, "what you're saying, Meg, is that the only way through from the Forest Road to Goldenwater is on the track that leads to your farm?"

"That's right, dear. I dare say you could put a track through Mr. Jenkins's land, but I don't think he'd let you. He keeps that land for pheasants.

Breeds them for the sport. Sport? Shooting the poor creatures. Funny idea of sport if you ask me."

"I can't believe it," Jack said thoughtfully, "to think that all that land was once part of our estate."

"And so it should have remained, dear. It should never have been sold. But, as I explained to you once before, my grandad was a terrible gambler and eventually, as must always happen, his debts caught him up and found him out and he died a ruined man—as did my father after him." Meg shivered and rubbed her hands.

At this moment, Stephanie started to cry and Phoebe went and lifted her out of the cot, rocking her gently and soothing her.

"You'd better be going, Jack," she said, over her shoulder. "Or else you'll be late for Meg's appointment."

"What appointment?" William asked.

"I telephoned this solicitor who's written to me. He said for me to go in this evening. He seems in a great hurry to see me. I can't figure it out."

"Come back with Jack and have supper with us, Meg," Phoebe said, still gently rocking the baby as she spoke.

"Oh, yes," Mary said eagerly. "Then we can find out what happens."

"And we can run you home later," Jack offered.

"Thank you, dear. That would be kind. But no need to run me home. I can walk back and check on the sett on my way. I did the milking before I came down here, so there's nothing to worry about. What can it mean?" she mused, following Jack to the back door. "Mutual benefit? I don't like the sound of it at all . . ." and, still talking, she disappeared out into the yard.

After she had gone, the children told Phoebe they'd go up to their rooms at the top of the house. William challenged Alice to a game of Spite and Malice, their favorite card game, and Mary said she was going to write a letter to their parents.

This could have been the truth. The children's mother and father had recently been moved from the hospital in Ethiopia, where they were both working as doctors with the Red Cross, to one of the refugee camps. The children only heard from them occasionally, because letters didn't always make it in either direction. But Mary still liked to write every week, because it made her feel in touch with them. However, as soon as they left the kitchen the children decided to go up to the secret room instead and made for the huge inglenook fireplace on the other side of the hall. Once there, they glanced back over their shoulders, to make sure that Phoebe hadn't followed them and then, moving quickly, they climbed up the protruding stones on the left of the hearth to the ledge and squeezed their way round the corner at the back to where the concealed steps commenced their spiraling ascent up the inside of the chimney.

As they disappeared from view Spot nosed his way out through the kitchen door and stood, tail wagging slowly and head tilted sideways in an inquiring position, scanning the hall. He looked up the staircase to the landing and then, nose twitching as he caught a whiff of the children's scent, he padded across the hall into the fireplace and followed them up into the dark.

# 3

# An Unexpected Visitor

To their surprise the Magician was waiting for them when they reached the secret room. He was standing looking out of the back window and didn't even turn as they appeared in the doorway behind him.

"Come in," he said, "I was expecting you."

The children moved into the empty room, their feet ringing hollowly on the bare boards of the floor. The light was dim, for the front window was closed and shuttered and the candle sconces had not been lit. A thin veil of dust moved on the evening air and a spider darted for a fly in a cobweb beside the old man's head, as he continued to gaze at the scene outside the window. The sun was setting in a riot of pink and gold. The colors streaked the sky above the valley side, staining the clouds purple and suffusing the woods with soft honeyed light.

Spot had followed the children in from the

stairs, his tongue hanging out as he panted. He sat down in the doorway and scratched his stomach with one of his hind legs, then he licked a paw, yawned and, with a sigh, flopped down on the floor and watched what was going on through hooded eyes.

Not that there was much to watch. The scene within the room remained peculiarly static; the Magician staring out of the window at the darkening sky and the children standing behind him, as if they had been summoned to his presence, without knowing why, and were awaiting his instructions.

Then somewhere, distantly outside the window, an owl hooted. Still the Magician remained motionless. He seemed not to have heard the sound, but Mary took a step toward the window, expectantly.

"Jasper!" she cried.

Stephen Tyler held up a hand, silencing her, and a moment later, the great owl descended out of the bowl of inky sky onto the rim of the window with a fluttering of wings. Once safely perched, he blinked, preened his feathers, turned his head, as if on a pivot, and glared at the Magician.

"What have you discovered, my bird?" Stephen Tyler said and, as he spoke, he raised his hand and stroked the owl's neck feathers with the back of his fingers.

"The fox, Cinnabar, and the otter, Lutra, have seen men up at the Water with measuring sticks and plans."

"Plans?" the Magician said, sounding immediately cross. "What are these plans?"

"Rolls of paper, Master, over which they ponder and upon which they write innumerable notes."

"Impertinence!" the old man exclaimed crossly. "Children, we have a most serious situation here." And, as he spoke, he turned away from the window, and walked toward the center of the room. "It is essential that you act swiftly to put a stop to this outrage. Otherwise all my endeavors—a lifetime's work—will be reduced to nothing." He shook his head and rapped the floor with his silver cane, angrily. "The greed of men! It will be my undoing. You, boy, you are the oldest. What have you discovered for me? Who has taken my land?"

William cleared his throat and repeated, as well as he could remember, all that Meg had told them down in the kitchen. During this the Magician listened closely, sometimes nodding as if he half remembered. Then, as the account was drawing to an end, he raised his good arm, holding the silver cane above his head, stopping William in midsentence.

"Good," he said, speaking more kindly and with less anger now. "You have done well." Then he turned and looked at the owl. "Crawden?" he continued. "The name Crawden is familiar. What do I know about this Crawden, Jasper?"

The owl had been listening silently from his perch on the window opening. Now, being addressed, he flew into the room, his wings moving the air so that it swirled the dust and struck cold on their faces. Reaching with his claws, he landed on one of the candle sconces and stared down at them.

"It was a Crawden who took the house from Jonas Lewis," he trilled sternly.

"Jonas Lewis," the old man repeated thoughtfully.

"He got into debt," William said, not wishing to be outdone by the owl. "He had been experimenting with alchemy. I think you'd been helping him . . ."

"Jonas?" the Magician said the name again, broodingly. "Yes, I remember, Jonas. He was a good pupil. But he misused his powers. What did he do?" He fired the question at the children, as though it was part of an examination.

"He made gold," Mary replied nervously.

"That is correct. He made gold." His words were like a drumroll. "Gold," he repeated the word with contempt. Then, after a moment's silence, another thought occurred to him. "What do you know about this?"

"Only what you've told us," Alice said.

"But we first read about it in a book that Uncle Jack borrowed from a lady in the town, last Christmas," William reminded them. "A sort of diary, written by Jonas Lewis himself."

"Meg knows something about it, as well," Mary added. "She's Jonas Lewis's granddaughter, you see . . ."

"Is she? The badger woman? The woman who caused me this injury." As he said the words, he moved his arm in its sling and winced at the pain.

"It wasn't her fault," Alice said, leaping to Meg's defense. "She didn't want the badger baiters to come. It was one of their dogs who did it."

The Magician smiled at her.

"I like a person who stands up for her friends. I hope you will do that for me one day . . . Minimus." He said the name so gently, lovingly almost, that Alice rather liked it. "So this woman is Lewis's granddaughter," he continued thoughtfully. "Mmmh! Interesting," and he walked over and stared at the owl.

"Lewis sold the house to Crawden when his debts overwhelmed him," the owl murmured, almost as though he was prompting the old man's memory.

"Yes, yes, I recall," Stephen Tyler snapped, making the owl sigh with resignation. "I am not so old that my memory has quite gone, thank you, Jasper!"

"No, Master," the owl trilled, and he blinked patiently.

"He was in debt," the Magician continued, "because he was working every hour that God gave him at the Alchemical Arts. That is correct, isn't it?"

"Yes, Master," the owl murmured.

"Perhaps, dear bird, one day you will forget. I hope you have somebody kind," he said the word ruefully, "to help you in your hour of need."

"I try, Master."

"But must you always sound so superior?" the old man asked.

"I cannot help my tone, Master."

The bird and the old man glared at each other for a moment.

"Now you've made me forget what we were talking about."

"Jonas Lewis," the owl said, in his most superior voice.

The Magician sighed and then smiled at Jasper. Reaching up, he stroked the owl's chest feathers; it was a gesture full of love and admiration. The bird puffed out its chest and whistled quietly. Then Stephen Tyler turned back to the children and began to speak in a confident voice.

"Jonas was not a wealthy man. He made a modest living from farming, but he was a scholar at heart. The two attributes do not sit happily together. A farmer must farm; a scholar must study. However, both such men must eat. Lewis had no private income." He sighed and shook his head. "That was his trouble. But he was a diligent scholar. That's why I chose him . . . He learned well, and quickly. I introduced him to the chemistry. That was my mistake. It didn't do at all. He became obsessed. Working all hours. The house still echoes with his pacing footsteps—back and forth, back and forth—and with his wife's pathetic cries. It ruined them. He took to gambling to finance his experiments." Stephen Tyler threw up his good arm, in a gesture of disgust. "He lost everything he owned and, worse, he put an end to his studies. As for me, I lost a good pupil. It was most annoying. After all the time I'd spent on him. But a pupil is essential to the work. So I determined that the next one should be a child. I'd had enough of men with their set ideas. The innocent mind, that's what was needed. Something fresh and unsullied to work on. But, of course, I had not expected that there should be three of you. Nor that you would be so very young. I am not good with children. I never had one of my own. . . ." and he stopped speaking suddenly, remembering sad times, and, producing a large square of material from the voluminous folds of his coat, he blew his nose loudly.

During all this time Spot had been lying on the floor, just inside the doorway. He appeared to have fallen asleep. But now, suddenly, he raised his head, his ears pricked forward and his nose twitching. Then rising quickly to his feet, he started to growl and the hairs on the back of his neck stood up.

"What is it, Sirius?" the Magician asked, irritated by this interruption.

Spot ignored him. He started frantically sniffing the floorboards, moving quickly round the room, darting from corner to corner.

"He's got the scent of something," Alice said, watching the animal in a perplexed way.

"Spot, what is it? What's wrong?" William asked.

"Someone else in the room," Spot muttered. "Not a strong scent. Someone small. Not a friendly smell."

Jasper sat very erect, his eyes flashing, his head jerking from side to side, listening.

"The assistant?" he hissed.

"Morden? Here?" the Magician demanded in amazement. "Where?"

"No," Spot replied, his nose still working, "not the assistant. But . . . one of his spies . . ." and, as he finished speaking, he rose up on his hind legs, leaning with his front paws on the sloping ceiling, immediately beneath the circular window beside which Jasper was sitting.

"Something outside the window?" Stephen Tyler exclaimed.

"The spinner . . ." Spot yelped, excitedly, his

tail wagging and his paws scratching at the sloping surface in his eagerness to catch his prey.

They all saw the spider at the same moment. It was poised in the center of its web, its legs spread on gossamer threads so fine that it seemed to be suspended on the air.

"The spider!" William cried, hurling himself past the Magician in the direction of the window.

But Jasper was nearest and quickest.

"Mine, I think," he whistled and, darting forward, he snapped the spider from its web and swallowed it whole.

"Ugh!" Alice gasped. "He ate it!"

"All gone!" the bird said, settling himself once more on his perch and looking down with a disdainful expression.

"Ugh!" Alice said again and she shuddered and pulled a face of revulsion.

Mary also stared in horror at the bird. She was remembering the mouse he had eaten at Christmas and, for a moment, she thought she was going to be sick.

"How could you, Jasper?" Alice exclaimed.

"Little girl," the owl hooted. "You eat sausages."

"Yes," she replied quickly. "But they're not alive and they don't wriggle."

"No," Jasper agreed with her, "I've never fancied eating dead stuff myself—not if it can be possibly avoided." And dismissing the subject, he picked delicately with his beak at one of his claws.

The Magician, meanwhile, was brooding.

"I must go," he said, speaking more to himself than to the others. "Too much is happening that I do not fully understand."

"That's how it always is for us!" William exclaimed. "You never tell us what's really going on. You expect us to do things without ever knowing why we have to do them."

The Magician turned and looked at him.

"Is this rebellion, William?" he asked, sounding almost amused.

"Not exactly, no," William replied. "But you say you want us to help you. You say we have work to do. . . . But you never tell us what it is."

The Magician sighed.

"A just accusation," he said. "But you see, boy, I trusted Jonas Lewis and my trust destroyed him. He was corrupted . . . by me."

"Then," William argued, "that's maybe why it's a good thing there are three of us. We can stop each other from . . . getting greedy and . . . Oh, please tell us what it's all about."

For a moment there was silence in the room as the old man thought about what William had asked.

"You'd have to come to my study for me to show you everything. I would need my books and my drawings at hand. I cannot think without my desk."

"But I thought this was your study," Mary said.

"Yes, yes, yes!" the old man snapped. "But I

mean my study in my own time. This is just a room—a study is books and paper and—a study is where a man can take his intellect down off the shelf, blow the dust off it and . . . apply it."

"The very first time we found this room," Alice volunteered, "last Christmas. You remember? When we first met you . . . I'm sure there was furniture here then. I'm sure there was."

The Magician glared at her.

"I thought I met you at the station," he said.

"No, you only met William there. Mary and I didn't really believe you existed."

"Impertinence!" the old man said, and then he chuckled. "I hope you have no doubt about it now?"

"Of course not," Alice said. Then she continued, pressing home her point, "But—where did the furniture go? Why could we see it then, if we can't see it now?"

"Easy!" the Magician exclaimed. "D'you ride a horse?"

Alice shook her head.

"I don't like them much," she said, "they're too high up." Then she added helpfully, "I do ride a bike."

"A bike?" Stephen Tyler asked, looking perplexed. Then, before any of them could attempt an explanation, he raised his hand. "Never mind. When a person first starts to ride—usually on a pony—they get on and trot along, as easy as anything. Then . . . they fall off. And, after that, it takes them ages to regain the skill and the confidence to . . . just ride." He emphasized the last two words. "Well, it is precisely the same with time-traveling. When you first came up here, you were all so . . ." he searched for the right words, "so . . . ready for anything . . . that you entered my world as much as I was entering yours. It was almost a mistake. You didn't know how you did it. You didn't even know what it was that had happened. Now—you want to time-travel. That requires serious knowledge . . . and a lot of practice. You are not ready for it yet."

"And yet, they can inhabit, Master," Jasper hooted quietly. "The girl has flown with me. They have all traveled in the kestrel. There are innumerable examples of them inhabiting. Ask the dog . . ."

"So?" Stephen Tyler rapped the question at the owl. "What has inhabiting to do with it?"

Jasper shrugged.

"If the assistant can use his spies in this time, without being able to time-travel himself . . . why shouldn't the children be able to do likewise."

The Magician thought about this for a long moment.

"Maybe. But it would be most irregular," he said at last. "I do not like to rush things." Then he turned and held out his good arm to them all. "Dear children. It is not that I don't trust you. You have proved your worth to me. It is just that I am so . . . concerned that nothing wrong should occur. And yet"—he sighed—"if Morden is progressing so fast, I may need you sooner than I thought. And, of course, *tempus fugit!* Who knows how much longer I have got? I will give this my serious consid . . ." And there, in the middle of the sentence, he disappeared from them back into his own time.

"He's tired," Jasper explained. "He forgets he's an old man." Then the owl looked out of the window at the gathering dusk. "Suppertime. Anyone want to come?"

But, strangely enough, all the children declined. Suddenly Phoebe's vegetarian cooking seemed very attractive to them.

# 4

# Some Very Bad News

Jack returned from the town on his own. He was so late that Phoebe had decided that they should start supper without him. They were halfway through the meal when they heard the Land-Rover drive into the yard.

"Here they are!" Phoebe exclaimed with relief. She had been concerned about them, because they'd been away so long.

But it was only Jack who walked through the door, and the look on his face told them that he had had some very bad news.

"What is it? What's happened?" Phoebe asked.

"Where's Meg?" Mary inquired at the same moment.

"I dropped her back at Four Fields," Jack said, crossing into the scullery and returning with a glass of beer.

"Jack?" Phoebe said again, spooning food onto

a plate for him. "There's something wrong. What's happened?"

"That man!" Jack exclaimed. He was so angry that he could scarcely speak. Sitting down at his place at the table, he took a long drink of beer, then, shaking his head, he looked round the room. "Where's Steph?" he asked.

"Sleeping—upstairs," Phoebe told him. "It's very late. It's all right. I've switched on the baby monitor. We'll hear her if she needs us. Jack, what is it? What's happened?"

Jack sighed and took another gulp of beer. It was as though he was steadying himself before doing something that he dreaded.

"That man!" he said again. "That dreadful man!"

Alice felt a cold shiver go down her back. Spot, who had been sleeping under her chair, sat up, listening, with his head on one side. Alice, almost without thinking, put her hand down and rested it lightly on his back.

"Which man?" Phoebe asked.

"The solicitor, Martin Marsh . . . Sorry, it's all been a bit of a shock!"

"But—not for us, surely?" Phoebe said. "Whatever's happened .. it's got nothing to do with us . . . has it?"

"A holiday leisure center at Goldenwater? An amusement park? Speedboats on the lake? Holiday chalets and community rooms? Ad-

venture tracks through the forest . . . including a
'Wild West Trail'. . . ?" he said this last item with
particular bitterness.

"An amusement park?" Phoebe repeated, her
voice filled with disbelief. "Holiday chalets?
Where? What are you talking about?"

"At Goldenwater," Jack snapped at her. "I
thought I'd made it perfectly clear."

"Please don't lose your temper, Jack. Not with
me. I wasn't there. This is all new to us."

Jack sighed and ran his hands over his face.

"Sorry," he said. "It's been a bit of a shock."

"They want to build a leisure park at
Goldenwater?" Phoebe said, trying to compre-
hend just what it was he was saying. "I don't
believe it. They can't do this."

"They think they can," Jack said, pushing away
the plate of food that Phoebe had served him,
without having touched a morsel. "What's more
they say their research shows that the project will
be very popular in the area. It will bring in jobs
and 'life' to the place," he said, emphasizing the
word *life*.

"Life?" Phoebe cried, appalled at the statement. "What life? It's teeming with life up there.
Birds and butterflies and . . . What about the life
that's already there? What about the badgers?"
she cried, clutching now at straws.

"The badgers?" Jack exclaimed sardonically.
"Oh, don't you worry! The badgers instantly

became part of their grand scheme. Meg had only to mention them and Mr. Marsh leaped at the idea. We mustn't worry our heads about them. The badgers will be left safe and secure. They'll become one of the features of the park. A regular badger watch will be organized for the guests. Parties of people led by a warden—like a safari park in Africa. Oh, yes—he was very enthusiastic when the badgers were mentioned. He said his clients would be delighted."

"Who are these people—his clients?" Phoebe demanded, her temper rising. "What are their names?"

"A firm called Playco UK. Martin Marsh has become their legal representative in this area. Playco!" he spat the name. "Moneygrubbing greedy little men." Then he took a deep breath and tried to speak more calmly. "They're a new company apparently. Their aim is to introduce the holiday theme park to this country as it has never been seen before. America's Disneyland will pale into insignificance by comparison. And Goldenwater has been chosen to be their first project."

There was a moment of stunned silence in the kitchen as they each considered Jack's words.

"But . . . they can't. They can't change Goldenwater. . . ." William said. "They mustn't!"

"Can we stop them, Uncle Jack?" Mary asked.

"Not us. They claim that what they propose won't affect us in the least. Marsh had the nerve to say that we, having applied and got permission to run our hotel, have opened up the area. He said the theme park can only increase our trade and add to our success. In fact, he's making it appear that our plans for this place are what first alerted Playco to the potential of the area."

"How dare they?" Phoebe exclaimed. "What a load of nonsense! Our plans? I can't see how a country hotel—where people can come and be refreshed in the quiet beauty of Golden Valley—is in any way comparable to their vulgar funfair ideas." Then she suddenly had another thought. "But—why did they want to see Meg?"

"Ah, that's the clincher, really. Meg's land is in their way. They want to buy her out, so that they can put a road through. It's the only suitable access to the site."

"Then that's all right!" Phoebe cried, trying to smile. "Meg will never sell to them."

"Yes," Jack agreed grimly. "That's what she told them."

"Well then, Jack?"

"Do you have any idea how old Meg is?" Jack asked her, almost losing his temper with her again.

Phoebe shook her head as though she could see what was coming.

"Seventy-three," Jack replied quietly.

"I thought she was just in her sixties," Phoebe said. "She doesn't look that old."

"How much longer can a seventy-three-year-old woman hope to survive on her own," Jack continued, "with no heating, no water, animals to feed—a farm to run? Besides, they told her they are prepared to wait, if they must. The money they're offering for her land will certainly tempt the next owners if it doesn't in the end tempt her."

"Money!" Phoebe cried, her temper flaring. "Always money! We must stop these people. If they build at Goldenwater, then there's no sense nor justice left in this country. What's the next step? We've got to fight them, Jack."

"They're a vast company, darling. They'll have all the lawyers and all the backing. . . . We don't stand a chance."

"We won't if that's going to be your attitude from the start," Phoebe spat at him. "If that's how you're going to react, we may as well pack our bags now. Let's sell them Golden House as well. They can run Ghost Hunts here and Magic Evenings. They can have Elizabethan Banquets and Medieval Jousts . . ."

"Don't suggest it to them!" Jack said, reaching out a hand and smiling as he touched her arm. "They'll leap at the ideas. And maybe they'll make us an offer that *we* can't refuse."

"There is no such offer," Phoebe cried. "I will not have people coming and ruining this place."

"I thought you didn't like it here," Jack said quietly.

"I suddenly do," Phoebe spluttered the words and then took a deep breath, steadying herself.

"You mean . . . people can really do this?" William asked, horrified.

"I've always wanted to go to Disney World,'" Alice whispered.

"Well, if you wait here long enough, it seems your wish will be granted. You'll only have to set foot out of the door!" Phoebe shouted at her, her temper blazing again.

Alice looked at the table, and pushed out her lip. The attack was so sudden and unexpected it was as if she'd been struck in the face by Phoebe.

"Hey!" Jack cut in. "We mustn't start fighting among ourselves. That won't solve anything. We must save all our energies for the big fight."

"I'm sorry, Ally!" Phoebe exclaimed, sounding close to tears herself.

"It's all right," Alice said, in a small voice.

"What'll happen next, Uncle Jack?" William asked.

"There's a public meeting in the town next week," Jack replied.

"We must go to it," Phoebe said at once. "But— Meg will never sell," she added, clutching at straws again.

"She doesn't want to, of course, but they've offered her a lot of money," Jack said quietly. "Enough to buy a little cottage in a village and be safe and secure for the rest of her life. She has nothing of her own. I can't help feeling it would be a wise thing for her to do."

"But—what would happen to her cows?" Alice asked sadly.

"And the badgers . . . and everything?" Mary said in a dejected voice.

"She'd never leave the badgers," William agreed.

They were all silent, as they each contemplated the unexpected and terrible news that Jack had brought them.

# 5

# Taking Sides

The proposed plans for Goldenwater were revealed in the local paper later that week. The headline on the front page read: HOLIDAY CENTER WILL BRING JOBS TO THE AREA.

Dan, the younger of the two builders working on the house, had a copy tucked into the back pocket of his jeans and showed it to Jack as they went into the kitchen for coffee break. The children were already there, preparing a picnic with Phoebe's help. They were going to spend the day up at the lake again and, this time, Phoebe and Stephanie were to accompany them.

"It's all right for some!" Arthur, the older builder, said, referring to their lives of leisure, as he sucked noisily at a mug of tea.

Jack was reading the article in the paper with increasing anger, but Dan told them he thought the plan was a good idea.

"We need something going on round here,"

he said. "There's nothing for us young people to do."

"You mean you want to go on Wild West Trails through the forest?" Phoebe asked him in disbelief.

"Well, maybe not that exactly," he agreed. "But a bowling alley and . . ." he peered over Jack's shoulder, reading from the paper, "speedboats on the lake . . ."

"There are supposed to be otters in that lake," Phoebe told him. "How d'you think they'll enjoy your speedboats?"

Dan was a bit put out by this but argued that otters hadn't been seen there for years.

"Anyway," he continued, "what's the difference between you running this place as a hotel and these other people opening up Goldenwater as a holiday camp? I don't see the difference."

"You don't mean you're in favor of Goldenwater being turned into a theme park, Dan?" William asked him, his voice sounding shocked. "You can't be."

" 'Course I am," Dan replied. "That's what I've been saying, isn't it? 'Bout time something happened around here. It's so dozy you have to kick yourself to know if you're still alive or not."

"But—when the badger baiters were in the valley, you couldn't wait to get at them. You were on our side then!" William exclaimed.

"Side?" Dan asked, frowning. "What side? There aren't sides. There are just different opinions. You lot see it one way—and I see it another. We can all have our opinions. Besides, what have the badger baiters got to do with it? I'm against cruelty. That's why I hated the baiters. I don't see your argument. There's nothing cruel about opening a holiday camp, is there?"

"Except that half the wildlife will be wiped out and the place will cease to exist in the way that it has done for centuries," Phoebe said. "Isn't that a form of cruelty?"

"They'll look after the wildlife," Dan said, pointing at the paper, which was now spread on the table in front of them. "It says so here . . ." He leaned over, reading slowly from the page, " 'the natural beauty of the place will be preserved and the animal and bird life will be encouraged, giving countless holiday-makers the chance to observe at close quarters and in a natural habitat the wonders of nature. . . .' "

"Can't keep a place to yourself, you know," Arthur said. "That's selfish, that is."

"So instead," Phoebe argued, "you're going to side with some city businessmen, who've hit on a way of lining their wallets at the expense of destroying one of the last really wild and natural areas in the country?"

"Places can't stand still," Arthur blustered. "You have to move with the times. . . ."

"Oh, give me strength!" Phoebe said, and she went quickly out of the kitchen.

"Besides," Dan said in the silence that followed her departure, "we don't know the final plans yet. We don't know exactly what they're intending. It's just a planning application. They won't be able to do anything we don't like. . . ."

"Anything who doesn't like?" Jack demanded.

"They can't put up any buildings," Dan said, "or chop down trees or . . . anything, without us having a say. That's democracy. That's the law of this country. The people speak."

"Politics!" Arthur grumbled, blowing his nose loudly on a dirty handkerchief. "Nothing but trouble!" He raised a finger to stab home his considered opinion: "Politics, the law and religion are at the bottom of every disagreement that ever was. No good comes of them." And then he blew his nose again.

"Well, it looks as though we're going to be on different sides over the next few months then, Dan," Jack said mildly, stretching and scratching the back of his neck. "Because there's no way I can sit back and let this happen without a fight."

Dan shrugged. "I don't want to fight with anyone. All I'm saying is it sounds like a good idea to me. They say it could rival Disney World. Nothing wrong with that. Bring a lot of trade to the area. Everyone'll profit from it. Including you, Mr. Green . . ."

"Dan . . ." Jack groaned.

"You will, though. Just think about it. Your hotel will be right on the doorstep."

"I don't want it on the doorstep!" Jack bellowed.

"So—because you don't want it, you think you have the right to stop it for everyone else?" Dan jeered, scoring a point. "That sounds really selfish to me, that does."

Jack sighed and threw up his hands.

"Let's drop the subject. We're getting nowhere," he said wearily. And, rising from the table, he started to clear away the mugs, putting them on the draining board, beside the sink.

"I've always fancied going to Disney World," Dan said, speaking more to himself than to any of the others.

Alice stared at her hands and said nothing. She felt a bit embarrassed that he was voicing precisely her own thoughts on the subject. Although she hadn't joined in the discussions much, since the night Jack and Meg had first heard the plans from the solicitor, she had listened carefully to all that had been said. And, if she were asked, she would have to admit that she still thought the idea of having an amusement park so close to them was exciting.

She hadn't said anything to William about her feelings, because he was obviously against the scheme. But she'd tried once to talk to Mary about it. It was the evening after Jack had seen the solicitor. She and Mary had been sitting in the walled garden. Mary was drawing and Alice was bored.

"I think Disney World would be fun," she'd said. "Better than just sitting around all the time, doing nothing."

"Read a book," Mary had said, her voice off-hand as she concentrated on trying to get a bit of perspective right.

"I don't want to read a book," Alice had complained. "I want to go on a really exciting big dipper. Or one of those bomber things that make me feel sick. You know the one I mean, Mare . . ."

Mary had turned and looked at her.

"Why d'you want to make yourself feel sick?" she'd asked.

"I don't. But I'm bored," Alice had complained.

"We can't be bored," Mary had said quietly. "More things happen to us than they do to anyone else I know."

"You mean because of the Magician?" Alice had said, throwing a pebble at a stone. "But when he isn't here—then it's boring."

The girls relapsed into silence again, until Alice couldn't bear it any longer.

"I'd still like to go on a big dipper," she said, in a sulky voice. "Or . . . a ghost ride!" The thought cheered her up at once. "Yes, that's what I'd really like. I want to go on a really scary ride. . . . You know the sort of thing. When you have to have your eyes closed half the time and creepy things come out of the dark and brush your cheeks. And things jump out and make you scream . . ." And she'd gotten so carried away by her fantasy that she'd made herself scared just sitting there in the garden.

Now, as they prepared to go for the picnic and another day spent swimming and lying in the sun up at Goldenwater, she still thought she'd prefer to be setting off for the best funfair in the world and that, once there, what she'd like most would be to go on a really scary ghost ride. "It's just one of those things I enjoy," she thought with a shrug, "being so scared that shivers run down my back and I wish like anything that it would stop. I can't help it. It's the way I am. I like being scared!"

# 6

# Ducks and Drakes

It was William who started it.

The children were lying on the flat stone beside the lake, where they usually picnicked. When they'd finished eating Phoebe decided to take Stephanie to Four Fields, to visit Meg. The sun was hot and she was worried that the baby was getting too much of it on her delicate skin. Meg's little farm was only a short distance from the lake, through the woods behind where they'd all been sitting. It would be cooler walking in the forest, she said, and she hadn't seen Meg since the night of the solicitor's meeting and wanted to know that she was all right.

Spot got up from the shade of a bush, where he'd been lying with his tongue hanging out, and followed Phoebe. Alice almost decided to go with them as well, but she was feeling lazy and said that, although she might join them later, for the moment she was feeling so full she couldn't possibly move, not even if she wanted to.

"Perhaps," William suggested, as he stretched out on a flat piece of ground and put his empty backpack behind his head for a pillow, "perhaps if we just wait here, the Magician will come and we can tell him what we've discovered. That'd be best, don't you think?" And he sighed blissfully.

"So long as he doesn't come too soon," Mary agreed. Mary, who liked nothing better than lying in the warm sun, was already drifting off into that delightful state, halfway between waking and sleeping, where sounds recede and dreams hover on the edge of consciousness.

So, as the food and the heat worked on them, making them drowsier and sending each of them into a delicious, hazy sleep, William—whose mind always took longer to surrender than his sisters'—said dreamily: "There isn't a river." And that's how it began.

"A river?" Mary murmured, without any real interest. "A river—where?"

"Out of the lake," William said, sounding more alert and sitting up as he spoke. "There must be."

"Oh, William!" Mary protested. "Stop thinking and go to sleep."

"No, listen a minute!" William insisted, scanning the view with shaded eyes.

"What, Will?" Alice asked, yawning and then sitting up reluctantly.

"The water comes in at the top of the lake,

right?" William said, using his working-out voice. "Where that waterfall is . . ."

"Shall we go and look?" Alice asked eagerly. "We still haven't explored up there."

"Just a minute, Al," William said frowning and looking, not in the direction of the waterfall, but toward the standing stone and the distant outline of the yew tree at the bottom end of the lake. "That really is very odd," he said, speaking to himself.

"What is?" Mary asked, getting drawn in against her will.

"Well, the water comes in . . . but it doesn't go out anywhere."

"It must do," Mary told him, sitting up and scanning the shoreline.

"It'd overflow otherwise," Alice said, scratching her cheek. "Like leaving the tap running into a bath, when the plug's in."

"So—where does the water empty out of the lake then?" William asked in a puzzled voice.

"Somewhere over on the other side," Mary suggested, but even as she spoke she could see that that wasn't possible. The far shore revealed an undulating landscape of rising ground, covered with dark fir trees.

"No, I don't think so. It's got to be the bottom end, Mare," William told her. "That's the only place where the ground is fairly flat. Although, come to look at it, even there it rises toward the yew tree." Then he turned and stared at the girls. "In fact," he continued, in a surprised voice, "this lake is surrounded by higher ground. It's in a complete hollow." He rose to his feet. "This lake isn't possible."

"Oh, William, don't be silly," Alice said. "Of course it's possible. We can see it, can't we?"

"Was there a current?" Mary asked, getting up and standing beside her brother. "When you swam far out—the other day, when we thought you'd disappeared."

"I don't think so. I mean, not particularly," William replied. "Why?"

"Because it would show which way the water is flowing."

"Well, it must be flowing away from the water-fall," her brother said, beginning to sound irritated.

"The best way to find out," Mary said thoughtfully, moving away from him, "would be to walk right round the edge of the lake. Sooner or later we'd be bound to find where the water flows out. It shouldn't take too long. It isn't very big."

But it took them longer than they thought. For one thing, the heat was intense. It bounced off the ground and shimmered over the surface of the water. There was no breeze and every step they took was exhausting.

"Do we really want to know?" Alice complained, after they'd only gone a short distance.

"You don't have to come, if you don't want to," William told her.

But Alice didn't want to be left behind in case something interesting was discovered and so she continued to trail along behind them, complaining about the heat and sighing a lot.

After a short while they reached the bottom end of the lake. Here the ground rose gradually toward the standing stone and the yew tree.

"D'you remember the line?" Mary said.

"What line?" Alice asked.

"When we first came up here last holiday. We noticed that the tree and the stone and the lake were in a straight line with the dovecote and the house down in the valley and . . . there were other things as well, weren't there? I can't remember them all."

"Yes, that's right," William said. "I'd forgotten all that. There was a gap in the trees as well . . ." and, as he spoke, he turned and scanned the distant skyline above the waterfall at the top end of the lake. "There!" he cried, pointing. "There's the gap."

The girls turned, looking in the direction of his finger. Just visible at the top of the cliff, immediately above the waterfall, there was a break in the trees.

"Funny how you get things all confused until you know the lay of the land," William observed. "That gap up there is probably where the stream flows that becomes the waterfall, that fills the lake . . ."

"It's still in a straight line, though," Mary insisted. "And," she continued, warming to her subject, "the Magician told us there were three lines up here. There was the Silver Path . . ."

"The Dark and Dreadful Path," Alice murmured, remembering the night of the badger bait. "It was me who made it silver again."

"We all did, Alice," William said, grumpily and, as he spoke, he picked up a flat stone and flicked it, skimming and jumping, across the smooth water of the lake.

"You weren't there," Alice said defiantly. It had been her deed. The Magician had said so. He'd said she was brave. He'd said he was proud of her. It was so typical of William to make out it was all of them.

"It really was Alice mostly," Mary said, springing to her sister's defense and adding to William's annoyance. She watched him as he picked up another stone and bent his body to throw it. "And there was a golden path, as well, wasn't there?" she continued. "That was over toward Four Fields, where Meg lives. Then, between those two paths . . ." William's stone skipped twice and sank. He selected another and aimed again. ". . . between them, the Magician said there was a third path without a name, marked by all these things in a straight line . . ."

William's stone skidded across the surface of the water and then, in midair . . . it disappeared.

"Oh!" Mary gasped.

William turned and looked at her, an equally surprised look on his own face.

"Did you see that?" he asked.

"Do it again, Will," Mary said.

"What? Do what? What happened?" Alice asked.

"Don't tell her, Will. Just watch, Alice. See if it happens for you."

Alice turned and stared at the lake.

"Watch what?"

"William's stone."

William took another stone and flicked it across the surface of the lake. The direction it went was at an angle, crossing their line of vision. As the stone, in midair between two skips, crossed the invisible line that ran the length of the lake from the waterfall to the standing stone and the yew tree behind it . . . it vanished from their view.

"It's done it again," William whispered.

"What did you see, Al?" Mary asked.

Alice pulled a thoughtful face and scratched her cheek.

"Well?" Mary prompted her.

"It disappeared," Alice replied, making the fact almost sound ordinary. Then she turned and looked at her brother and sister. "That's exactly what happened to you, William."

"What?" William asked. "When?"

"William, she's right!" Mary gasped. "When you were swimming the other day . . ."

"I told you, I went underwater."

"Yes, that's what you probably did. . . ." Mary agreed reluctantly.

"But all the same, to us," Alice insisted, "you just . . . disappeared."

A splash caught their attentions, making them all look once more at the surface of the lake. A series of tiny disturbances on the surface plopped away into the distance.

"Fish jumping," William remarked to himself.

Then, as they were all watching, not far out from the shore, a stone fell from nowhere onto the surface of the water and ducked and draked, the hops getting weaker, until it sank from view. And immediately another stone appeared, followed almost at once by a third and then a fourth.

"Where are they coming from?" Alice gasped, searching the shoreline to see if there was anyone there, throwing the stones.

"Out of nowhere," Mary whispered.

"But always appearing at the same point!" William cried, excitedly. "You see? They appear in the air at exactly the same point. . . ."

"How d'you mean, Will?" Alice asked.

"Watch! Where my stones disappear . . . the others appear," and as he spoke, he picked up another flat piece of rock and flicked it out over the water. It skimmed the surface until it reached the imaginary line . . . and then went . . .

"Where?" William asked, his voice hoarse with frustration.

"Maybe into another time," Mary said simply. "The Magician's time. Why not? We've got quite used to the Magician coming and going—why should we be so surprised if a stone can do it."

"But how?" William cried desperately, his face creased with the effort of trying to understand what was going on.

"We're not supposed to ask 'how.' We're supposed to just let things happen," Alice said, a little smugly. It was a lesson that she had learned well on their last visit.

But this wasn't good enough for William.

"No, Al. That might be right for you. But it isn't for me. It's not good enough—just to say it's magic. I have to know how it works. There must be some logical explanation . . . there must be rules that the magic obeys. . . . There must be some reason to it. . . ."

During this exchange, Mary had been silent. She turned her back on the lake and looked at the standing stone. Then, staring at it thoughtfully, she walked up the gently rising ground toward it.

The stone was as tall as a man and leaned sideways into a holly bush that seemed almost to be supporting it. There was no carving on it. It was just a single slim pillar of rock, roughly squared into an oblong. Any hard edges that might once have been fashioned by the stonemason's tools had long ago been worn away by centuries of wind and rain and frost.

"Where are you going?" Alice called.

"Just thinking," Mary answered, going round behind the stone and disappearing from Alice's view.

"Mary?" Alice called.

For a moment there was no reply. Alice felt her heart beating faster and making her gasp for breath.

"Will," she whispered.

William turned quickly and looked in the direction of the stone.

"Mary!" he called.

"What?" she asked, coming into view from behind the holly bush.

"Oh, cupcakes!" Alice exclaimed. "I thought you'd disappeared as well."

"Well, she had for a minute, hadn't she?" William said thoughtfully.

"No—she'd just gone out of sight. That's different," Alice protested.

"I'm sure it's got something to do with this line thing," Mary said, walking slowly round the standing stone, staring at it solemnly. Then, reaching out, she put the palm of her hand flat against the rough surface.

"Yes! It has a lot to do with the line," Stephen Tyler said, appearing round the side of the stone, making Mary jump with surprise.

"Oh!" she gasped. "You startled me."

He was leaning heavily on his silver stick and his other arm was still in the sling. He was more bent than usual and looked tired and old.

"Sssh!" he whispered, gesturing to her to be silent. Then he surveyed the lake, solemnly, as though he was watching something that the children couldn't see.

The children remained quiet, scanning the lake in the hope of seeing whatever it was that was so fascinating the Magician.

"Interesting!" he said at last. And then he continued in a more animated voice, "I'm sorry about that. I was in the middle of watching my assistant when I became aware of your presence. It's all the fault of old age," and, as he spoke, he sounded irritated. "I can't keep my mind on things like I used to. It is of extreme importance to the alchemical arts to have a still, silent mind. Mine pops about and brays like a young donkey." He shook his head, as though clearing his thoughts. "So, so. Here we all are. What have you been up to?"

"Were you playing Ducks and Drakes?" William asked.

"Ducks and Drakes?" Stephen Tyler said, in a puzzled voice.

"You know, skimming a stone across the surface of the water," William told him.

"Not I, no. But my assistant. He has too much free time."

"He's here?" William gasped. "Morden is here?" He looked round, searching along the side of the lake.

"No, no, no! Here—but in his own time," the Magician said patiently. "In my time!" Then he smiled. "Poor William," he said gently, "how you do suffer in your head! It is just a question of time again. Once you understand that—it will all seem perfectly simple, I promise you! And you really are making great strides forward. I am very pleased with you all."

The old man nodded thoughtfully. He looked at each of the children in turn, peering at them almost as though he were seeing them for the first time. Then he nodded thoughtfully again.

"Fascinating!" he said. "I should go. I didn't intend to come. My concentration!" He shook his head sadly. "There is much to do. Keep working! You won't have me forever, you know. . . ."

"Please," William cut in, "where does the water go?"

Tyler looked at him sharply.

"Go?"

"From the lake," William explained.

"I'll tell you about water, William," the old man said, forgetting at once that he had intended to leave and turning instead toward them. "Water is the nearest man can get to understanding the eternal principle." Then he nodded, emphatically, as though he had just imparted a gem of knowledge.

William frowned, Mary looked at her feet and Alice sighed.

"There! What d'you think of that, then?" the Magician asked delightedly.

"I haven't a clue what it means," Alice said, without hesitation.

"William?" the old man asked.

"I don't know what it means, either," William had to admit.

"What d'you know about water?" the Magician asked him. "Where does it come from?"

"From rain," Alice announced.

"Where does the rain come from?"

"From evaporated water being drawn up into the upper atmosphere," William replied.

"Good! Where does the water come from?"

"From rain," Alice said again and then she frowned, puzzled by the answer she had just given. "But—where does the rain first come from?"

"Precisely," the Magician said, after a moment, and he nodded. "The time has come for you to understand about water. Wait there . . ." and, as he walked quickly away from them, leaning heavily on his stick, he disappeared once more from their view.

"Now what?" William murmured, searching the space that the old man had just vacated.

"Oh," Alice sighed. "I hope we're not going to have another lecture . . ." and, as she said the words, a rowing boat slid into view on the margin of the lake. It was being pulled by the Magician.

"You ask me where does the water go? I must show you Blackwater Sluice."

Alice looked doubtful. "Blackwater Sluice," she called. "What's that?"

"An exciting ride, Alice. Isn't that what you wanted?" the Magician answered her, and Alice felt her cheeks burning as she blushed. The old man had obviously been reading her thoughts again. It was a habit of his that she particularly distrusted. She considered it unfair—like cheating at cards.

"Oh, do you indeed?" Stephen Tyler said, looking at her severely.

"I didn't say anything," Alice said, in an innocent voice.

"Your thoughts are very noisy, Minimus. They deafen me sometimes. So, come along. Get in all of you," he said, steadying the boat. "One of you will have to row. This confounded arm is preventing me doing half the things I enjoy."

# 7

# Lutra

"I take it you do know how to row?" he said as they jostled for seats and the boat bobbed and wobbled on the surface of the water. "William, you and Mary take an oar each and, Alice, you come and sit beside me. But—carefully!" he cried, as they all moved at once and the boat tipped so much to one side that they almost capsized.

"Water," the Magician told them, "is a tricky element. It must be treated with respect." Then he settled into the seat at the back of the boat and motioned to Alice to sit beside him. "Ah!" he sighed, "this is very pleasant. Row on!" and, trailing his good hand in the water, he closed his eyes and soon was snoring quietly.

Alice started to giggle. She also closed her eyes and snored loudly. The Magician immediately opened one eye, glared at her through it, and then scooped some water from the surface of the lake and splashed it into her face.

"Hey!" she shrieked. "That was freezing!"

"Don't snore then!" the old man said, and he closed his eyes again.

William and Mary sat side by side on the center bench, facing Alice and the Magician. Then, each taking an oar, they dipped them in the water and pulled together. The boat slid silently away from the shore.

"But where are we going?" Mary asked.

"It's not a very big lake," the Magician said, still with his eyes closed. "You can't get lost."

"Where did this boat come from?" William asked. "It looks too modern to be from your time."

"Don't ask unimportant questions. I found it," the old man replied.

"But—where? That's all I'm asking," William insisted. "You disappeared and came back and . . . oh," he shook his head, tense with frustration. "It's all so confusing. . . ."

When William next looked up, as he pulled backward on his oar, he saw that the Magician's eyes were open and that they were staring piercingly at him.

"Well . . ." William protested at the old man's accusing stare. "I can't help it. I've got the sort of mind that likes to work things out. . . ."

"Poor William," Stephen Tyler murmured. "What happens when you meet the incomprehensible? What then? When you are faced by something beyond your understanding? We are mere mortals, William. Would you want to be God?"

"And anyway, it's all such a waste of time," Mary suddenly said. "That's what you always do, William. You get bogged down in little details and forget the really important things."

The Magician swiveled his eyes so that he was now staring at Mary.

"And what do you do, Mary?" he inquired quietly.

"Do?" she asked nervously. She didn't like the attention that, with her words, she had called upon herself.

"You have, very precisely, summed up your brother's chief characteristic. What, I wonder, do you think yours might be?"

Mary blushed and remained silent.

"Falling in love!" Alice said in a bored voice. "She's always doing it."

"And you disapprove?" the Magician demanded, turning suddenly to look at her.

Alice shrugged.

"It's boring!" she said.

"All I meant," Mary said, quickly changing the subject, "is that we've discovered all sorts of things that we've got to tell you and William goes and asks you an unimportant question about where the water goes. . . ."

"But sometimes," the Magician told her, "the seemingly unimportant turns out to be crucial."

And, reaching over the back of the seat, he took hold of the small tiller and guided the boat out toward the center of the lake.

William and Mary continued to dip the oars and the boat slipped across the water, cutting the perfect reflection of the surrounding scenery so that it seemed as if they were sailing across a pale, watery sky. Dimly, through the gloom below, fish moved languorously and the sunlight dappled the surface of the lake, flashing and sparkling.

The Magician stared down at the water as it slowly flowed past, his hand creating a tiny ripple that swirled and eddied and then was lost across the smooth, silky surface. He sighed and when he next spoke his voice was gentle and far away, as if he was remembering distant thoughts.

"The water, here at Goldenwater, has always been a mystery to people," he said. "As William has so correctly observed, there is no apparent outlet for it. Not from the surface, at least. Many years ago—before my time; before the time of the monks; before even the time of the Roman invaders—a mighty race of people lived here who understood the world of nature and were able to harness her powers to their own ends. Rather as the people in your time are harnessing nature— but with one vital difference. In your time, people harness and destroy; they take and don't give back. They believe that all things are for their personal use. The people I am talking about lived in harmony with their world. They took nothing, expected nothing, and harmed nothing. They learned many miraculous skills, long since forgotten. They moved mountains and yet left the mountains where they had always been. The Standing Stone is witness to their power. It came many hundreds of miles, brought here by unknown means and was placed precisely at the center of the energy field that has sustained this valley and the surrounding countryside since the great age of ice first shaped these hills and vales and fashioned our known world."

"What's an energy field?" William asked.

The Magician sighed. "You ask such difficult questions," he said, gazing thoughtfully across the water. "Can I, perhaps, pursue that at a later date?"

William shrugged.

"All right," he said. "But just tell me about these people then. Where did they go? What happened to them?"

"They were conquered by the weak and by the cunning. They lost to the greedy and to the mean. They did not understand what it meant to fight for their existence. They welcomed all beings as part of the natural world. They had no word in their language to cover hate, because they had never experienced that emotion."

Again Stephen Tyler sighed.

"Move slowly now," he said, raising a hand. "We are almost at the center."

William and Mary dipped their oars gently once more and then, as the boat slid forward, they rested them on the sides of the craft where they dripped sparkling drops of water onto the floor near Alice's and Stephen Tyler's feet.

As the boat came in line with the standing stone at one end of the lake and the waterfall at the other, the Magician swung the tiller, slowing the movement so that, at last, it came to rest, bobbing from side to side, crossing the imaginary line at an acute angle.

"Watch," he said and, rummaging in the folds of his coat, he produced a smooth nugget of gold, hanging on a fine golden chain.

"What is it?" Alice asked him, her eyes shining as she gazed at it.

"My pendulum," the old man replied. As he spoke, he lifted the chain, holding it tightly between his thumb and index finger, the piece of gold suspended motionless below. "With my pendulum I measure the earth's energy. Here, at the center of Goldenwater, it is extremely strong. See!" The piece of gold started to turn slowly in a circle although Stephen Tyler made no movement and there wasn't a breath of wind. At first it made only a slow circle but then, as the motion gathered strength, the gold moved faster and faster, pulling at the thin golden chain until it was flying at an angle of forty-five degrees from the old man's hand.

"What does it mean?" Mary asked, watching in amazement. "Why is it doing that?"

"We are on the middle way," Stephen Tyler replied and gathering the pendulum back into his hand, he returned it to his pocket. "When you asked where the water went, William," he continued, "you touched on the great mystery. That was the question that must first have drawn our forefathers to this place. That is where the power comes from. Beneath us here—deep, deep down; fathoms below—there is an opening in the hard rock of the wall of this flooded basin. The water flows through it into unimaginable caverns. It is known to the locals hereabouts as Blackwater Sluice. Few men have been there, though many have tried and failed. The opening is very narrow. Only a child could squeeze through it. And the depth is so great that breathing apparatus would be required just to reach the place."

"How do you know so much about it?" William asked in a hushed voice. "You speak about it as though you've been there."

The Magician looked at him for a long moment and then he smiled.

"Lutra!" he called. It was a soft, gentle sound. "Come to me, my Lutra." And, raising his hand, he pointed across the surface of the lake. The children all turned to look in that direction.

"Lutra!" he called again. It was the sound that the wind makes as it whispers through trees; the sound of the song of a whale. "Lutra!" It was sad and happy, soft and strong. It was a sound full of love.

"Look!" Alice cried, and she also pointed in the same direction as the Magician.

Now they could all see, coming toward them across the thin, colorless, moving expanse of water a V-shaped point of ripples, traveling fast, like an arrow, pointing straight at them.

"Come, my Lutra!" Stephen Tyler said, speaking almost brusquely and leaning toward the water as if guiding the ripples toward him. "You are well met!" he cried and, at that moment, a head popped up out of the water. The face was sleek and shining, the eyes twinkling, the nose a bright black button with a set of fine gray whiskers sticking out below it.

"What is it?" Alice said.

"This is Lutra!" Stephen Tyler exclaimed. "My Lutra."

"But . . . what is it?" Alice insisted. She had never seen a creature quite like it before.

"Have you never met an otter?" Stephen asked her, amazed at her ignorance.

Alice pulled a face and shrugged. "Don't think so," she said. "Have I, Will?"

William shook his head and Mary, who was sitting on the side of the boat nearest to the creature, leaned forward and held out her hand to it.

"Lutra, my dear," the Magician said softly. "I want to show my friends Blackwater Sluice."

The otter turned his twinkling eyes and darted a look at the Magician. "Spare them nothing," the old man continued. "They are my good and constant friends. They must understand everything. . . ."

As he finished speaking the otter turned, and with a plop, it disappeared from view down below the surface, right beside the boat.

"Oh, don't go!" Alice called, leaning over the edge of the boat, searching the dark below her. Then, almost before she had time to snatch a breath, the ice-cold of Goldenwater enveloped her and she felt herself being dragged, gasping, down into its twilight depths.

# 8

# Blackwater Sluice

Everything happened so fast that Alice was never quite sure what had actually taken place. One moment, it seemed, she was leaning over the side of the rowing boat, looking down into the deep water at the disappearing shadow of the otter and the next . . . she was in the water herself and it was incredibly cold as it slipped round her body, pulling her down below the surface.

The light began to fade and then, like a submarine preparing to dive, Alice's body reacted to some unheard command. All sound disappeared as she closed her ears. She flicked with her thick tail and felt even colder, darker water enveloping her. At the same moment she closed her nostrils and eyes. Like a craft battened down for a storm, she sped through the water, going down and down until, at last, she could feel the tug of a current.

Her lungs were at bursting point. The

immense pressure of the water that surrounded her squeezed her body. She wanted to open her eyes, but the lids seemed to be sealed. She couldn't move them. Nor was there any way that she could turn and aim for the surface of the water. As if drawn by a magnet, her course led her deeper and deeper, to the very bottom of Goldenwater.

The current that she had felt was growing stronger and, with it, she careered toward the rocky wall of the submerged valley that formed the bowl in which the lake was held.

Reaching out with webbed claws she felt the rock beneath her and, like a blind person, she probed across the rough surface, the pull of the current dragging her closer and closer to the narrow outlet through which the water was surging.

The force of the current was so strong now that it buffeted her body knocking her sideways and making her gasp. As she did so, she opened her mouth, and swallowed a mouthful of icy water. She choked, coughing and spluttering and making herself sick. A tight band encircled her lungs, squeezing the breath out of her. She could see strange lights flashing in front of her eyes.

The eerie silence that had accompanied her from the surface of the lake was suddenly shattered by the terrible sound of tearing water as it crashed and sucked and roared its way through the narrow opening.

"Blackwater Sluice," a voice in her head whispered. "I hates this place as much as anywheres I knows. I only ever comes here when he makes me—and once when I was a young cub and that was by mistake. Hold on now, Minimus . . . We's going through."

With a sickening lurch, Alice felt herself falling headfirst into a bottomless pit. All around her sharp cold water was tearing at her body and the sound was so deafening that it made her want to scream. Spikes of stone tore at her fur and she knocked the side of her head against a protruding rock. Then, almost before she had time to feel the pain, the falling sensation altered to a spin. Turning and squirming and horribly sick, Alice was sucked through the black water until, as if shot from a gun, she found herself free of the water and flying through cold, damp air.

A moment later she landed with a jolt on a stony spit of land beside which she could hear the water churning and raging as it rushed on into the black.

It was the darkness that she noticed most. It was more intense than any night. It hemmed her in on every side. It was so thick and impenetrable that it felt solid, like a wall. She realized that up until then she had never really known true darkness before. Always in the past, however black the night, once her eyes had grown accustomed to where she was there had been a lessening of the dark until, gradually at first, vague objects had begun to materialize in front of her. But here, now, the darkness remained; however long she waited, it wouldn't go away.

Her shoulder hurt where she'd landed on it. She was freezing cold and wet. She started to shiver violently. The sound of the water rushing through the narrow opening was deafening. She put webbed claws to her ears, blocking out the sound, and as she did so, she felt the sleek, oily fur that covered her body. This discovery—the unfamiliar feel of her body, so foreign to her that she couldn't even recognize what it was she had changed into—was too much for Alice. She crouched down on the cold, wet ground and started to sob pitifully.

"Alice!" Mary shrieked, making a dart for her sister's body. But she was too late. Alice was leaning too far out over the side of the boat and, just as Mary's hand brushed her shoulder, she toppled out and hit the water with a gasp of surprise and fear, before disappearing under the surface.

"William!" Mary screamed, turning back to look at him.

William was standing up, beside Mary, swaying giddily. He'd leaned forward also, trying to grab at Alice as she was falling. Now, with his youngest sister's weight suddenly removed, the small craft rocked back and bobbed about on the disturbed water. William, still leaning forward in a most precarious position was thrown off balance. With his arms flailing and legs kicking, he fell, back first, into the lake on the other side of the boat.

William was a very good swimmer. But the sudden shock of the cold took him unawares. His thin shirt billowed and his shorts grew heavy as the water soaked the material, weighing him down. His sandals had an unfamiliar feel in the water; they made his feet clumsy. He wanted to get rid of them, but they were too firmly attached for him to be able to kick them off.

The weight of his clothes and his thrashing feet forced William backward farther down into the water. He could see the light receding above him and his arms and feet reaching toward it as though in some desperate way he was trying to hold on to the outside world and to pull himself back up toward it.

On first impact, he must have swallowed a lot of water. He was choking and spluttering. Gasping, he inadvertently took another mouthful. He started to panic and this panic made him thrash his arms and legs with renewed vigor, exhausting his energy and doing nothing toward helping him back to the surface of the lake.

"Easy," a voice whispered in his head. "That's no way to treats the water. Yous do it my way."

Later he would claim that he saw the otter swimming toward him through the green half-light before they merged and became one. But he could never be sure. All he was aware of was seeing his arms and legs, still reaching out toward the distant surface of the lake, shrink into claw-ended stubs and a thick, flat, wonderful tail came into view.

"I like the tail best!" he whispered and he beat it powerfully. At once he shot through the water, his body turning and diving as he propelled himself forward. This newfound skill fascinated William. He wanted to beat the tail forever. It was such fun driving through the water. But a voice in his head whispered severely:

"Leaves all the moving to me, if yous don't mind. Besides, we let the water do mosts of the work."

"That's what we were told in life-saving," William suddenly remembered. "Let the water do the work."

"All that tails wagging only makes yous tired. I's don't want to be tired. Do yous?"

"I suppose not," William thought. But he couldn't help feeling disappointed. The tail wagging had been fun.

"Yous not here for fun," the voice whispered sternly. "Where we's going isn't fun. We needs our strength for Blackwater Sluice, I don't mind yous knowing. I hates this place. I only ever comes for him—except once when I was a little pup and came by mistake. . . ."

The tug of the current was strong now. The otter stretched his paws in front and behind, making his body into a long, sleek cigar-shape from the tip of his whiskered nose to the end of his tail. Opening the eyes a little, they were able to see, through the murk, a narrow crack in the rocky side of the deep cleft into which they were being dragged. The force of the water, driving through this cleft was so strong that it seemed not to move at all. It appeared instead like a solid substance, black and hard. As the otter's body connected with this water, William felt a huge surge of energy. It was as though he had reached out and taken hold of a swiftly moving vehicle and now, having been whipped off his feet, was being dragged along at an alarming speed.

"Here we go!" the otter-voice in his head whispered and then with a piercing "Aaaahhhh!" of desperate sound, which William suspected was more of his making than the otter's, they both, as one, hurtled toward the narrow opening.

"We'll never make it!" William screamed, mentally ducking his head and trying to avoid the hard, jagged rocks that sped toward them.

The sound of the water roared in his ears. The rock closed in, tighter and tighter, all around his otter-body. They turned and dodged and flicked and spiraled down and through the solid earth.

"Blackwater Sluice!" a voice screamed in his head and, a moment later, William heard Alice's terrified voice, shouting:

"William! William!"

"I'm here," he told her. "It's all right," and, as he spoke, panting and gasping for breath, the otter-body left him and he saw his own arms, reaching through the water, to where Alice was thrashing and shouting on the surface of the lake.

As William went overboard, the boat rocked horribly. Mary managed to grasp hold with a hand on each side and to hang on, as if she was on a roller coaster at a funfair. If she hadn't she would certainly have landed in the water as well.

The boat meanwhile was pitching backward and forward and from side to side, throwing her in all directions, as though it were trying to shake her off. Great drafts of water slapped into the shallow trough beneath her feet, dragging the boat lower into the water with its weight. The surface of the lake crept closer and closer. It seemed inevitable that they would sink.

But Mary forced herself to keep calm. She took deep breaths and clung onto the sides of the boat, willing it to become still and steady once more. Gradually peace returned to the gleaming surface of Goldenwater.

As soon as she was able, Mary turned, looking over her shoulder, searching for any sign of William or of Alice. The pale reflection of the encircling hills was as flat and as clear as a mirror.

She swung round, panic grabbing at her, and searched the water in the other direction.

Then, with a gasp, she realized she was alone in the boat. The Magician had also disappeared. Where he had gone to, she didn't know. When he had gone was an equal mystery. Why he had gone seemed almost unimportant.

"Typical!" Mary said, out loud. "Just when we need you!" and then, as she spoke, she felt a terrible wave of nausea and fear sweep over her. "William!" she shouted. Kneeling in the cold water at her feet, she leaned over the side of the boat, staring down into the depths of the lake. "Alice!" she yelled.

But she knew it was pointless. She had seen Alice disappear over the side and, a moment later, she'd heard William cry out as he fell backward into the water behind her. Now, gazing at the unbroken surface of the lake, she could only suppose that they were both drowned. She covered her face with her hands and felt the hot tears that sprang from her eyes.

She didn't know how long she remained kneeling in the wet, but eventually, a strange jerking motion caught her attention. Opening her eyes, she was surprised to discover that the boat was moving. As if drawn by invisible hands, it was being pulled slowly across the water.

Scrambling forward to the prow, Mary looked over the side. The length of rope that Stephen Tyler had used to pull the boat along the shore was now pointing at an angle down into the water a few feet ahead of the boat and, as Mary watched, she saw the wet, gleaming head of an otter break the surface, the end of the rope firmly clenched between its teeth.

The otter was dragging the boat slowly toward the shore. As Mary saw it, so it turned and looked back at her.

"Had enough for one day?" the familiar voice of the Magician whispered in her head.

"Oh, please," Mary sobbed. "Where are William and Alice?"

"We took them to Blackwater Sluice," the otter told her, leaning back in the water and holding the rope between his two big claws as he spoke.

"But where are they now?" Mary asked.

Then, before the otter could reply, she heard William calling to her from the shore.

"Mary!" she heard him say. "Are you all right?"

Looking up, Mary saw William, wet and bedraggled, but seemingly unhurt, standing in the shallow water at the edge of the lake.

"Where's Alice?" she yelled.

"She's here. Didn't you see me? I just helped her ashore," and, as he spoke, Mary saw Alice kneeling on the ground behind her brother.

"Is she all right?" Mary yelled.

" 'Course she is," William replied. "I got a badge for life-saving, didn't I? What's the matter with you?"

"Nothing," Mary replied quietly, and, taking the oars she started to row the boat slowly toward the shore, tears of relief and tiredness running silently down her cheeks.

The otter swam for a moment beside her. It raised its head out of the water and watched her with bright, twinkling eyes.

"Don't cries, little girl," the otter called, his voice a high, fluting whistle. "It's all over now. All's safe again. I hates Blackwater Sluice. . . ." and before he'd finished the sentence he dived out of sight, surfacing a moment later with a silver fish caught between his jaws.

The sun beat down. William and Alice were draped in their swimming towels, and their wet clothes were spread out beside them, drying in the hot air.

Mary beached the boat farther along the shore and waded through the shallow water to dry land. Then, turning, she pulled the boat up after her onto the shingle.

As she was about to leave, something glinted on the long seat, catching her attention. The back of the boat was still bobbing in the water, and Mary waded back out to discover what it was. The Magician's golden pendulum was lying on the wooden seat. Mary reached over and picked it up, gathering the thin chain into her hand. As she did so, she thought that without this proof she would almost have believed that he had never been there at all; that they had only imagined him.

"That's so often how it is," she thought and, placing the pendulum in the pocket of her jeans, she turned and hurried along the beach toward William and Alice.

"Are you both all right?" she called.

"Yes!" Alice replied, sounding cross. "Don't fuss, Mary. I just nearly drowned, that's all!" and she shrugged and made a face, as though nearly drowning was the sort of thing she did every day.

"Thank goodness you were there, Will," Mary said, kneeling down between them. "I'd never have been able to save her."

"I could have swum you know," Alice said, and then she shivered and hugged herself.

William was sitting cross-legged, tossing a pebble from one hand to the other, staring out across the lake.

"What happened?" Mary asked.

"I fell in," Alice replied, sounding petulant again.

"But after that. Did you see Blackwater Sluice?"

"Oh, stop Mary!" Alice whispered, clamping her hands over her ears. "I don't ever want to think of that place again."

William took the stone and threw it as far as he could out into the lake.

"Will?" Mary pleaded. "Please tell me."

"What?" William asked, trying to sound brave.

"What happened?" his sister repeated, anxiously.

William shrugged. "You tell me," he said.

"Well, one minute we were all looking at the otter and the next you and Alice were in the water and you seemed to have completely disappeared and the boat nearly sank and then . . . you turned up here on the shore. Oh!—and the otter. I saw the otter again . . ." She frowned, as she remembered, scarcely believing what she was saying. "It was pulling the boat along."

"That's all that happened?" William asked, looking at her.

"So far as I know," Mary replied.

"How long did all this take?"

"I don't know," Mary replied. "Not very long. Why?"

William shook his head and frowned.

"There's something else, isn't there?" Mary asked him, looking at him closely. "Please tell me the rest, Will. Please."

"I think," her brother replied, speaking slowly, "that Alice was drowning and I went to save her . . . Just like you said. That's all."

"Yes, that's all," Alice said, and for a moment she and William stared at each other.

"It isn't!" Mary cried. "There's something that you're not telling me. There's been some magic, hasn't there? Something happened—and I was left out. Why? Why do I always miss out on things? Why?"

"Oh, Mare," Alice said in a small voice. "It wasn't very nice magic. . . ." and she and her brother started, between them, to try to describe what had happened to each of them.

"It was horrible," Alice gasped as she came to the end of her story. "I never want to go on a ride like that again. Not ever."

"It's not fair," Mary said, ignoring this last remark. "I always miss out on things," and, lying back, she closed her eyes to hide from them the fact that she was crying again.

# 9

# William Works Things Out

The secret room was bathed in late afternoon light. The rays of a pale apricot sun streamed in through the back window, coloring the steeply sloping ceiling, the walls, the floor, and even the dusty air, with gold. Birds were singing that strange, expectant chorus that heralds the night. Distantly, across the valley, the low drone of nature, the buzzing and humming, the sighing and breathing, the long chord of creation, echoed through the trees of the forest and the high lands beyond. A tiny breeze stirred, sighing across the outer roof, bringing the scent of roses and the toasted smell of herbs from the walled garden below.

Mary couldn't stop crying. Not that noisy, sobbing, painful crying that comes with despair; but silent tears, caused as much by the beauty of the scene that she watched through the circular window as by her own state of mind. She had been vaguely sad since the afternoon at the lake. But she hadn't spoken about it to the others. She hadn't wanted to share the feeling with anyone. She would scarcely have been able to put it into words. It was no more than a slight, nagging sense of rejection. She felt as though she'd been left out. Magic had taken place and she hadn't been a part of it. Why? Was it because she wasn't good enough for it? Or ready for it? Or . . . why? She shrugged, wiping her cheeks with her hands, and sighed deeply.

Maybe the best thing to do would be to just not bother—as she wasn't bothering about Dan anymore. What was the point of wasting time trying to put herself in places where he was bound to see her if, when he did see her, he just treated her as a kid and wouldn't talk seriously to her? He was just like the magic, really. He left her out too. And this view . . . Even this view through the window . . . She wasn't really a part of it. She was only an outsider, watching, looking, removed. Even the view excluded her. She felt as if she didn't belong anywhere; as though she were invisible; or didn't exist. She was tired of only looking, tired of feeling, but tired most of never seeming to belong anywhere.

They had returned from the lake via Four Fields where Phoebe and Steph and Spot had been waiting for them. Meg had given them tea in thick, chipped mugs and big wedges of shop fruit-

cake, which William and Alice had devoured rav-
enously. They had, of course, none of them
breathed a word about what had happened,
although William did ask Meg if there was a boat
at the lake.

"No, dear. There used to be one, I think. But
not now that I know of," Meg told him. She
seemed subdued herself and Phoebe soon suggested that she and the children should be getting home.

At supper that night Phoebe had told them
that Meg was sorely tempted by the offer to sell
Four Fields.

"What should I do, dear?" she said. "I never
thought to be offered money for Four Fields. I
mean, it isn't good land and the house is falling
down. Of course I don't want to move, I never
even contemplated such a thing. Never thought
I'd be able. Thought I'd live and die at Four
Fields. But with the money they're offering, I
could buy a little cottage in a village. I'm not getting any younger, dearie. And the life here is
hard. . . . Hard for an old woman like me. . . .
One fall of a bad winter's day and then where
would I be? Who'd milk the cows then? Who'd
even know? There are days on end when the
snow's lying, when I don't see a soul. I could lie
for a week. I wasn't fit last winter. But I kept
myself going. You have to think about these
things. This place . . . Well . . . It's all right when

you're young. Not quite so good when you're past your time."

The children had all been horrified at the news, though Jack seemed to understand it.

"But . . ." Alice had exclaimed, "she can't want to leave Four Fields. We'll visit her every day. Would that help?"

"And what about when you're at school?" Phoebe had reasoned with her. "And when your Mum and Dad return from Africa and you're not living here anymore?"

"But we'll always visit," Alice had protested, suddenly appalled at the thought of not living at Golden House, even although she missed her mother and father.

"But if she sells," William had said, "those horrible people will take the place and tear down the cottage and plow up the fields. Meg couldn't let that happen."

"Who's to say it won't happen after her death anyway?" Jack asked.

"She has no one to leave the place to," Phoebe said. "She told me today that she has no family."

"She could leave it to us," Alice had cried eagerly.

Phoebe had smiled. "She was thinking of doing just that," she told her. "Meg thinks of you as her family."

"There, then," Alice said, blushing slightly and helping herself to another spoonful of Lemon Snow. "That's settled."

"And what would you do with Four Fields?" Phoebe asked. "You're not going to farm it."

"I might," Alice had replied, with her mouth full. But she knew in her heart that farming would bore her and, being honest, she'd screwed up her face and sighed. "No. What I really like is Meg farming it and me being able to go and see her when I'm in the mood."

"I thought you were the one who welcomed the theme park idea, Alice," Jack said.

But Alice had shaken her head and shuddered glancing fearfully at William.

"No. I've gone off that," she'd told them, and then she'd stared glumly at her plate and refused to say anything more.

And indeed none of them had spoken about the boating accident even to each other. Alice was too scared to want to think about it. Mary felt rejected and William . . .

William's head had been in a turmoil. He had to work it out. Now, as he sat cross-legged on the floor of the secret room, doodling with his finger in the dust, his brow was still knitted into a frown as he went over and over the events of that afternoon.

Alice and Spot were sitting together under the mirror. Spot was trying to persuade Alice to play "try and catch me"—a really boring game that he was partial to, which consisted of Alice making a dive for him and he jumping away backward, tail wagging and always just out of her grasp. (The only way that she sometimes won was to get him trapped in a corner and then they always ended up fighting, although however much Spot bit her, he never actually hurt her.)

It was William who'd suggested that they should come up to the room. He had a lot of questions for the Magician. But of course, when he was needed, Stephen Tyler very seldom appeared.

"I think," William said aloud, his voice making the others jump. "I think that what happened was—you fell out of the boat Alice and I dived in to rescue you."

"No, you didn't, William," Mary said indignantly. "You fell in—and what's more, you yelled as you did so."

"Well, anyway, that's not important, Mary. . . ."

"Trying to make yourself out a hero," Mary muttered.

"I was awfully glad you came, though," Alice admitted.

"And anyway—that doesn't explain you both going through that horrible tunnel thing and the otter experience . . ." Mary said.

"But, Mare," William insisted. "You say that the whole thing was over in a moment. There wasn't time for everything to happen that Alice and I think happened. And," he emphasized, stopping Mary from interrupting him, "Alice thought she went in Lutra—or whatever the otter was called—

and I thought I went in him . . . but we weren't in him together . . . and at the same time *you* saw him pulling the boat toward the shore. . . ."

"Maybe there were three otters," Alice chimed in.

"I don't think so," William said, shaking his head.

"So what *do* you think?" Mary asked.

William paused for a moment and stared at the floor.

"I think it's all in our minds," he said.

"Oh, terrific!" Mary exclaimed sardonically. "That's really cleared everything up for us, hasn't it?"

"All right. You explain it, Mary, if you're so brilliant," her brother snapped.

"I can't, can I? It didn't happen to me, did it?" Mary answered.

" 'Course, there's one way to find out. . . ." William said, deep in thought again.

"Find out what?" Alice asked.

"If Blackwater Sluice was imagined by us or if we really went there. . . ."

"How?" Mary asked.

"Well—if we ever go there again," William replied quietly, "Alice and I will recognize the place, won't we?"

Alice put an arm round Spot's shoulder and hugged him to her.

"You see—we were told that the magic is what

we believe in. You said that, didn't you Spot?" William asked.

But the dog merely yawned and put on his haughty look. He had a habit of doing that.

"I think," Alice said, looking at him, "that you put on that face when you don't know the answer."

"We wouldn't have known about Blackwater Sluice if Mr. Tyler hadn't just told us about it," William persisted with his working out.

"So?" Mary said, seeing where it was leading.

"He put the idea in our heads."

"But . . . when we found this room . . . we hadn't even met him then," Mary argued.

"But this room isn't magic. It's real. What happens here sometimes is magic. . . . Or is it all real, really. What did he mean by the energy field? What did that mean . . . ?"

They became silent again. William retired inside his head, trying to make sense of his jumbled thoughts. Alice stroked Spot, who lay back beside her and yawned and pretended to go to sleep. Mary walked back to the window and looked out at the gradually gathering dusk.

"We should go down," she said, more to herself than to the others. "It'll be dark soon."

Behind her, William suddenly looked up.

"What did you say?"

"It's late," Mary explained.

"No!" William cried, a look of dawning recognition spreading across his face. "Of course," he cried. "That's it!"

"What, Will?" Mary said, moving toward him. "What's it?"

"What you said about the dark," he said. "It's getting dark. . . . Oh, thank you, Mary! That's it!" he exclaimed, jumping up. "If it gets dark—what do we do?"

"Switch on the light," Alice replied facetiously—William was getting boring again. But this time he clapped his hands and hugged her.

"That's right, Alice. Electricity. That's it!" He was so excited that he was bouncing up and down.

"What is?" Mary demanded.

"The energy field—what Stephen Tyler was talking about. The energy . . . it must be something like electricity. How does electricity work?"

Mary frowned and shrugged. Alice shrugged and yawned.

"You just switch it on," she said.

"Then what happens?"

"Light comes on."

"How?"

Alice sighed. "I don't know," she said grumpily. "It's just one of those things that happens."

"Like magic . . ." William agreed quietly. "Except it isn't. It's scientific. Uncle Jack could tell us. It's something to do with a positive force and a negative force and a neutral force.

"Oh, that's really clear, William!" Mary sneered. "We all know about electricity now, don't we?"

"No. Of course we don't. It's really difficult. It's electrons and protons and all that stuff. . . ."

"All what stuff?" Alice protested, in a sudden bad temper. "You're getting as bad as the Magician. He's always using long words. . . . What's the point of long words? They just stop you understanding anything."

"And a magnet," William continued thoughtfully, having failed to hear a word his sister had said. "A magnet's the same sort of thing. . . . Magic and mysterious—and yet real. You know that piece of gold he had—on the chain? What was it he called it? His pendulum . . . It was picking up . . ." He searched for a word to describe what he was feeling for, "waves . . . energy . . . electricity. Oh, I don't know . . ." He sighed, covering his head with his arms, utterly defeated by the struggle in his mind. "If only he wouldn't go off when we need him. If only he'd help . . . Why is it all so difficult?" And he sounded so desperate that Mary crossed to him, wanting to comfort him.

"Will," she said gently. And, to her amazement, as he turned away from her, she saw that there were tears on his cheeks.

"Go away, Mary. I'm all right," he said, his voice breaking.

Mary sighed and, putting her hands in her

jeans pockets, she walked back toward the window. As she did so her fingers wrapped round an unfamiliar object in one of the pockets. She couldn't for a moment work out what it was. Then she remembered.

"Oh, William!" she cried. "He hasn't quite abandoned us. He left us this." And, as she spoke, she turned to the other two producing from her pocket the golden pendulum.

# 10

# Jasper Comes to Help

William and Alice stared at the piece of gold on the thin chain that Mary was holding out toward them.

"But what's it for?" Alice asked. "I mean, so it went round in a circle. So what?" Then she sighed. "It's very difficult being the youngest, you know," she said. "I haven't had time to know as much as you both do."

"I don't know what it's for either, Al," William told her. As he spoke he reached out to the piece of gold and then pulled back, as if he were afraid to touch it. "Maybe you shouldn't have taken it, Mary," he said.

"But it was lying there. Mr. Tyler must have dropped it. He'd be furious if he'd lost it. It's obviously important to him."

As she spoke, she picked at the chain with the thumb and forefinger of her other hand. Then, slowly, she lifted the pendulum and let it dangle in front of them.

"Why a pendulum, anyway?" she said, staring at it thoughtfully. "A pendulum's what you have in a grandfather clock." She swung the gold piece backward and forward. "Tick tock. Tick tock," she whispered.

"I'm sure we're not supposed to touch it," William said, moving away from her.

"Why are you afraid of it, Will?" Alice asked in a quiet voice.

"I'm not afraid," William said, without much conviction. "It's just . . . Well, it belongs to the Magician. It comes from another time. It's the first thing of his that's remained behind when he wasn't here himself. . . ."

"Apart from the mirror, of course," Mary said, walking across to the corner where the round, convex mirror was attached to the wall. As she drew closer to the mirror, the pendulum—which was still dangling in front of her—started to sway. "It's moving," she said.

"Only because you are, Mary," William told her, following her.

But as Mary reached a point just in front of the mirror, the piece of gold shot forward, as if it were being pulled. It took Mary so by surprise that the chain almost slipped free of her grasp. She had to nip her thumb and finger tightly together to stop it flying free.

"It's really strong now," she said.

Then, as they all continued to watch closely,

the gold piece started to describe a circle in the air between Mary and the mirror—like a propeller, it whizzed round and round.

"Are you making that happen?" Alice whispered.

'No," Mary cried. "Honestly I'm not." Her voice sounded anxious and she shied away from the whirling pendulum as though she were afraid it would hit her. "I don't like it, William. What's happening?"

"Don't know," William said, sounding equally alarmed.

"Spot," Alice called. "Help us! Tell us what to do."

The dog had risen from the floor and was standing watching the pendulum, with his head on one side and his tail between his legs.

"Morden!" he growled.

"Where?" William cried.

"Through the mirror," the dog growled again. Then, barking loudly, he sprang at the mirror, jumping up as if trying to reach it, snarling and biting. The hairs on the back of his neck were standing up and he seemed angry and dangerous.

The strength of whatever it was that had been attracting the gold piece diminished at once. The whirling became weaker until finally the pendulum was hanging downward again from Mary's outstretched hand.

"How d'you know that was Morden?" William asked Spot.

But the dog ignored his question. He was energetically sniffing the floor in front of the mirror, his tail moving slowly, his nose flat on the floor. Suddenly the dog jumped, as if he'd been stung. He turned in midair, looking toward the window. Then, springing forward, he started to bark again.

"Morden! Morden! Morden!" he seemed to say.

"Where?" William cried, desperately scanning the shadowy corners of the room.

Alice and Mary hung back, and Alice slipped a hand into Mary's for reassurance.

"What is it, Spot? Please tell us," William pleaded. Now Spot had made for the window, and was standing up on his hind legs, trying to see over the high sill.

"Morden!" he barked again, a long, wailing, agitated sound.

Then he was silent—and in the pause that followed they all heard a crow squawking somewhere outside the room.

"What was that?" Alice hissed, ducking behind Mary and covering her eyes with her hands—a sign that now she was really scared.

"Bird!" Mary whispered.

"Crow!" William exclaimed and, as he spoke, he brushed a fly away from his face. It buzzed noisily, landed on the candle sconce in front of the open widow and sleeked its head with its two front legs.

"Is Morden in the crow, Spot?" Mary asked, stepping out of the corner toward him and William.

"Don't know," the dog answered. He was still standing on his hind legs, supporting himself against the sloping ceiling under the window with one front paw. The other was poised in an elegant fashion and, as he spoke, he looked back over his shoulder, sniffing the air of the room. His nose twitched, the hair on the back of his neck bristled again. Turning his body, Spot dropped down onto all fours once more and silently padded round the room, sniffing in the corners and going out onto the landing at the top of the spiral stairs.

"He's not still here, is he?" Alice whispered, her hands clamped over her eyes.

"Don't know," Spot growled, returning to the room.

"What is wrong, Spot?"

"Something bad," he muttered.

"Is it another spider?" Mary asked, searching in the fading light for a web.

Spot sat down in the middle of the room, yawned and scratched with a back leg behind his ear.

"Scent's too weak now," he told them, as a gust of perfumed breeze blew in from the world outside.

William, who had been silent, crossed and squatted on the floor in front of the dog.

"Spot . . ." he started, using his working-out voice. The dog yawned again and, having finished scratching, shook his head vigorously.

"You know when, sometimes, Alice is in you . . . or, when the Magician is in you . . ." William continued. Spot stared at him, his head moving slowly from side to side, as though he were listening carefully to the words. "Well," William continued, "what really happens? I mean—what does it feel like, to you?"

"Don't ask a dog," a voice hooted behind them and, with a flapping of wings, the owl sailed in over the sill and settled on the candle sconce. As his claws gripped the metal, the fly that had settled there buzzed away from him, up toward the apex of the roof, where it landed, upside down, and continued to watch the scene below through its single eye. The owl, distracted by this, watched the flight with more than a little interest. Then it hunched its shoulders, whistled loudly, and glared down at the children.

"A pupil is only as good as his or her teacher," Jasper continued. "If you have serious questions, don't waste them on the dog."

Alice put her arm round Spot and hugged him toward her. But he didn't seem unduly upset by the owl's remark. He yawned, licked Alice, and then slid down onto the floor, still half leaning against her, and gnawed at his haunch where he had an irritating tickle.

"Owls are all brain," he said in a contented voice. "You listen to the owl. He'll talk and talk . . . and send you off to sleep in no time," and he proceeded to fall asleep himself, with a contented sigh.

"What is it you want to know?" Jasper asked, looking at one of his talons closely and then sucking off a little piece of mouse flesh that he'd missed from a recent meal.

"What I really want to know," William said, his brow creased by a frown, "is . . . if Morden never comes here to our time—how does he get animals . . . well, the rat anyway . . . on his side and to do his work for him?"

The owl stared and blinked.

"The mind," he fluted, after a moment, "is much easier to move about than the body. He sends his mind. Because he isn't nearly as clever as the Magician, he hasn't found a way of sending his body yet. He projects his mind. . . ."

William sighed. It was another of those impossible answers.

"But," the owl added, "what he doesn't realize is that he is close—very close—to moving his body as well. All he has to do now . . ." Jasper continued, lowering his voice and looking over his shoulder out of the window, "is . . ." he hissed the word, turning his head once more and blinking at them. Then, with a sudden movement, he launched off his perch and soared up toward the raftered ceiling.

The fly was taken completely by surprise. Jasper snapped it up into his beak and swallowed it down.

"What happened?" Alice gasped.

"Fly," Jasper replied. And he returned to his perch. "What was I saying?"

"What Morden had to do in order to bring his body to our time," William prompted him.

"Oh yes!" the owl hooted. "That got his interest!"

"Whose?"

"Morden's of course!"

"Where?" William cried, beginning to lose his patience.

"The fly," Jasper told him in a weary voice.

"You mean, Morden was hiding in the fly?"

"No, William!" Jasper trilled irritably. "Only his mind."

"Like before," Mary gasped, remembering, "with the spider?"

"Precisely," the owl hooted. "Stupid man! You should never use the same trick twice."

"So now—you've just eaten Morden?" William demanded, trying so hard to work it all out.

"Of course I haven't," Jasper whistled.

"But . . ."

"I have merely blocked his attention. I keep telling you . . ."

"So what will have happened to Morden?"

"Nothing!" the owl cried. "Except that he won't

now be hearing our conversation; he won't now be witnessing our time."

"But—when the Magician was inside the badger at Blackscar Quarry and was attacked by Fang," William insisted, "his arm was hurt—it's still bad in fact, months later."

"Because the Master has managed to travel his body, not only his imagination . . . his attention . . . The Master brings his entire self . . . sometimes . . ." The owl shrugged and looked wide-eyed and thoughtful for a moment. "At other times, of course, only his mind is here."

"Like now?" Mary asked, in a whisper.

Jasper looked at her and blinked.

"Oh, I don't understand!" William groaned. "It's all too difficult for me."

"That's because you concern yourself with the wrong questions . . . you're trying to understand all the wrong things, William," the owl said. "But, I'll give you the answers, if that's what you want. Listen. Don't try to work things out. Just . . . Listen."

The word crackled on the air and was followed by a long silence. Jasper stared at William with such piercing eyes that he seemed to be trying to see right into his head.

"Now," he whispered at last, "just listen to me, William. All right?"

William nodded and swallowed nervously. He wasn't at all sure what was being asked of him.

After all, he was listening. He wasn't interrupting what was being said. He wasn't talking instead. What else was he supposed to do? . . . Then he realized that the owl was already speaking and that so far he hadn't heard a word that was being said, so he tried to stop thinking and to attend.

". . . Magician's assistant has discovered that he can allow his mind to travel across time in certain creatures," Jasper was explaining in a slow voice. "He doesn't come himself . . . but his thoughts, his awareness, can travel . . . As the mind travels in dreams. Or in the imagination. When you imagine being in a different place—you are almost there, aren't you? You smell and sense the new place and, for a time, you become oblivious of where you are. . . . You understand?" The owl shifted his feet on the candle sconce and rotated his head, thoughtfully. "The fly existed in your time," he continued, "and also then, in Morden's."

"The same fly?" William demanded.

"Of course not—and yet, perhaps . . . Yes—why not? There are an awful lot of flies—silly creatures!" Jasper shivered "Not only flies, of course. The owl too is common to both times . . . and the fox . . . the badger . . . the blackbird . . . otter . . . fish . . . Most of us exist in both times." Then he stared at them coldly. "Although," he added, "in this age, some of us are becoming scarce, not to say lonely," and he shivered again and trilled. "Yes, I have to say that my family is not as abun-

dant now as it used to be. And that would make a
difference. For example—the Magician would
not now choose to travel here in a wolf—because,
sadly, the wolf has gone from these woods; or a
bear—because there are no bears. . . ."

Alice yawned and cuddled closer to Spot.
Jasper's fluting voice was making her sleepy. She
placed her head on the dog's gently breathing
body and closed her eyes.

"But," Mary said, "there are human beings in
the Magician's time—and human beings now.
Why doesn't he come in one of us?"

"Doesn't he?" the owl whispered.

Mary frowned.

"Sometimes I sort of . . . think his voice," she
admitted.

"Or do you hear his ideas. . . ?"

"Well, yes—I suppose that's it," Mary said with
a shrug, not quite sure that she saw the difference.

"Dear Mary," Jasper said kindly. "You have a
natural ability not to dwell on problems. . . ."

"So . . ." William cut in, not wanting the subject
to change before he'd at least tried to understand, "what you're saying is that it *is* all in the
mind?"

"Everything is in the mind, yes. Everything you
see, everything you hear, everything you touch,
smell, taste . . . All interpreted through the mind.
But it's more than that, William. Your mind and

Mary's mind are now linked, as you both join in this discussion. . . ."

"But Mary might be thinking quite different things from me," William observed. "We may be hearing the same words and yet thinking totally different things about them."

"Precisely," the owl hooted excitedly. "That is why the essential step on the journey is the stilling of the mind. Just as in making gold you must first hold still the mercury, so with true alchemy the mind must be silent before realization can begin." The bird raised a claw, stopping William from interrupting him. "Listen to me, boy!" it hooted severely. "If you and Mary were now free of your own individual thoughts . . . If you were both able to listen to me entirely, without any disturbance at all in each of your minds . . . What would happen?"

The children shook their heads. They didn't know what answer was expected of them.

"Would you not be linked. . . ? Joined. . . ? United. . . ?"

"It would be like when I go in Spot," Alice said, in a sleepy voice. "That's all that happens, really. I see through him, hear through him, and all that. . . ."

"Yes," the owl agreed, "and at the same time, we are seeing and hearing, through each of you. The mind, William. The mind. When it is still and silent and empty of all your thinking . . . Then it is free to go anywhere."

"But," William cried, "how do we get the mind to become still?"

"Just by giving up," Jasper said, "by stopping asking questions, by not trying to think . . . by allowing ideas to come and go without immediately pouncing on them and worrying them to death. . . ."

"Oh, William!" Mary exclaimed. "I can't see that ever happening for you."

"I'm starving for a mouse," Jasper said, his voice changing as he looked over his shoulder at the gathering night outside the window. "Any of you want to go hunting?"

"No, thank you," Mary replied quickly. She'd been hunting with Jasper once before. The memory still haunted her.

Jasper stared at her and blinked.

"You mortals are strange creatures. You eat all manner of rubbish and scoff at a nice little mouse. I'm off. All this talking has made me feel peckish!"

# 11

# The Public Meeting

The following evening a meeting was held to discuss the planning application for the development at Goldenwater. The hall where it was to take place was already crowded when the party from Golden House arrived. The audience was made up, for the most part, of people they didn't recognize, but Mary picked out Dan sitting near the front. Mr. Jenkins, the farmer from the Moor Road, was there with his wife and gave them a wave and Miss Prewett, the librarian at the local museum, actually squeezed out of her row and came to stand beside them at the back.

"Oh, I am so glad you came, Mr. Brown," she whispered to Jack. "This concerns you as much as anyone. It's an outrage, you know. Have you seen the plans?" she asked, handing him a folder of papers. "Look at the expense they've gone to already—preparing all this. They mean business, I'm afraid, Mr. Brown . . . it is Brown, isn't it?"

"Green," Jack corrected her, in the narrow gap she left between two sentences.

"Green, of course! How stupid of me. Now, what was I saying? Oh yes, if they've already forked out this much money on presentation—they're not going to give up the fight in a hurry. . . ."

Miss Prewett would have continued to talk all night, but three people now climbed up onto the small stage at the end of the hall and one of them, a woman, was trying to silence all the chattering. Jack drew Miss Prewett's attention to this fact and she whispered:

"That's Mrs. Sutcliffe—our local M.P. I don't trust her one little bit. She has absolutely no interest in history. Never trust a person who doesn't like history!"

Mrs. Sutcliffe was a short, fat woman with very black hair and bright red lips. She was wearing a blue summer dress that was too tight for her and carried a handbag hanging over one arm. She started the meeting by introducing "the two other members of the panel who have come here tonight to tell us all the exciting plans they have for our lovely area. On my left is Mr. Martin Marsh, who I'm sure many of you will recognize. Mr. Marsh is, of course, a much respected local solicitor, who has lived in the town most of his life. And on my right is Mr. Charles Crawden, son of Sir Henry Crawden, who is, I need hardly tell any of you, the owner of much of the forest land around here. The Crawdens are a fine old local family and are themselves part of our heritage and our history. I think I'm right in saying that there have been members of the Crawden family living in these parts since the first Elizabeth was on the throne. So that means they go back a good few years!"

Miss Prewett nudged Jack and raised her eyebrows as much as to say "you see what I mean?"

Martin Marsh now rose to address the meeting, producing from his briefcase a set of notes on which his speech was written. A thin man, with thin hair and even thinner lips, Martin Marsh wore a permanently mournful expression—"like death warmed up" was how Meg described him, which made Alice giggle. He was dressed in a dark, pinstripe suit and an old school tie. It was difficult to guess how old he was because he had the air of someone who had always looked middle-aged.

He first thanked Mrs. Sutcliffe for "giving up her valuable time to come here tonight." Then he went on to explain that Playco UK was a new company and that they were all very lucky that Charles Crawden, one of its directors, was a local man, otherwise "the potential of the Goldenwater site could have been totally overlooked."

The other man on the stage beamed and smiled and nodded at this mention. Charles

Crawden had a shiny face with a lot of tight, light brown curls above it. Mary thought he looked like an overgrown baby, with his plump body encased in a brown tweed jacket and plus-fours. He leaned his elbows on the table in front of him and rested his several chins on his pudgy pink fingers, apparently listening with rapt attention to all that was being said.

"Obviously," Martin Marsh continued, referring to his notes as he spoke, "any development in this area will be welcomed by us all; not only because it will bring much needed job opportunities but also because it may help to save a once-thriving community from stagnation and ultimate death." There was a great deal of clapping from the audience at this, which seemed to encourage Mr. Marsh. "For any business to survive in the present economic climate it is necessary for the directors and the workforce to pull together. We here in this room are both the directors and the workforce and this," he stretched his arms out as he spoke, "our glorious countryside, is the family business. The picture is far from reassuring. Farming is in decline, the Forestry Commission has had to cut back on expenditure, industry has deserted us, local mining is a thing of the past, and the small businesses of the town are closing down one by one due to lack of patronage. Is it any wonder that we feel we belong to a forgotten corner of the British Isles? Well, so be it. If

Whitehall won't help us—we must set to and help ourselves."

More clapping welcomed this statement, during which Phoebe turned to Jack, shaking her head:

"How is destroying the Goldenwater supposed to help?" she whispered.

"Idiotic man!" Jack said aloud, making one or two of the people near to him look round.

"It must be clear to us all," Martin Marsh's voice droned on, after he'd taken a sip of water from the glass in front of him, "that our real asset is our scenic and historic heritage. But this must be made to pay. We cannot live on our past. We have to make our past into our future. For this reason alone, I welcome Playco UK and its scheme wholeheartedly and pledge them my support. My reasons must be obvious, not only for the short term, but also in the long term. We are speaking here tonight about the future; the future for our children and our children's children." He paused, dramatically, allowing a scatter of applause. "Playco-Gold—the proposed name of the Goldenwater development—will put us not only firmly on the map of England, but of Europe and the entire civilized world. We live in the age of the tourist. I can see a time, in the not too distant future, when Americans and Japanese will be rubbing shoulders in our market square, their plastic cards at the ready! Now, thanks to Playco, the spenders will be coming to us. Like apples ripe for picking—the harvest will be ours!"

Martin Marsh returned to his seat and Mrs. Sutcliffe rose again. She thanked him for opening the debate so stirringly. Then she turned to face the audience.

"Our reason for being here tonight is our natural concern for our community. There may be some of you who will be opposed to what Playco UK proposes. But perhaps now Mr. Crawden could be prevailed upon to answer any questions that might arise? Mr. Crawden?"

"I would be delighted," Charles Crawden replied. His voice was silky smooth and he smiled radiantly at the audience, without rising from his seat. "Not that I'm an expert on all matters, of course. . . ."

There was an awkward pause, while he looked round the hall, waiting for someone to speak.

"Don't be shy. I'm sure someone must have a question."

A woman halfway down the hall rose to her feet.

"Can you tell us," she said, in a nervous voice, "will there be a hotel in the development?"

"It's all in this pamphlet," Charles Crawden replied, holding up a copy of the prospectus that Miss Prewett had handed to Jack. "The details are quite complicated. But yes, there will be a large hotel up at Goldenwater. There will also be holiday chalets and a Wildlife Lodge has also now been incorporated into the scheme, where guests will be able to observe the nocturnal activities of the large badger sett that is situated up there."

Meg glanced at William and whispered:

"They didn't waste much time, did they, dear? They didn't know about the badgers till I told them."

"But in that case," the woman who had asked the question continued, her voice getting strong, "isn't there a possibility that this scheme, far from helping local businesses, will take custom away from them?"

"Are you in business yourself?" Charles Crawden asked, his smile beginning to set on his face.

"Yes," the woman replied. "I run a registered boardinghouse."

"Then I'm sure that you won't suffer from a little competition?" Charles Crawden said, his voice becoming crisper. "If you run a good boarding-house," he said the words as though they were somehow distasteful to him, "you will no doubt keep your regular patrons. Playco-Gold can only increase your guests' enjoyment and add to their holiday experience. At the very least it will give them somewhere else to visit. It will add an extra dimension to their holiday."

"My guests are not the sort of people who go to funfairs. They are mainly walkers. They come here to enjoy the freedom of the forest. . . ."

"Yes, that, of course, is another point that I

think I should raise," Charles Crawden said, cutting across her speech. "My father, as the owner of the Goldenwater estate, has been extremely patient with trespassers in the past. But the land is privately owned and, as such, people are only permitted there through the goodwill of my family."

"That's absolute nonsense," an elderly man said, getting up from his seat and introducing himself as though he were used to public meetings. "Colonel Dearing, Ramblers' Association. The whole of the forest area is covered with a network of bridleways and footpaths. The public have every right to be there."

Charles Crawden shrugged and beamed.

"Obviously I don't have all the facts at my fingertips, Colonel. But I think you'll find that the lake itself should not be used. My family have fished it in the past and my son has every intention of doing so this summer. . . ."

"Oh, that's odd, isn't it?" Colonel Dearing said sarcastically. "The Crawden family haven't been near the place for forty years and now, suddenly, your son wants to go fishing there?"

"There is no law, so far as I am aware, Colonel," Charles Crawden replied, still smiling but with a cold edge to his voice, "that states when a man should and should not inhabit his estate. Unless of course you subscribe to squatter's rights?"

"No, of course I don't. If you don't want people to fish there, you should put up a notice."

"And how does your son purpose to get to his fishing lake?" Mr. Jenkins, Jack and Phoebe's neighbor, asked, rising to his feet.

"And you are . . . ?" Crawden asked, his eyes narrowing and the smile now so stuck to his face it looked as if it would crack.

"Jenkins, local farmer. From the Moor Road. Your lot have already been in touch with me. I own some of the land you want."

"Ah, yes. Now I recall. Well, Mr. Jenkins, as the last speaker so ably pointed out, there are public rights of way. . . ."

"Footpaths, yes. But not roadways. What about your future customers? Are you expecting them to walk from the Moor Road to this holiday camp you're going to build?" Mr. Jenkins said. "You can study any ordinance survey, you'll find no roads running across my land. The only track my side of Goldenwater leads to Four Fields. I'm right about that, aren't I, Miss Lewis?"

"Yes," Meg replied shyly. "When my grandfather sold the estate to the Crawden family it was all private land. He kept back Four Fields and made the cart track through the forest at that time."

"There is, I believe, vehicular access to the forestry land beyond your smallholding, Miss Lewis?" Martin Marsh said, referring to a map that he had produced from his briefcase.

"There is a track, yes. But not as far as Goldenwater."

"These are all matters that will have to be looked into and ironed out," Mr. Marsh said, folding the map once more.

"Are there any other questions?" Mrs. Sutcliffe asked, as though she were anxious to change the subject.

"Yes, I have one," Miss Prewett said, making all eyes turn toward where the Golden House party were standing.

"Yes, Miss Prewett?" Mrs. Sutcliffe said. Then turning to Charles Crawden she said in an audible whisper, "This is the local historian I was telling you about, Charles."

"Ah yes!" Crawden said, turning and beaming in the direction of Miss Prewett. "Fire away."

"Do you have proof that your family actually owns the land?" Miss Prewett asked in a clear voice.

Her question caused a ripple of interest to stir through the assembled audience. Charles Crawden was obviously so nonplussed by the question that he turned and leaned across Mrs. Sutcliffe to consult with his solicitor. Martin Marsh, meanwhile, was riffling through the contents of his briefcase.

"What an extraordinary question," he muttered. "I haven't actually got the deeds on me. But, yes, of course the land belongs to the Crawden family."

"Why do you ask, Miss Prewett?" Charles Crawden inquired.

"Casual interest, Mr. Crawden," she replied. "I am a historian, you see. These things are an abiding fascination. One so often finds, in my line of work, that assumptions have been made and that, as the years have passed, those assumptions have become accepted as fact."

"Well, I assure you that, in this case, the facts are the facts. Goldenwater is on Crawden land. Who else could it possibly belong to?"

Mr. Crawden was asking a rhetorical question and turned away, not expecting an answer.

"Well," Miss Prewett replied, her voice ringing out, "if the land was not sold with Golden House to your family, then it would still belong to the Golden House estate—as it has done ever since it was purchased from the Crown Estates, during the last year of the reign of Edward the Sixth. The land had originally belonged to the Abbey of Llangarren—which was dissolved in 1539 . . ."

"Thank you, Miss Prewett," Mrs. Sutcliffe cut in. "But we are not here for one of your endless history lessons. . . ."

Her remark received some good-humored laughter from the hall, but it did nothing to stop Miss Prewett, who was now on her favorite topic and seemed unaware of the interruption.

"The details of this transaction," she continued, "are in the museum library. The Quiet House, as it was known, in Gelden Valley had already fallen into disrepair long before the purchaser, Stephen Tyler, took possession in 1552. . . ."

To hear Stephen Tyler's name mentioned was a shock for the three children. But it also had the most spectacular effect on Charles Crawden. He swung round, rising up out of his chair, and faced Miss Prewett. His face changed from baby-pink to a strong scarlet and he was not smiling anymore.

"Stephen Tyler?" he roared. "What has the legend of a magician got to do with the twentieth century? Please don't waste my time with red herrings, woman! The Crawden family own Goldenwater and we intend to develop it. That is the end of the matter."

There was a moment of stunned silence and then a lot of voices started speaking at once. Martin Marsh closed his eyes and covered his face with his hands. Mrs. Sutcliffe tried to regain order and Crawden sat down, looking flushed and flummoxed and obviously aware of what a foolish thing he had done with his outburst.

Mrs. Sutcliffe seemed incapable of controlling the audience now. After a hurried conversation with her colleagues on the platform and a feeble attempt to call for order, she declared the meeting closed, and the three speakers left the stage and hurried out of the hall through a door in the back wall.

As Jack drove Miss Prewett back to her home

he asked her what had prompted her question about ownership.

"Just a hunch, Mr. Brown," she replied. "Oh, what a pity your grandfather wasn't still with us, Miss Lewis . . . you see, I remember your name," she said, almost embracing Meg in her enthusiasm, "because you're part of our history. If only we could go back in time." The children glanced at each other, but remained silent. "I have a feeling that the only thing the Crawdens bought from your family was the house," Miss Prewett continued, without seeming to pause for breath. "It's all in that book. The one your grandfather wrote. I must look it up again. I'm sure there's something in it about the estate. But you, Mr. . . . oh, what is your name?"

"Why don't you call me Jack?" he asked, with a laugh.

"Because I'd probably end up calling you Tom! That's why!" Miss Prewett replied. "Here we are!" she cried, as Jack nearly missed her cottage gate. Climbing out of the Land-Rover, she thanked them for the lift and then called, "You should check your deeds, as well, Mr. . . ."

"Green!" the children all called in unison.

"Yes, quite!" Miss Prewett said. "That's precisely what I was going to say. Good night to you all. I'll look up that book as soon as I have a minute. I just have a hunch . . ." and, still talking, she disappeared up the dark path to her front door.

# 12

# In the Tree House

The house deeds revealed nothing that they didn't already know. The original was with the mortgage company, but Jack had a photocopy. With them he was able to establish that Golden House, together with two acres of land, lying mainly to the east, west, and south of the property, had been transferred to his possession. There was no mention at all of the lake, nor of the land that surrounded it.

"Mind you," Jack explained, "these deeds only go back as far as nineteen hundred— when the Crawdens purchased the property from the Lewis family. I asked my solicitor about that, when we were buying the house. It's all quite legal—but not very satisfactory. There is a covering letter, explaining that new deeds had to be drawn up, as the previous ones had been destroyed in a house fire. . . . I think that's what it said. I haven't a copy here. My solicitor's got it."

"But in that case," Phoebe observed, "surely

the land could still belong to Meg. D'you see what I mean, Jack? If her grandfather had sold the Crawdens all the land—then surely it would appear in the deeds."

"Yes, you'd think so. But the Crawdens must have some proof of ownership. They'd never have gone this far without being sure of their case."

"I think Miss Prewett was just clutching at straws," Phoebe said glumly.

"We'll see what she turns up in that book," Jack told them. "I'll call in at the museum, next time I'm in town." Not for the first time they all wished that Golden House had a telephone. "We are supposed to be getting a line put through—but, as you know, we're in 'the forgotten corner of England'!" Jack said, quoting from Martin Marsh's speech, with a grin.

Then, as so often happens, the drama of the planning application faded into the background as other pressing events took over.

Dan and Arthur had been working on an out-house in the yard, when the roof caved in and they both narrowly escaped being crushed by the debris. It was nobody's fault, but Arthur made a lot of noise about compensation and danger money and Jack lost his temper. Arthur immediately went into a sulk and threatened to walk out and Jack was forced to apologize. He explained that Stephanie had developed a bad cough and that he'd been up all night and . . .

"It really wasn't my fault the roof caved in, Arthur."

"I'm not saying it was your fault, Mr. Green. I'm merely pointing out that I am flesh and blood, and you're very lucky that my flesh and blood isn't now squashed all over your backyard. That's what I'm saying."

"And I am apologizing," Jack said.

"Well, that's as maybe," Arthur grumbled. "But I can't spend your apology, can I? What good's your apology?"

"But—nothing happened to you, Arthur. . . !" Jack exclaimed, almost losing his temper again.

"Could have, Mr. Green, that's the point. Think what could have happened."

"Oh, come on, Arthur," Dan said quietly. "It was our fault. Mr. Green might just as well ask us to compensate him for knocking down his outhouse."

"Whose side are you on, lad?" Arthur had moaned. Then, with a lot more protesting, he'd gradually let the matter drop.

After a couple of days Phoebe decided to take Stephanie to the doctor. She and Jack had both been up most of each night nursing the baby. Consequently they were both lacking sleep and got bad-tempered with each other and with the children.

"I'll call in at the museum," Phoebe said at breakfast that morning, "and see what Miss Prewett has discovered."

She asked the children if they wanted to drive into the town with her, but they all agreed that it was too hot and that they'd prefer to go to the lake.

"D'you think it's still all right to go up to Goldenwater?" Mary asked.

"Yes," Jack said. "The worst that can happen is that you'll be told to leave. But, as was pointed out by that man from the Ramblers' Association, there are masses of rights of way up there."

So the children packed a simple picnic—it was too hot to carry more than some fruit and a packet of biscuits—and they set out soon after breakfast, accompanied by Spot, who panted a great deal in protest at the weather.

"It's all right for you," he'd told Alice. "You're not covered in fur, are you? Besides, panting cools me down."

They walked slowly up through the forest, climbing the steep path that led to the badger sett and the yew tree on the heights above Golden Valley. The sun bore down, blasting them with heat whenever they came out of the shade of the trees.

Up above in the cloudless sky a solitary black bird wheeled and turned.

"Could it be the Magician?" Alice called to the others, hopefully. "Like when he was in the kestrel? What d'you think, Mare?"

Mary shaded her eyes and looked up at the bird. Then she shrugged.

"Don't know. It's too far away to see what kind of bird it is."

"What difference would that make?" Alice said. "The Magician can be in anything."

"Well, he wouldn't be in a rat, would he? Or in a spider. Or in a fly. I mean, those are the kind of creatures that Morden uses."

"But this is a bird, Mary," Alice said, as though she was speaking to an imbecile.

"I know that, Alice," Mary snapped back, the heat making them both irritable. "But Morden might go in birds as well. Horrible ones like . . . vultures and . . ." She shrugged. "I don't know. There are some birds that frighten me, like rats do you."

"I like birds," Alice said, comfortably. "I've been in a blackbird and a swallow . . ."

"Shut up, Alice!" Mary warned.

". . . and we all went in the kestrel," Alice continued, beginning to smile. "You don't like birds, Mary, because you were scared when Jasper took you hunting at Christmas and you had to eat that mouse."

"Alice!" Mary said, her voice sounding dangerous.

"There was all blood everywhere, wasn't there?" Alice gloated, warming to her subject and enjoying making Mary squirm. "You could taste the blood, couldn't you? And it dribbled down your face and you had to lick it off your chin. . . ."

"I said shut up!" Mary said, really losing her temper. "I mean it, Alice. Shut up!"

Alice sighed and brushed her hair away from her face. It was too hot to fight. She stared up at the black dot of a bird again, wheeling up above them. "Spot. Is that Mr. Tyler up there?" she asked.

But the dog didn't even bother to look up.

"Stop talking!" he growled. "It's far too hot for that."

As they neared the yew tree Alice, who was trailing behind, called to the others to wait for her.

"I'm going up to the tree house, anyway," William said, speaking for the first time since they'd started out.

William had been silent a lot since their last visit to the room at the top of the chimney. Mary had once or twice challenged him to "stop working things out, William," which had made him irritable and proved that he was doing just that. Now, as he hurried ahead and disappeared into the cool depths of the yew branches, it seemed to Mary that he was trying to get away and to be on his own.

"Where's Will?" Alice asked, puffing into view, red-faced and exhausted, followed by Spot.

"Gone up to the tree house," Mary replied, sounding glum.

"Ugh!" Alice groaned, sinking to the ground

and lying flat on her back. "I hope they put an elevator in!"

"Who? Where?" Mary asked, without much interest.

"Those people—when they build the adventure park or whatever it is. I hope they put an elevator from the bottom of the valley up to here."

"You're impossible, Alice," Mary said. "You really don't care, do you?"

"Not now, I don't," Alice replied, closing her eyes. "It's too hot to care."

Spot, meanwhile, crawled toward the welcome shade of some bushes and lay down with his tongue hanging out and his eyes closed.

Up above them the black bird circled, it wings creaking on the torpid air.

"Listen," Mary said, looking up and again shading her eyes. "Can you hear its wings beating?"

Alice squinted at the sky. As she did so, for a moment, she saw a small girl, lying on the parched grass, looking up at her. Slowly turning on outstretched wings, she stared down at the girl beneath her. Then, as a single rough sound rose in her throat and broke as a croaking squawk, echoing and reverberating on the hot air, so she tilted her wings and stretched her head, pointing her sharp beak toward the earth.

"Oh!" Alice gasped, sitting up and automatically protecting her face with outstretched hands.

"What?" Mary asked.

Alice saw only the dusty treetops disappearing over the side of the valley in front of her and the hot, languid morning that surrounded them. Spot was asleep under the bush and Mary had turned to look at her with concern.

"Alice?" she said, sounding alarmed. "What happened?"

"I don't know," her sister replied in a small, fearful voice. Then she looked up at the sky again, seeing the bird retreating on a long upward spiral into the blue haze.

"Al?" Mary said, more gently. "Something happened to you. Are you all right?"

Alice looked at her sister. "I think so," she said. Then, kneeling, she searched the dense foliage of the tree, looking for any sign of the hidden room. "William," she called.

"What?" a voice above her asked.

"What are you doing?"

"Watching that bird," William replied.

"Did you see what happened?" she called, then she got up and ran through the branches to the dark interior of the yew.

It was cooler under the tree, but dry and airless. She found the first foothold and started to climb up the trunk. Reaching the iron ring, she grasped hold, stretched across to the platform and hauled herself up, panting and perspiring. Then she edged her way round the trunk, ducked under the spreading branch, and saw, ahead of her, light spilling out of the door of the tree house.

William was sitting on the solitary chair in front of an open window. The other windows had their shutters closed, but the light from this single opening was so dazzling that it blinded Alice and made her shield her eyes.

William was sitting as motionless as a statue, staring out. As Alice ran toward him, he seemed scarcely to be aware of her presence.

"William," she said breathlessly.

"What?" he asked.

"What are you doing?"

"I told you—watching that bird."

Alice stood back from him, watching. Then, putting her hands in the pockets of her shorts, she waited. William didn't move. He was so still that he seemed to be hardly breathing. His eyes stared, unblinkingly, into the light.

"You're up to something, aren't you?" Alice whispered at last.

"Alice!" William protested.

"What?" she nagged.

"Oh, you are impossible!" her brother snapped, turning to glare at her.

"Why? What?" Alice protested.

"I was trying to stop my mind," William explained.

"Stop it?" Alice exclaimed. "How?"

"I'm not quite sure. It's very difficult. Thoughts keep coming."

"Listen, Will," Alice whispered, interrupting him. "That bird. I think I saw through its eyes for a moment."

"Well, that's happened before, hasn't it?"

"Yes," she answered doubtfully. "Only this time it was like . . . like as if I was seeing myself . . . like a hunter would see me."

"What d'you mean?" William asked.

"Just that. It was like as if at any minute I'd swoop down and . . ." Alice shuddered and shook her head. "It wasn't nice, William."

William turned and looked out of the window again and, as he did so, the black bird that had been slowly flying round and round in the sky above the tree, suddenly swooped, making again the terrible squawking sound that Alice had felt in her own throat earlier.

"Watch out!" William yelled, ducking down. "It's coming for us."

As he finished speaking the window opening in front of them was filled by the body of the crow. Its wings beat fiercely and the sound of its deep, angry, croaking voice filled the small room as it alighted on the sill and stared at them through piercing eyes.

The bird was entirely black; as black as the blackest night. Even its bill was black; even its claws. It stared with such intensity that Alice could feel her legs beginning to shake. William, who had been sitting on the chair in front of her, had slid off as the bird flew at them and was now crouching on the floor. Slowly he looked up at the bird.

"Go away," he said. "Go away!"

The crow remained, staring deeply.

"Mr. Tyler?" Alice whispered hopefully.

"Squawk!" the bird screamed.

"Not Mr. Tyler," Alice whispered, shaking her head.

Very slowly William rose from the floor until he was standing immediately in front of the crow. Alice watched her brother as he took a long, deep, steadying breath. His eyes were as unblinking as the bird's eyes; his body as tense and as motionless.

"Go away!" William said, his voice shaking with emotion.

The bird glared silently, as if trying to stare William out. But William was equally strong. He seemed to Alice, as she watched, standing slightly to the side and behind him, to be so enclosed in stillness that he was like a stone.

"Go away!" he said again. And this time his voice was quiet and very calm. It had almost a conversational tone, as if he were having a long discussion with the bird of which Alice had only been able to hear those two words.

The bird blinked and, as it did so, it seemed to lose some of its power. William didn't move. For a moment longer the crow hesitated, darting its head from side to side, blinking and staring at him. Then, shrugging its wings and hooding its eyes, it turned away and launched itself off the sill, out into the hot morning light.

"It's gone," Alice whispered.

"Poor bird!" William said—his voice still sounding unfamiliar to Alice; distant and calm and strong.

"It was a horrible bird," Alice said. "I think it wanted to eat me."

"Yes," her brother said, quietly. "I think it probably did." Then, turning his back on the light, he suddenly shivered.

"Are you all right?" Mary asked, stepping into the room from the platform outside the door.

"I didn't know you were there," William said, sounding now, not only like himself once more, but also a little bit afraid.

"I was watching. I didn't dare come in," Mary explained. "It was Morden, wasn't it?"

"I think so," William said, quietly. "Not exactly in person, you know—but like Jasper told us . . . Morden was filling the bird's mind. I couldn't get in. . . ."

"But you did," Mary said. "You sent the bird away."

William shook his head and frowned.

"The bird went of its own accord—once Morden had left its mind."

"And did you make Morden leave, Will?" Alice asked, not at all sure what had really been going on.

"I don't know," William replied with a shrug. His voice sounded tired now. "I didn't really do anything. I just tried not to think. Tried to be still and empty. No. I didn't even really try. I just did nothing."

"Well," Mary said, looking at him thoughtfully, "whatever you did or didn't do—it seemed to work."

"How d'you mean—work?" he asked.

"The bird obeyed you," she told him. "It did what you told it to do. It went away."

"I'm glad," Alice said. "It was a horrible bird."

"No," William said, losing his temper. "It wasn't horrible itself. It was being made to be horrible. But why? Why does Morden hate us so? Why?"

"There you go again," Mary said, glad to be able to criticize him. "Asking questions!" And she turned and led the way out of the tree house.

# 13

# Crow

The heat shimmered over the lake, crinkling the view. The water seemed to ripple up into the air and the reflection on the surface had no beginning and no end. William sat, cross-legged, on the pebble strand and stared silently at the moving light glittering and dancing in front of him.

Mary was lying on the parched grass behind him, soaking up the sun, and Alice and Spot were paddling along the edge of the lake, not far away.

For a long time nobody had spoken and the only sounds had been the distant lazy singing of a bird and the occasional plop as a fish jumped for a fly.

Then Mary suddenly sat up, saying, "I wonder what happened to the boat," and shading her eyes, she searched the shoreline along beyond where Alice was now bending down, watching some tiny fish swimming round her legs beneath the water.

"Alice," Mary called.

"What?" she yelled, without turning around.

"You can't see the boat, can you?"

"What boat?"

"The rowing boat. The one we went in the other day," Mary said irritably. Alice had a habit of being deliberately obtuse, sometimes.

"Can't see it," she called, looking along the shore in front of her and shaking her head. "It's probably hidden somewhere."

"But who would have hidden it? We left it over there on the shore where we were picnicking," Mary said.

"Don't know," Alice replied, sounding far from interested. She looked up, shading her eyes, and slowly moved her head, scanning the whole lake and the high dome of milk-blue sky above it.

The black crow sailed on a thermal of warm air, looking down.

"That bird's still there," she called nervously.

Mary squinted up into the dazzling light.

"I know," she said. Then she turned her attention to William, sitting in front of her, as still as a rock.

"William—did you hear?" she asked. "That crow's watching us."

William remained silent.

"William," Mary repeated. "That bird's flying overhead still. . . ."

"Oh, shut up Mary! Please," William begged her.

"Why? What are you doing?"

"Trying to stop thinking," William replied.

"How?"

"By not listening to you, for one thing, and by trying to stop any thoughts from coming into my head—which is very difficult, with you nagging all the time."

"Boring!" Mary muttered, lying back on the ground. "If that bird attacks me, it will be entirely your fault!" Then, closing her eyes, she allowed her mind to slide once more toward that delicious state, on the edge of sleep, where sound and dreams merge.

In her mind she saw a picture of William and herself dipping the oars in and out of the water as they rowed Stephen Tyler and Alice slowly across the lake. She saw Stephen Tyler swing the small tiller round, so that they were crossing the imaginary line down the center of the lake. Still in her half-dreaming mind she saw, as if from the boat, the distant edge of the lake and the standing stone, with the yew tree behind it and, beyond, far across the unseen space that contained Golden Valley, the V in the trees that marked the continuation of the mysterious, invisible line toward the east.

Mary sighed contentedly and stretched, enjoying the warm sun on her body. Then, gradually at first, but soon growing in intensity, she began to hear the sound of running water. It was so real that it didn't seem to belong to a dream at all. As she sank deeper into sleep, the sound of this tumbling, boiling, bubbling water, filled and deluged her mind.

"Goldenspring," a voice whispered. "Meet me at Goldenspring."

"Oh!" Mary exclaimed, waking, sitting up and looking round at the same moment. There was no one there, of course, and yet the voice had sounded real enough.

"Dreaming!" Mary said, and she was about to lie down again when she noticed a spider weaving a web between two stiff stalks of rush grass beside her.

She turned and lay on her stomach, resting her chin on her hands, and watched the tiny insect as it busily knitted the gossamer threads with its legs. It worked with great precision, all its energy and concentration directed on the task. At one moment it fell, seemingly without any support, and then started to climb up the air again as it returned, supported on an invisible strand of its own making.

"Go to Goldenspring," the voice whispered again and, as she heard it, the spider stopped working for a moment and looked at her.

"Mr. Tyler?" Mary whispered excitedly.

"Where?" William said, turning round and seeing his sister, lying on her stomach, gazing with rapt attention at a blade of grass.

Mary didn't answer him. She seemed scarcely to have even heard him.

"Mary?" William said, crawling toward her and pushing straight through the rushy grass where the spider had been making its web.

"Oh, William!" Mary cried.

"Now what?" he asked, exasperated.

"The spider. You've broken its web.

"Is that all? I thought you'd seen Stephen Tyler."

"Maybe I did," she said, after a moment ". . . in a way." Then she frowned. "Except—the funny thing is—he seems to be everywhere, doesn't he? I mean, it isn't so much that we see him as that all the creatures seem to be part of him." She scratched her head. "It is very confusing—and I hate spiders usually. . . .

"You know what you were saying about that boat . . ." William said.

"What about it?" Mary asked, searching for signs of the spider.

". . . I think he brought it from the past—Mr. Tyler, I mean . . ." Then another thought occurred to him. "Hey, Mare!" he said. "Have you still got his pendulum thing?"

"Of course I have," Mary said, rising and crossing toward him, producing the gold nugget on the chain from her jeans pocket.

"Can I hold it?" William asked her.

"Yes," his sister replied with a shrug. "It isn't mine, you know. I just happened to find it."

William held the pendulum by its golden chain. It swung slowly backward and forward then gradually became still. William stared at it thoughtfully.

"Nothing's happening," he said but then, almost before he'd finished speaking, everything started to happen very fast.

They saw Alice running along the side of the lake toward them, waving her arms to attract their attention. Distracted for an instant, William took his eyes off the pendulum. As he did so, it started to rotate, going so fast that it all but disappeared. The crow, which had been circling slowly above them, dropped out of the sky, making straight for William's outstretched hand.

"William!" Mary shrieked and, as she did so, she grabbed hold of her brother and pulled him toward her.

With a terrible squawk, the crow flew at William and Mary then, beating its wings to slow its flight, it hovered for a moment in front of them and pecked the pendulum out of William's still outstretched hand. They felt the air fanned into a cold draft as the bird beat its wings once more, making for the sky.

William threw himself at the bird, reaching out with both his hands, grabbing at the flapping wings. He almost managed to catch it, but when he fell forward onto the ground he was holding only a single tail feather in his clenched fist.

"It's taken the pendulum," he gasped, looking up to where the crow was now flying away from them, the glittering gold chain dangling from its beak.

"William! Mary!" Alice gasped breathlessly, as she raced toward them, followed by Spot. "There are men coming through the trees over there. I don't think they saw me."

"It's all right," Mary said, catching Alice's agitation, "I mean, we're not doing anything wrong. We've a right to be here. . . ."

"No, you don't understand," Alice hissed. "It's them. . . . The men from the meeting."

William was still watching the crow. It flew toward the standing stone and landed on top of it. Then it turned and glared at the three children, fixing them with its bright, black eyes. The golden nugget dangled from its beak and flashed in the sunlight.

William took in a long, slow breath of air. As he did so he straightened his back and shook his head. Then, just as the bird was stretching its wings to fly off, he glared at it again, with piercing, unblinking eyes.

The crow, taken by surprise, seemed unable to look away. It raised first one foot and then the other and flapped its wings. But William's eyes seemed to be holding it, as if by some invisible thread.

Still maintaining this look, William walked toward the standing stone. . . .

He saw the boy walking slowly toward him. He even recognized the boy as himself. At the same moment he knew that he had entered the crow's mind and was seeing through the crow's eyes. It seemed a most natural state of affairs.

A movement, just beyond the edge of his sight, made him look to the left. The color of the grass was suddenly brighter and more lush. The distant trees were heavy with summer leaf. The lake rippled, reflecting a cloudless sky. . . .

Standing below him on the grass was a young man. He was wearing an open-necked jerkin of a dull red color, baggy shorts, nipped in at the knees, and thin stockings that clung to his legs. His black hair reached almost to his shoulders. He had dark eyes beneath black brows and a very pale complexion.

"Give it to me, crow!" the man said and, as he did so, he reached out his hand and walked toward the stone on the top of which William was standing.

William bent forward and dropped the golden nugget on its chain from his beak onto the surface of the stone in front of him. Then, hunching his feathered shoulders, he stared down once more at the man.

"Give it to me!" the man repeated, holding out his hand and willing the bird to obey.

William felt his mind being filled with half-formed thoughts and ideas, each of them clamoring to be heard. The desire to give in to them was very strong—particularly for William who liked to be in control of what went on in his head. He sensed the thoughts tempting him to give them his attention. Each thought needed to be considered and each idea to be worked out. It was like being in a room with the door closed and hearing voices at a distance; not being able to distinguish the words being said, there was a strong desire to reach out mentally and try to listen. But he knew that if he did so he would lose his advantage. He had to keep his mind still and empty. He took in another deep breath and stared into the man's eyes.

"What's happening, crow?" the man asked, his voice trembling with intensity.

"Morden," William croaked. It was half a question and half a statement.

The man gasped and raised his hands in front of his face, as if warding off an attack.

"Morden," William said again.

"Who are you?" the man whispered.

"Why are you attacking us?" William asked.

Morden gasped and took a step backward.

"Why are you interfering with the Magician's work? Why won't you leave us alone? Why?" William demanded.

"You? You have come from that time?" Morden whispered. "I don't believe this. It is my mind playing tricks. It isn't possible for you to have traveled. You are ignorant children. This is some sort of trap. Now, crow," and as he said the word, so the man's voice grew shrill with indignation, "give me the pendulum!"

William stared at the man he called Morden. He felt no fear. He was in command.

"If you want it, come and get it," he croaked.

But the man was obviously not impressed by this implied threat. His thin lips curled into a smile and he threw back his head.

"Think we're clever, do we, little boy? Think we've learned the ancient secrets? You know no more about anything than that stone!"

"I agree," William said. "But I've only just started to learn. Just give me time."

"Oh, yes! You think you're so clever," Morden mocked him. "You think you're safe because you have the Master working for you. But what will happen when he goes, little boy? What then? You'll be lost without him. You'll be nothing."

"Why are you fighting us, Morden?" William said, ignoring the man's insinuation. "Why? What have we done to you?"

"Give me that pendulum!" Morden yelled, his voice shaking with anger.

"No," William said. "You're a bad, wicked person. You use rats to frighten us. You tried to stop Stephanie being born. When the badgers were being killed . . . you could have helped us, but you didn't. I expect you were even glad. You associate yourself with all that's horrible and cruel in the world. Now, when men are thinking of spoiling this place, you could be working with us and the Magician. Instead you let it happen . . . you want it to happen. Why? What's in it for you?"

Morden stared coldly up at the crow on top of the standing stone. His eyes were so penetrating that William felt himself being held by them. He could sense the other man's mind fighting for supremacy over his. A moment of panic seized him. He saw Morden take the advantage. William breathed again deeply, tensing his crow claws on the hard rock beneath him.

"Power?" William said at last. The word had come into his head, but he scarcely understood what it meant. "Is that what it means for you? Power?"

"Yes," Morden answered. "Power, little boy . . . and much more. Soon the Master will die. He's an old man. He's already beyond his time. When that happens, I must inherit all this. I've worked for it. Not only the estate, but also his magic and his knowledge. He has trained me himself. He is unable to stop it. I am his creation. When he dies, little boy, I will be the master here. I will be your magician. You will need me. I will show you all the wonders of the art. Together we will make gold. Not . . ." he raised a finger and wagged it ". . . not like the pathetic Lewis. This time we will get it right. You and I, little boy. Together, you in your

time and I in mine, we will be supreme. We will be
all-powerful. We will hold the secret that all men
crave. Riches and power in abundance. Gold." As
he said the word, he shivered with excitement.
"Gold, little boy. Unlimited gold. No man will be
our equal then. We will be invincible, you and I.
Now give me the pendulum!" And as he said the
last words, he jumped at the stone, trying to reach
up to where William was standing.

With a squawk of rage, William launched himself into the air and dived at Morden. His beak
closed over the skin on the back of the outstretched hand. Morden immediately pulled
away, with a cry of pain, and William saw blood
ooze from the wound that he'd inflicted.

"God's blood!" Morden yelled.

William flew at him again, his wings beating
and his beak and claws aiming at the man's
upturned face. Morden raised his arms above his
head, beating savagely, trying to ward off the
attack. William's claws sank into his shoulder and
he managed to nip one of Morden's ears. Then
he was knocked off balance and had to flap away,
out of the man's reach, before turning once more
into the attack.

"Crow!" Morden screamed. "Crow! Obey me!"

But William was in crow's mind and, for now,
crow was William's bird. He flew again at the man,
squawking savagely. Morden took a step back,
looking desperately over his shoulder, searching

for a place to hide. As he turned to run, William beat his wings and reached forward with his claws, winding them in Morden's flowing hair. With a piercing cry of rage and fear Morden knocked the bird away again. Then, abandoning the fight, he ran, arms flailing above his head, toward the shelter of the distant beech forest.

"Little boy!" he shouted. "I will be even with you. You have made Morden your enemy. The day will come when you will wish you had not been born."

"Squawk!" William replied.

"Little boy!" he heard a voice call again. "No point hiding, we know you're there!"

As William watched he saw the crow flying in pursuit of Morden . . . Then the beech trees toward which they were heading merged and changed into dark, dull firs. . . . The bright grass became parched and brown. . . . The heat was intense. . . .

"Come on, little boy, come out from there," he heard the voice say.

William walked out from his hiding place behind the standing stone and looked toward the lake. He was confronted by a strange group of people. Alice and Mary were there, with Spot beside them, his hackles up and growling quietly. They were standing between two men from the public meeting—the solicitor, Martin Marsh, and Charles Crawden with his pink, shiny face. In the middle of the group an ancient man, wrapped in a tartan rug—although it was such a hot summer day—sat in a wheelchair. He was glaring at William, leaning forward out of his chair on an ebony walking stick.

"Well, come on," he said. "Come here where I can see you!"

As if in a dream William walked toward them. He looked once again across the lake at the dark fir forest that so recently had been bright woodland.

"It's a dream," he thought.

Then he looked again at his sisters and the men. They didn't look real either. None of it seemed real.

"Which is the dream?" his mind whispered.

He knew, without any doubt, that, briefly, he had seen into Tudor England, four hundred years in the past. Now he was back in what he called the present. The transition between these two times, these two worlds, had been as smooth, as uncomplicated, as uneventful, as the blink of an eye.

"Maybe it's all a dream?" his mind questioned.

"Come here, boy," the old man said. "I want to look at you."

Up above, in the bright sky, a solitary crow wheeled and turned, squawking.

# 14

# Sír Henry Crawden

The man in the wheelchair stared at William.

"Go on then, cat got your tongue, boy? Name? Reason for being here? Bit of your history? Relationship to these two? Hurry up! I am a very old person. Time is precious to me."

William forced his mind back into the present. He was finding it as hard now to listen to the man's questions as, moments before, he had found it hard not to attend to the thoughts in his head. He glanced over his shoulder again, looking at the far side of the lake, reassuring himself that what he could see there was indeed fir forest and not beech wood. He swallowed. His heart was beating too fast and his mouth was strangely dry. It was almost like being afraid, this sensation he was experiencing, but without any panic. He was calm and frightened at the same time. He wanted, more than anything, to be alone with Mary and Alice so that he could tell them what had just happened. He wanted to shout out: "I've just seen through the crow's eyes— and what I saw was another age, another time. I've just managed, somehow, to travel back in time. Not me—but my mind. My mind has seen into the past." But now he had to focus instead on this old man in front of him, who seemed in a bad temper, and was staring at him with hostile eyes.

"Are you going to answer me, or are we going to have to wait here all day?" the man said.

William felt suddenly enraged by the man's behavior. How dare anybody, let alone a complete stranger, address him like that? He remembered how, when the crow had glared at him with just the same hostile eyes as this bad-tempered old man, he had forced his mind not to panic, not to be overawed.

William took a deep breath and straightened his back. Then, in a clear, calm voice he said:

"I'm William Constant. My sisters and I are staying with our uncle in Golden House. That's the big house down in the valley . . ." he explained, turning and pointing in the direction of Golden Valley.

"Yes, yes," the man interrupted him, testily. "I do know where Golden House is. So you are the brother of these two, are you?" he said, nodding his head in the direction of Mary and Alice. "Well, I, young man, am Sir Henry Crawden," he continued, glaring at William as though he wanted to frighten him, "the owner of the land on which you are now standing." Then he nodded again and waved a hand. "Wheel me round, Charles. I want to look at the view."

Charles Crawden stepped forward and taking hold of the wheelchair he pulled it round so that the old man now had his back to William and was facing the lake with the distant high ground and the wooded shore on either side.

"What do you think of my son's plans for this place, William?" he said at last.

"I think they're horrible," William replied without a moment's hesitation.

Sir Henry's head jerked round as he tried to see William, then he beckoned to him impatiently.

"Come where I can see you," he said.

William crossed and stood beside the wheelchair. Mary and Alice moved in to stand on either side of him.

"You don't want a funfair here?" the old man asked in a conversational tone.

"It isn't going to be just a 'funfair,' Father," Charles Crawden protested. "You've seen the plans. This will be an enormous undertaking."

Henry Crawden shrugged.

"So? It will be a big funfair, then." He looked silently at the view. Birds were singing in the trees toward Four Fields and the surface of the lake was as flat and as still as a mirror. "I haven't been back here since the summer of 1940," the old man said, quietly. "Back from Dunkirk—on a bit of leave, you know? I could walk then. The legs got it in '45." As he spoke, he rapped his thighs with clenched fists. "Very useful things, legs. Look after them if you can." He was silent for a moment, remembering. "Aunt Crawden was still alive then," he continued. "But batty, of course. I rather dreaded visiting her. She became increasingly odd after Uncle Crawden died. But it was always necessary to keep in with her. That was the summer of 1940—and it was the last time I saw her. She died in '45. I lost the legs and Aunt Crawden lost her life . . . practically on the same day! I remember thinking that she might have got the better end of the deal. But now I'm not so sure—to be batty would be worse, I think." He shrugged, looking at the children. "Life without legs is merely . . . limiting . . ." He shook his head, lost in a memory. Then, with a shrug, he leaned forward on his stick and said, over his shoulder, "So, Charles, paint the picture for us all."

"Picture?" his son asked, surprised.

"That's what you brought me here for, wasn't it? To sell me the idea?" the old man snapped. "Well, now's your chance. Sell it, to us all! Convince us that this isn't another of your crackpot schemes."

"Shouldn't we get rid of these children first, Father?" Charles Crawden asked.

"Don't underestimate them, Charles. Play your cards right and they may very well be your first paying customers!" the old man said.

"Very well then," the son said, sounding haughty, "if you insist." His voice shook on a note of new authority. It sounded as though he was reciting something learned by heart: as though he was giving a lecture. "The site we will be utilizing is all to the right of the lake. As you know the land to the left belongs to the Forestry Commission. Down on the shoreline we plan to create a waterfront lido, for small craft—speedboats, pedaloes, canoes, etc. This will be constructed of breeze block faced with local stone—as far as possible. There's a disused quarry nearby which we intend to utilize. The lido will resemble a Cornish fishing harbor scene. Behind it will be situated a central square with shops and stalls; a supermarket, cafés, restaurants . . . an amusement arcade . . . a fountain in the middle. Flower beds. Places for people to sit." He was getting quite carried away with the wonder of his vision. "It is here that our Medieval and Tudor Experiences will be held on certain days each week. Jousts and Tournaments and . . . all that sort of thing. There will always be something going on. It will be the hub of the fun." He glanced nervously at his father. "We intend to call it 'Crawden Plaza'—in honor of you, Father."

Sir Henry's face remained impassive. His son cleared his throat nervously.

"Martin, did you bring the plans to show Father?" he asked. But at once his father interrupted him, irritably.

"I have seen the plans, Charles."

His son cleared his throat again and his hands were trembling.

"Go on, tell me more!" the old man rapped. "Make it live for me."

"The Hotel Crawden will be situated behind and to the side of the plaza. Here there will be gardens and a maze. . . . All the ground on this side of the plaza will be taken up with chalets—for self-catering holidays. The adventure playground will be through the woods over there. We will also build a safari lodge-style hotel on the edge of the cliffs behind us. . . ." As he spoke, he turned his father's chair so that they were all looking up the gently rising ground to the standing stone and the yew tree beyond. "This is a comparatively new idea and we have no plans to show you as yet."

"Where will it be?" the old man asked.

"Where the yew tree is, Father."

"I see. The tree will come down?"

"No!" Alice exclaimed. "You can't chop down the tree."

"That position affords the finest view across the valley," Charles Crawden told her, "and is also best suited for the guests to watch the badger sett from the lodge balcony."

"Mmmh! Badgers! What else have you planned for your guests?"

As Charles Crawden continued to speak, he slowly wheeled the old man round once more so that he was viewing the lake.

"Pony trekking in the Welsh hills. Forest trails. A Wild West expedition—complete with bears!" he made it sound like an amusing joke. "A cinema . . . and yes, I must admit, for the children, a 'funfair' as you call it, Father. Possibly a zoo—but that will be in phase two. And, depending on how well we do on phase one, we are thinking of constructing a monorail through the woods so that guests who do not feel energetic can enjoy the forest experience from the comfort of a chair. . . ." He was beginning to sound desperate now, longing as he was for his father to show signs of some real enthusiasm. "There are plans afoot to exploit some of the mine shafts that lie below ground level. We could have ghost rides . . . a 'journey to the center of the earth,' that sort of thing. Young people enjoy being frightened! We intend that there shall be so much going on to amuse the guests that they will never be bored. We intend to give them value for money."

"Well, Charles," the old man said when his son had finished speaking. "We're most impressed. Aren't we, children? It all sounds most exciting. You seem to have thought of everything. And, yes, you are of course right, it is an 'enormous under-taking.' Now—what are the snags?"

"That really is family business, Father. We'll discuss all that in private, I think."

"Nonsense," the old man said, waving aside the idea of secrecy. "Access? Is that it?"

"Mmmh, yes," his son replied. "We have offered the woman good money. But I'm not sure she will go for it."

"How will I be able to persuade her?"

"She said she wanted to speak to you in person," Charles Crawden said.

"Who is this woman?" his father demanded.

"Funny old bird, bit of a loner. Not quite all there, I should say. What is her name, Martin?"

"Lewis," Martin Marsh replied.

As soon as he uttered the name, Henry Crawden gasped.

"Lewis?" he whispered.

"Yes, Sir Henry. Margaret Lewis. She owns the property called Four Fields that lies between your land and the Moor Road."

"Meg Lewis," the old man sighed. "She is still alive? I somehow thought . . ." Then he shook his head. "No. I will not see her. Wheel me back to the car. . . ."

"She asked for you, Father. You may be our only hope."

"I will not see her, Charles. Let that be the end of it. Get your access through the forestry land. The Commission won't object, I'm sure. . . ."

"So—you approve of the plans?"

"I will not see that woman," Henry Crawden said. "As far as the rest is concerned that's for you younger people to decide."

Across the old man's head, Charles Crawden and Martin Marsh exchanged a look of relief.

"Splendid, Father. I'll get Martin to draw up all the necessary documents."

"Documents?"

"It would be more simple, Sir Henry," the solicitor said in a smooth, wheedling voice, "if the land was made over to your son. . . ."

"Yes, yes, of course," Henry Crawden said, seeming hardly to be interested in the matter. "Do what you like with it."

"But—if you have any suggestions, Father, we would of course value your advice."

"There is one," the old man said. "Why not use the original family name. It would be more in keeping with the place. After all, our family have been here since fifteen-ninety-odd."

"The original name?" William asked, speaking for the first time since Charles Crawden had started to reveal his plans.

"Yes," the old man said. "One of our forebears was a bit of a rogue, I'm afraid. Got into trouble with the church and state! We, being a sensible family, changed our name. We didn't want any of

his muck sticking to us, did we? Oh, this was centuries ago. We've been called Crawden almost
since the day of his death. Well—if there's a rot-
ten apple in the barrel you toss it out, don't you?
Though, to tell the truth, I've always rather
enjoyed the idea of having a wizard on the family
tree."

"A wizard?" Alice exclaimed.

"That's what they said he was. He was
drummed out of the county. Mind you, by that
time James the First had come to the throne—
and there were plenty of rumors that he was a bit
of a wizard himself! Sorcery was in vogue! But not
in these parts. The locals got very hot under the
collar! Had the poor chap sentenced and then
executed."

"The Wizard was . . . executed?" William
gasped.

"Are you sure?" Mary asked him, trying to stop
her voice from shaking.

"Absolutely certain," Sir Henry replied cheerfully. "We Crawdens have always been a colorful
lot . . . Until recently, that is," he added, glaring at
his son. "Oh yes," he continued, "the Crawdens
are only here in these parts thanks to the wheel-
ings and dealings of our family wizard. Perhaps
that's why Uncle Crawden was so desperate to win
the house back." The old man shook his head.
"Perhaps he had a sense of family? Not that it
brought him any luck either . . . he went as potty

as his sister. Both of them right round the twist! You want to watch out, Charles! Maybe we Crawdens are destined never to be happy here in the Goldenvale."

"Superstitious nonsense!" Charles Crawden exclaimed.

"Oh, quite!" his father agreed. Then he leaned over toward William in a conspiratorial way. "My son enjoys the other great Crawden family characteristic—he has an insatiable desire for riches! If there's any money to be made . . . he'll be there, regardless of the danger!" Then he straightened up once more. "I've had enough now, Charles. Take me home. Goodbye, you children. Enjoy the lake while you can. Poor lake! Poor countryside! Soon this will all be a 'funfair!' " and, once again, he said the word with relish, as if he enjoyed taunting his son with it. "Well, get a move on, Charles," he snapped irritably, "push me back to the car!"

"Sir Henry," William called, hurrying after them.

"What now?" the old man asked.

"What was the name of the wizard?"

"Oh, didn't I say? Stupid of me. It was a name not unlike our own, really," the old man told him, "we didn't change it much. The wizard in our family was called Morden. Matthew Morden— God rest his soul!"

# 15

# The Entrance
# to the Tunnel

The children watched silently as the Crawdens and Martin Marsh disappeared through the trees, heading in the direction of the Forestry Commission land lying above Four Fields.

Spot, who had settled on the ground at Alice's feet while Charles Crawden had been describing his plans, sat up and scratched his neck below one ear. Alice crouched down beside him and put an arm round him. She felt depressed and couldn't explain why.

"Matthew Morden," William whispered. "They're related to Morden."

"At first I thought he was talking about Stephen Tyler when he mentioned a wizard. . . ." Mary exclaimed.

"And I did, Mare," Alice agreed.

William walked away from them, deep in thought. He was remembering the man in the red doublet and hose that he'd seen running toward the beech woods that had crowded down to the edge of the lake on their left where now only somber firs stood in stiff straight lines. He shook his head. It was all so confusing now that time had passed and the event was only a memory and no longer a clear experience. "It couldn't have happened," his mind told him. "It isn't possible. There must be some other, reasonable explanation. Think, William; think!" his mind whispered. "Work it out, William. You know you can. Make some sense out of it all. . . ."

"NO!" he shouted out loud, shaking his head from side to side and punching the fist of one hand into the palm of the other.

"What, Will?" Mary asked, running to him alarmed. "What's the matter?"

"Nothing!" her brother answered tersely. "There's nothing the matter." Then quietly and calmly, after taking a couple of deep, steadying breaths, he started to tell them what had happened when he had looked through the eyes of the crow.

Mary and Alice listened in silence and even Spot sat at his feet and cocked his head on one side, staring up at him. When he had finished recounting all that he'd seen up to the point where he'd emerged from behind the standing stone and been discovered by Sir Henry and the others, William shivered, as if he were cold. Then he clasped his arms round his body and stared moodily at the ground, waiting for his sisters to respond.

Alice frowned and sniffed, then she scratched her cheek, thinking deeply.

"You mean—you time-traveled? Like the Magician does?" Mary asked.

"No. I don't think so," William replied. "Not exactly."

"Whatever happened," Alice said, "we couldn't see you."

"Couldn't see me?" William asked, surprised.

"No," Alice told him.

"But . . . what happened to me?"

"You hid," his youngest sister replied.

"Hid?"

"Yes. I came running to tell you both that I'd seen those men coming, pushing the pram thing—and as I did . . . you ran behind the stone. He did, didn't he, Mary?"

"Yes," Mary agreed with a nod. "I thought it was rather a funny thing to do. I mean—I thought you were scared or something."

"Did you actually see me run?" William asked.

"Um . . . No," Mary said at last. "But you must have done—because one moment you were standing beside me and the next you weren't. I heard Alice calling, looked round, and when I looked back—you'd disappeared."

"Alice," William asked.

"What?"

"Did you see me run behind the stone?"

"No. I'd looked back over my shoulder, pointing out where the men were coming from. But that's what must have happened—because that's where you came from when old Sir Thingey called you."

"So, you neither of you saw me from the moment that I started seeing through the eyes of the crow," William continued thoughtfully.

"Oh William! We've all done that," Alice groaned.

"Yes, I know. But usually it happens by chance. I made it happen."

"All right," Mary said, grudgingly. "Maybe you think you did. So—did you also make yourself see back into the past?"

"No," William agreed with a sigh. "I don't know how that came about . . . except . . . Oh! Why is the Magician never here when we need him?"

"Of course!" Mary exclaimed. "The spider. I'd forgotten about the spider! We have to go to Goldenspring. He said he'd meet us there," and, as she spoke she started to hurry along the shore of the lake in the direction of the distant high ground.

Spot bounded away in front of her, barking, glad to be on the move.

The sound of falling water grew steadily closer. The earth underfoot became spongy and wet. Boulders jutted out of the turf and pools of water reflected the sky. The ground began to rise more steeply until they were scrambling up the side of a hill, through sparse trees and great clumps of gorse that scratched their bare legs and arms.

Eventually they reached the side of a fast-flowing stream. The water bubbled and slid over stones and through narrow channels as it careered down toward the lake. Above them now the sound of falling water was almost deafening.

"Higher up, I think!" William yelled, pointing.

Mary turned and led the way again, scrambling up the steep grass and, in places, having to crawl on all fours up an almost vertical cliff. Above them a ridge of rock blocked out the view. But when they had pulled themselves up and over this edge they found another summit waiting just ahead of them.

After half an hour of strenuous climbing they reached the top of yet another jagged cliff. In front of them now they discovered a solid wall of rock over which the stream fell in a roaring sheet of glittering water. The power of the falls was so strong that it caused gusts of cold wind to blow at them and a fine spray filled the air and soaked through their clothes to their skins.

"Goldenspring!" William said, having to shout in order to be heard above the din of the water.

"We can't go any further, I don't think," Mary called, scanning the cliff face for any sign of a path leading upward.

"So—where is he?" Alice asked. "You said Mr. Tyler would be here, Mary. Where is he?"

Mary shrugged.

"Don't know," she replied. "Maybe we have to wait. He definitely said to meet him at Golden-spring."

"If it was him," William said.

"I'm sure of it," Mary called. "Who else would it have been?"

"It could have been Morden," William observed.

"No!" Mary said, defiantly. "I know it was the Magician. I just know it was."

"Well, I'm not going to hang around," William called. "I'm getting soaked."

"Which way, then?" Alice yelled.

"Back down," William replied, making for the path up which they'd climbed.

"Come on, Spot!" Alice shouted, following her brother.

But Spot's barking made her stop and look round. The dog had followed some invisible track right up to the edge of the stream halfway up the sheer side of the waterfall and was now standing, with his back to them, his tail wagging, barking excitedly.

"What's up with him?" William asked, looking back.

"Come on, Spot!" Alice called.

But the dog ignored her command and continued to bark and to claw at the earth as if he had discovered something very important.

"I think he wants us!" Mary shouted, retracing her steps.

William and Alice followed and, as they grew closer, so William pulled ahead of the other two, frowning slightly as he climbed up the steep ground toward the waterfall.

"What is it, boy?" he asked, when he reached Spot. "What's the matter?"

Spot whined excitedly and jumped up and down, barking.

"Tell me, then!" William commanded. Then, when the dog continued to whimper and bark, he turned his back on him and stared at the waterfall.

At first all he could see was the solid sheet of falling water. Then he noticed a ledge of rock that projected from where they were standing and, clinging to the sheer cliff, disappeared from view behind the water.

"I say," he called to the others, "there's a sort of path here." And, as he spoke, he started to edge sideways along the ledge, with his back pressed against the cliff.

"Be careful, William!" Alice called. "If you fall in, you'll be swept all the way down to the lake."

Spot was now following William out along the ledge.

"Come on," Mary said, grabbing Alice's hand. "I don't want to be left behind."

As she spoke, William disappeared from view.

"Oh!" Alice squealed. "He's gone behind the waterfall!"

"Don't look down!" Mary told her, making Alice immediately do just that. For a moment she felt giddy and almost lost her footing, but Mary grabbed her hand again and held her back.

"I said not to, you idiot!" she hissed in her sister's ear.

"Yes. All right!" Alice snapped nervously.

Side by side they edged along the ledge until the water was so close to them that they could touch it just by stretching out a hand. But, at the last moment, when it seemed that they would be sucked into its swirling midst, the rock face behind them veered away from the fall and they found themselves in a low passage with the water completely blocking the view in front of them.

"We're behind it!" Alice exclaimed.

The air was cold and damp and the noise extreme.

"Mary!" she shouted in her sister's ear. "We're behind the waterfall!"

"But where's William?" Mary yelled.

"And Spot?" Alice called, looking round Mary to where the ledge seemed to peter out against the face of the cliff.

A moment later William appeared in front of them, as if from nowhere.

"Oh!" Mary exclaimed with a start. "Where did you come from?"

"Look!" William called and, as he did so, the girls saw that beside where he was standing there was a narrow opening slanting sideways into the rock.

"It's a tunnel!" William yelled. "It seems to go quite a long way in."

# 16

# The Company
# of Friends

"I'm not going in there," Alice whispered, peering over Mary's shoulder into the dark opening.

"What d'you think, Will?" Mary asked. "Is it safe?"

William shrugged.

"Only one way to find out," he said and, as he spoke, he squeezed between the rocks and disappeared from their view.

"Oh, Will—do we have to?" Mary groaned. There was something maddening about William when he was trying to be macho. But as she spoke, Spot, who had been sitting at her feet, looked up at her, tail wagging. Then he turned and sprang through the cleft in the rock, following William.

"Come on, Mare," Alice whispered. "Spot seems to think it's all right." And, grasping each other firmly by the hand, they walked together into the cave.

As soon as they passed through the entrance

the sound of the waterfall faded until it was no more than a distant roar. They were in a narrow passage that seemed to have been cut through the solid rock. The floor, walls and roof overhead were all smooth hard stone. The small amount of light that filtered through the curtain of water behind them was scarcely able to reach more than a short distance and soon they were feeling their way in the dark.

"Will?" Mary called, nervously.

"I'm here," her brother answered, his voice coming from somewhere just ahead of them.

"Wouldn't it be more sensible to go back to the house and bring a torch?"

"Hang on a minute," he called and, a moment later, the girls heard him gasp.

"What is it?" Alice whispered, nervously, but then, before anyone had a chance to give her an answer, she was able to see for herself as she and Mary stepped out of the dark tunnel into a strange and eerie half-light. At once they could see William standing in front of them, with Spot at his side.

The place they had entered was no more than a broader, more spacious piece of the same tunnel through which they had just been stumbling. But here the roof was much higher and thin rays of light filtered down from a distant crack, somewhere up above them, which filled the space with a soft, green-tinged luminosity.

It took Mary and Alice a moment to adjust to this new light. Then, gradually, the gloom ahead of them sorted itself out into innumerable shapes and objects. The space was crowded with animals and birds. They sat on the floor and stood on boulders. They clung to the walls and perched on outcrops of rock.

Cinnabar, the fox, looked at them with burning, amber eyes. Bawson the badger, was near him and Jasper, the owl, was clinging to a spur of rock. A blackbird flew down from somewhere and alighted on Alice's shoulder.

"Merula?" she whispered, recognizing the bird with whom she had traveled up the Dark and Dreadful Path on the way to the badger baiting during the spring. But Merula didn't reply. He merely stared into her eyes for a moment, then turned and faced in the direction that all the creatures were looking.

Now, as their eyes grew increasingly accustomed to the light, the children could make out more of the details of their surroundings. The walls of the cave were lined with birds. They clung to every available cranny and were squashed together on the few ledges. There were swallows and swifts, blue tits and chaffinches, speckled thrushes and the tiny wren. A big black and white magpie stared down with baleful eyes and a green woodpecker looked sideways at them from a nearby perch. The brilliant blue of the kingfisher gleamed in a dark corner and a mallard duck shifted his weight from foot to foot on the floor not far from where they were standing.

A kestrel, seeing them arrive, called once—"Kee Kee"—a long, sad, haunted cry.

"It's Falco," Mary whispered. "You remember, Alice. You called him Kee Kee. . . ."

"Yous took your times," a voice lisped and, turning, they saw Lutra, the otter, standing up on his hind legs near to an unfamiliar squirrel.

"Sssh!" Jasper hissed, glaring down from his perch.

"What's going on, Jasper?" William whispered. But Jasper only blinked severely and made no answer.

"Wait!" Spot replied, putting a paw on William's arm, and, as he spoke, he turned and looked toward the center of the cave, in the same direction as all the other creatures.

A thin beam of light cut from the unseen opening up above and ended, like a spotlight, on the rough rock floor round which the company was gathered. William, Mary, and Alice, standing side by side with Spot, turned their gaze in this direction.

For a long time—or perhaps it took no time at all for time itself seemed not to matter or even to exist—nothing happened. Then, falling from the heights above them, stealthily, mysteriously, a tiny spider appeared, suspended on a gossamer thread. The silence in the cave was immense. The watching, intense. Every living, breathing creature was attending only to this smallest of beings.

The spider hung for a moment a few feet above the ground, slowly turning on its silver thread. Then, with a sudden, unexpected haste, it dropped from their sight and the silver thread was instantly replaced by a silver staff, surmounted by an emblem of twisting dragons and the sun and the moon and, even as this familiar emblem flashed in the gloom before them, Stephen Tyler appeared, standing in their midst, leaning heavily on the staff, with his other arm in a sling.

"So," he said after a long moment, speaking quietly, "you are all met." He looked slowly round at the gathered throng. "A full company, I think." Then, turning his eyes on the owl, he said in a light, conversational tone. "Jasper, my bird, what's to do?"

"To do . . ." the owl repeated, a reedy whistle.

"Speak for us, Jasper," Bawson, the badger growled.

"What has happened, Master?" Jasper said, in a soulful voice. "We're all afraid. Things are not as they usually are. Why have you called us all to this place? Tell us what has happened?"

"Happened?" the Magician repeated. "Life has happened. I am an old man, Jasper, and I have been pretending otherwise for too long. Old!" he said the word with fierce disgust, then he shook his head and smiled sadly. "The old forget—they forget how to fight; they even forget that they have grown old! But there, I admit it now. I am a foolish . . . old man." He sighed. "Children, come here," he said, beckoning William and Mary and Alice into the center of the floor. "Listen to me. There is no magic that can counter greed. Morden will win. I cannot stop him. . . ."

"What?" William gasped. "Why?"

"Because he is younger and fitter and I found you too late," Stephen Tyler replied.

"But you did find us!" Alice exclaimed. "We can't give up now."

"They stopped the men with the dogs from killing my people," Bawson, the badger, protested.

"When Morden tried to prevent the baby," Jasper hooted, "we won. The baby was born."

"Yes, yes. All true," Stephen Tyler nodded. "But now I'm tired—and this confounded arm hurts. And I do not have the strength. . . ."

"Then give us the strength," William cut in.

"Ah, William," the old man shook his head. "That's what Jonas Lewis said to me. What happened? He made gold for himself. He thought to use the magic for his own gain. And so he lost . . . everything. From that moment I should have seen where this endeavor would lead. Jonas Lewis forfeited the estate to the Crawdens. And because of him we find ourselves in the state that we are in now." The Magician paused, deep in thought. Then he shook his head and sighed once more. "Yet I cannot find it in my heart to blame Jonas. It was I who gave him the power."

"But it's different with us," William pleaded. "There are three of us for one thing, so we won't do things just for ourselves. And, besides, we don't want to make gold, do we?" he added, looking desperately at his sisters.

"What *do* you want, then?" the Magician asked him sharply, before Mary or Alice could reply.

William thought for a long moment.

"I don't know," he said at last. "I can only think of the things I don't want."

"And they are?"

"I don't want some horrible greedy people to come here and spoil everything. I don't want them to chop down the yew tree and put the badgers on show and build cages for animals in our forest."

"I don't want a pretend life," Mary said, speaking suddenly.

"Pretend life?" Stephen Tyler asked her, puzzled.

"That's what they're going to make this place into. A pretend place. People dressing up and pretending."

"So what would you rather have, Mary?"

"I want it to be real. I don't want to feel separate all the time. It's like television . . . I know you don't know what television is . . ."

"Pictures that move and come through the air. I remember. You told me once. I quite liked the sound of it," Stephen Tyler said.

"Yes . . . but . . ." Mary exclaimed. Then she shook her head, unable to explain what she was feeling.

"But?" the Magician asked gently.

"Mummy and Daddy are in Africa," Alice cut in. "And sometimes . . . we see pictures on the news . . . horrible pictures . . . of children dying. So thin . . . with flies on their faces and . . ."

"Yes?" the Magician asked, turning to look at her.

"They're starving." She shrugged. "But it doesn't really mean anything to me. Not really. I mean . . . I try to imagine what it must be like. I try to care. But, in the end . . . well, they're just pictures on television."

William moved and put his arm round Alice's shoulder.

"She's right. Often we see the news when we're having tea. Not here. Not at Golden House. But when we were at home. We'll be looking at pictures of people starving . . . and we'll be stuffing ourselves full of food at the same time."

"So?" the Magician asked again. "What is it that you want? To starve with these people?"

"No, of course not," Mary protested crossly. "But we should be able to feel something for them. I mean, really feel."

"And if we did," William added, "then maybe help would come to them."

"But your mother and father, they are helping, aren't they?"

William shrugged.

"Dad gets angry about it," he mumbled. "He says the famine shouldn't have been allowed to happen in the first place."

"And why has it happened, William?"

"Well, there are lots of reasons. Have you heard of global warming?"

The Magician frowned and shook his head.

"No. I didn't think you would have," William sighed. "Then there's civil war in the country, so lots of medical supplies don't get through. . . ."

"Greed, William," Stephen Tyler murmured. "Greed is making it happen. But you want to . . . stop this suffering?" the Magician asked him. "Is that what you're saying?"

"Not all the time, no. A lot of the time I don't even think about it."

"So what is it that you want?" the Magician insisted.

"I want the magic to go on," Alice said quickly.

"Ah!" Stephen Tyler sighed, sounding disappointed.

"But—is that wrong?"

"Not in itself. But if you want magic, you must want it for a purpose—and that's where the problems begin. Morden wants magic . . ."

"To make him powerful," William said, remembering.

"You know that?" the Magician said, turning to him. "How?"

"He told me," William answered.

"Told you?" Stephen Tyler thundered, clearly amazed. "How—told you? Have you seen him?" Then a great look of dismay came over his face. "He has been here? He has time-traveled."

"No," William said, wanting to reassure him. "I saw him in his own time. . . ."

As he said this all the animals and birds started to twitter and sigh and growl quietly. Only Spot seemed unperturbed. He stood up, with his tail wagging, and looked round proudly.

"You have time-traveled?" Stephen Tyler gasped.

"No, not exactly. At least, I don't think so," William said cheerfully. "I just sort of . . . saw . . . through the crow's eyes."

After a long moment the Magician said:

"Tell me what happened, William."

And so William recounted, as accurately as he could, all that had taken place at the standing stone.

Stephen Tyler listened to him in silence and when he had finished speaking he walked away, deep in thought.

"You entered the crow, Corvus, by your own will? Is that what you're saying?"

"Yes," William replied.

"This is very important, boy," the Magician continued, using a stern voice. "You must tell me how. How did you manage this transference?"

William frowned.

"Well, I'd been trying to stop thinking—because it's the thinking that gets in the way, isn't it?"

"Go on," the Magician murmured.

"But . . . when it happened . . . I was angry, I think. You remember your pendulum thing? The crow pinched it from me. I wanted it back. Yes, I was angry. You see the crow had attacked us already. It went for Alice and later, in the tree house, I think it would have gone for us both. But I stopped it."

"How did you do this?"

"I just sort of . . . told it to stop."

"And it obeyed you?"

"Yes, it did," Alice said. "I was there. I saw."

"It was vicious and evil, and I lost my temper with it. We hadn't done anything to it, you see. Then, when it took the pendulum out of my hand, well, I just wanted it back. That's all that happened." The Magician grunted, deep in thought. "But, I mean, we've seen through the animals before," William continued. "It was nothing particularly new. . . ."

"But you say you saw Morden . . . ?" Stephen Tyler said.

"Yes. The crow was on the standing stone and

so in a way was I—because I was seeing through the crow. We had the pendulum in our beak and . . . suddenly . . . I saw him—I suppose it was him. He was wearing red clothes and he had very black hair . . ."

"Yes!" the Magician cried joyfully. "You have achieved more than my assistant has done in eight years. But more than that—the magic is still here. It isn't too late. Well done, William! Well done all of you . . ."

Then he stopped talking in midsentence and swung round, looking severely at William.

"But you still haven't told me what it is that you want; really want."

"I don't want anything," William replied, breathlessly.

"In that case you won't achieve anything," the old man snapped. "Not good enough, idle pupil! Think again."

"I want to stop Morden," William said.

"And no doubt Morden wants to stop you. Not good enough. There you have only action and reaction. Again. What is it you want, William? Really want?"

William hung his head. Mary moved a little closer to him. She felt sorry for him and couldn't understand why the Magician was behaving so angrily.

"Minimus—you tell him! Go on," the Magician snapped, shaking his head as though he was disgusted with William.

Alice gasped.

"Me?" she exclaimed. "I don't know what he wants."

"Not him! You, child. What do you want? Listen to me. When you ventured alone up the Dark and Dreadful Path—what were you doing it for?"

"The badgers," Alice answered indignantly. "The men with the dogs were going to kill them."

"Good!" the Magician roared. "And—all of you—last Christmas, when the child was being born, why did you risk your lives in the blizzard? Why did you, Mary, alone and unaided, deliver a baby, when you'd never ever seen one being born before?"

"I wasn't alone. Jasper was with me. . . ."

"Don't quibble, child! Why did you do it?" the Magician cried.

"Well, isn't it obvious? Because somebody had to."

"At last!" the Magician hooted with pleasure. "You did it for the child's sake, didn't you?—for the sake of the badgers? That's right, isn't it? So . . . Now, one of you, please, tell me . . . why must we stop these people who would take over our beautiful valley and destroy it? Why, William? Why?"

"Because they only want to do it for their own good; so that they can make money . . ."

"Because they want to take this sacred place

and make it into gold for themselves," the Magician said quietly. "They have no thought for the animals, for the birds, for the fish in the lake. No care for the violet and the primrose, the bending cherry blossom and the soaring oaks. They see it as a place that they can own and change and destroy—for their own gain, regardless of the lives, the well-being, the very future of the inhabitants of the land or even of the land itself. So what is it that we are against, children? What is it that we have to fight? Selfish acts. That is all. Disregard for the common good. Think about it. Self-motivated behavior is at the root of all suffering. People kill for greed. People die for gold. Children starve . . . the earth is parched . . . all in the name of greed. This valley must not be allowed to be destroyed in this way. Because, if it goes, there will be one less place on this great globe that is as nature has intended it to be. Look here, at our company of friends." As he spoke he gestured to all the birds and animals that surrounded them. "Do they not also have the right to live in their land? And if we deny even one of these, our fellow creatures, then shall we not be in danger of being denied ourselves? He who destroys, shall be destroyed. He who causes suffering, shall suffer. It's a small thing I'm asking of you, William, and of you, Minimus, and also of you, Mary of the big heart—though I fancy your moment of true trial is still in my future. Make

Golden Valley safe for generations to come, and your task will be complete. Complete your task and the alchemy will be accomplished. Eschew personal gain; honor justice; act truthfully; that is all that is required. You have all that is needed. The pendulum I left for you will be your touchstone. Don't let it out of your safekeeping. Remember, to make gold, you need gold. The pendulum is your gold. The creatures will help you. They are your friends. Make the estate safe from greedy hands, so that I, in my time, may die content, knowing that my task is complete. Do it for my sake, children, not for yourselves. Do it for me and you will gain my constant gratitude. Constant? Your names, I think. You Constant children—now you have the chance to earn that great name. Call me, when all is accomplished . . ."

And there, in midsentence, he disappeared and the children were standing alone, surrounded by a thousand gleaming eyes.

"What do you want us to do, William?" Jasper hooted.

"Me?" William exclaimed. "I haven't a clue."

"That is often the way with the Master," Jasper trilled. "He leaves one speechless. But I have found, over the years, that he never asks one to do something that is not, in fact, within one's capability."

William looked desperate.

"I don't even know what we're supposed to do; where we're to start," he stammered.

"Use the pendulum," Spot whispered, scratching behind his ear, as though trying to hide the fact that he was prompting William.

But these words only made William look even more worried.

"Yes, well that's another thing," he said. "I haven't got it."

At this the company started to mutter and hiss and tweet and squawk.

"Haven't got it?" Jasper asked mournfully.

"No. I think it must still be on top of the standing stone," William said. "You see, that's where I dropped it, when I saw Morden. . . ."

"Then I suggest that that's where we should start," Cinnabar the fox, said. "Come on, Will," and, as he spoke, he sprang toward William, knocking him off his feet.

As William rose from the ground he stood on all four feet and felt his body tingle with energy. Then, with a swish of his red-brown tail, he darted toward the dark tunnel and the waterfall beyond.

# 17

# The Battle over Goldenwater

After the gloom inside the cave, the light was dazzling. The fox padded along the narrow rock ledge and then, when he reached the bank of the stream, he paused for a moment, feeling the fine spray from the waterfall soaking his pelt.

Looking over his shoulder, along the line of Cinnabar's sleek red back, William saw a crowd of birds of every description issuing from behind the falls. At the same time, running and hopping and scampering along the ledge, came stoats and rabbits, a squirrel, Bawson the badger lumbering slowly, a group of chattering field mice, a couple of toads and, in among this strange collection, Spot walking between Mary and Alice. The duck waddled past and, reaching the edge of the stream, took flight on heavy, flapping wings. A moment later Lutra appeared, running on his short, thick legs toward the bank.

"See yous all in Goldenwater," he called and,

with a cheerful wave, he dived over the edge and they saw his lithe body disappear into the foaming pool at the bottom of Goldenspring.

"Best be off, then," Cinnabar called. But, before he had turned, Jasper appeared, sailing slowly out from the cave on widespread wings.

"Wait, Fox!" he hooted. "We must have some plan."

"The plan," Cinnabar replied, "is to fetch the pendulum and then to make a plan!" And before the owl could argue with them, he and William turned as one and sped off down the steep hillside.

Spot pushed up close to Alice, nudging her impatiently with his snout.

"If we hang about here," he whispered in her mind, "we'll get stuck with Jasper—and he'll talk for hours."

"We're going with William, Mare," Alice said hurriedly and, reaching toward the dog, she saw her own paw hit the turf as she and Spot joined bodies. Together, they raced away over the green spongy ground in pursuit of the fox.

"This is all most irregular," Jasper hooted. "We are supposed to make plans."

"Maybe this time Cinnabar is right," Mary said, trying to be diplomatic. "We should get the pendulum back before somebody else finds it."

"Quite!" Jasper whistled petulantly. "Like the assistant, for instance. Who knows what might happen if it fell into his hands."

"Mary!" a harsh, guttural voice called, making her look up with surprise. "You come with me!" the voice croaked and the big, black and white magpie that she had first noticed in the cave flapped its wings and landed at her feet.

"Mary," Jasper said, sounding slightly haughty, "this bird is the Magician's magpie. The Master calls him Pica. He uses him for doubtful purposes."

"They're not doubtful at all, you stuck up owl! He uses me to collect things. I am particularly good at finding gold. You will be very glad to know me. Now, come on Mary . . ."

"Well . . ." Mary said doubtfully.

"You don't want us to miss the fun, do you? If the assistant's friends are about, anything could happen." He chuckled gleefully. "I feel in the mood for a bit of a fight!"

"Another thing you should know about Pica," Jasper hooted witheringly, "is that he's a bit of a thug. He's always picking fights."

"And you're always glad when I come to your rescue—you miserable old rat-catcher! Come on, Mary. Let's leave the old windbag!"

"No," Mary said, doubtfully. "I really should stay with Jasper, he's my friend."

"Please don't stay on my account," the owl hooted.

"Oh, come on," Pica grumbled. "Anything could be happening while we stand here arguing."

"Well . . ." Mary said again.

"Actually, perhaps you should go with Pica, Mary," Jasper said in a mournful voice. "I am not at my best in the daylight."

"Well . . ." Mary repeated for the third time.

"Well?" the voice rasped in her head. "Quite well, thank you. And how are you today?" And with a harsh, mirthless chuckle Pica stretched his feathered wings, lifting them both up off the ground into the misty air.

"Oh!" Mary exclaimed, as the ground beneath her receded. "You won't go too high, will you?"

"High?" Pica croaked. "Don't you like flying?"

"To tell the truth, I don't do it very often," she whispered and then she closed her eyes as Pica banked into a current of air making the whole of Goldenwater tilt sideways in a most unpleasant manner, that made her feel quite sick.

"Just relax," the bird whispered in her head. "There is no finer experience than sailing through the bright air. Oh-oh!" he suddenly exclaimed and, as he did so, Mary felt her body swing round and her wings beat as she and Pica climbed together high above the lake.

"What?" Mary gasped.

"Company!" Pica croaked.

As he spoke Mary saw the crow flying toward them.

"Is it Morden?" Mary asked.

"Difficult to tell," Pica answered. "Best be a bit evasive, I think." And he winged his way in a great arc, dropping down once more toward the water. Below them now, they could see Cinnabar and Spot racing along the shore of the lake. Above and behind them, Mary could hear the crow squawking. Pica looked back over his shoulder, and Mary saw the big black bird floating on a pocket of air, his head turned toward the far shore of the lake. Again he squawked, an ugly sound. But this time, faintly at first, came an answering call. And then another . . . and another. A whole chorus of squawking sounds was coming from the direction of the dark fir forest that spread as far as the distant horizon. And, even as Mary and Pica turned their attention to that tree line, a black cloud detached itself from the cover of the firs and rose into the air, moving swiftly toward them.

"What is it?"

"Reinforcements," Pica replied grimly and as he spoke he turned and headed for the end of the lake where the standing stone was just visible, with the yew tree behind it at the top of the hill.

Behind them the crow continued to squawk ominously. Now his call seemed to be answered by a terrible buzzing sound, coming from the beech woods on the Four Fields side of the lake.

"Now what?" Mary gasped.

"More of Morden's friends," Pica whispered.

Cinnabar was almost at the end of the lake when the hornets attacked. They came out of the beech woods in an angry, buzzing swarm, flying round his head and diving at his eyes.

"What are they?" William screamed.

"Wasps—sort of wasps. Hornets in fact," Cinnabar answered. Then he flinched as one of the insects managed to sting through his thick fur.

"Ow! That hurt!" William exclaimed, kicking a back leg painfully as he tried to shake off another hornet that had just stung them.

"We'll have to make for the water!" Cinnabar shouted.

"Can foxes swim?" William wondered.

"If we have to," Cinnabar answered in his head and a moment later, as if to prove the point, he dived into the icy water, shaking the dreadful crawling insects off his back and legs.

Spot, who was still a little way behind Cinnabar, saw the swarm of hornets and quickly swerved, making for the gorse and broom bushes that edged the beech woods.

"What's happening, Spot?" Alice whispered in her head.

"Shhh," the dog hissed gently, then, lying on his stomach, he wriggled under the cover of the dense foliage, turning as he did so, in order to look out toward the lake.

They could see Cinnabar being attacked by the buzzing horde and watched as he turned and made for the water.

"Morden's doing," Spot thought.

Then Pica's desperate cries made them look up into the sky.

The magpie was surrounded by several crows who flew at him in turn, beating their wings and alternately snapping with their beaks and striking with their claws.

"That's Pica," Spot said grimly.

"Is he one of us?" Alice asked.

"Pica?" Spot sounded surprised. "Pica is the Magician's magpie. The Master thinks very highly of him. We must try to do something."

"But what?" Alice cried. Then, as Spot crawled forward a little, she looked back along the shore of the lake. "I wonder where Mary is?" she thought.

"Pica! Behind us," Mary screamed, as she and the bird dived away from the claws of one of the crows.

Pica looked back in the direction that Mary was indicating. The sky was black with birds.

"Oh, no!" he groaned. "Starlings. I really hate starlings. They fight dirty."

As he spoke the first of the starlings arrived, diving toward them, chattering gleefully as it aimed its beak at the vulnerable underside of Pica's wing. Pica kicked it away with his foot and dived lower, skimming along the surface of the lake, making one of the crows who was coming in for a renewed attack, miss his mark and hit the water with a smack.

"Good, Pica!" Mary squealed. Then she had to save her strength as they batted off two more starlings.

"We need reinforcements ourselves," Pica muttered. "Sirius!" he croaked. "Hey, Sirius!"

Spot stood up, hearing his name, and bounded down to the edge of the lake.

"What?" he yelped excitedly.

"Bark, damn it!" Pica yelled. "Let the others know they're needed! Bark like hell, Sirius!"

"Right!" Spot muttered. "That's something I can do. Are you ready for this, Al? My barking can cause quite a headache!"

"No, wait . . ." Alice cried urgently. She had just seen William wading out of the lake, swatting hornets and tearing his shirt off. Cinnabar was swimming far out now, and it looked as if William had returned to the shallows to draw the insects away from the fox.

"William!" Alice called and, as she did so, she saw Spot lift up his head and start to bark, a loud, incessant sound.

Alice, once separated, ran toward William, who was making swiftly for the standing stone.

"Al!" he shouted, looking over his shoulder as he ran. "I'll need your help."

Alice caught her brother up as he was running

up the sloping ground toward the stone. Some hornets were still buzzing around, but they seemed to be losing interest in him and they didn't bother to attack Alice at all.

"I won't be able to reach the top of the stone," William gasped, fighting for breath. "You'll have to stand on my shoulders. Can you do it?"

"I expect so," Alice replied doubtfully.

William crouched down, facing the stone and Alice, after a couple of false attempts, managed to stand on his shoulders, while hanging onto the stone with both her hands. Slowly, using the stone as a support, William started to stand up.

"When you can reach the top," he gasped, "feel with your hands. The pendulum should be in a sort of hollow right in he middle of the stone."

"Yes," Alice whispered, "I'll try. . . ." Then the last word turned into a desperate yelp, as she almost fell off his shoulders. She grabbed at the stone, steadying herself.

"All right?" William asked.

"All right-ish," she replied, in a tense voice.

Pica saw the chain glinting as he rose once more into the upper air, moving away from the surface of the water, pursued by three mean little starlings, who snapped and chattered and would not let him go.

"There it is," he thought, and Mary, seeing

through his eyes, was dazzled by the brilliant gleam of sunlight on gold.

"Go for it, Pica," she shouted. "Go for it."

Like an arrow from a bow, Pica shot toward the standing stone with the starlings in close attendance. At that moment, while both his and Mary's attention was distracted by the sight of the pendulum, they failed to notice the big crow, Corvus, dropping out of the sky toward them.

"Squawk!" he yelled, turning in the direction they were heading and seeing the flashing sunrays on the sliver of gold. Corvus knew he was nearer to the stone. He had the advantage. He laughed as he dived, cutting Pica off, reaching forward with his beak and claws.

Alice, shaking like a leaf, stretched up, clinging to the stone. Inch by inch she grew closer, until the top came into view.

"I'm here, Will!" she cried triumphantly and, putting one arm round the stone to give herself a secure hold, she reached across the surface, feeling for the pendulum.

"Squawk!" Corvus screamed in her ear and, with a gasp, Alice swung her head round to discover the big crow inches away from her face.

"This time it's mine, I think," the crow rasped, and, raising a claw, it scratched the length of Alice's hand just as her fingers wrapped round the smooth nugget of gold.

Alice gasped. The pain on her hand was awful. It felt as though a scalding steel knife had been ripped into her flesh.

"Al?" William cried out desperately from below, unable to see what was happening and with all her weight pressing down on his shoulders. "Alice? Are you all right? What's happening?"

Alice gritted her teeth, biting back tears. A sudden terrible anger possessed her.

"Get off!" she yelled, hitting out at the black bird with her free hand, while still gripping the nugget of gold in her fingers.

The crow turned, eyes blazing, and pecked viciously at Alice, stabbing his beak into her arm and her hand. With a cry of pain, she pulled away, releasing as she did so her hold on the pendulum. It slipped out of her grasp and fell back onto the top of the standing stone.

But this distraction gave Pica his opportunity. Seizing his chance while Corvus was attacking Alice, he dived for the stone and snapped up the golden chain by a single link. Then, putting all his strength into his wings, he raised himself up vertically off the stone, making for the upper air.

The pendulum hung down from Pica's beak, flashing and glinting as it swung in the sunlight. Corvus, looking up, saw the great nugget of gold within easy reach and opening his beak, he snapped the chain into his mouth. The two birds were now linked together by the pendulum.

Locked together by the chain, they rose into the air, wings beating, necks and heads straining away from each other as they both tried desperately to gain supremacy.

Pica, with a determined effort, turned and headed in the direction of the lake. But he couldn't shake Corvus off, nor could he get him to release his hold on the chain.

Falco heard Spot's urgent, incessant barking as he was lazily hovering over the great green forest, casually looking for a snack. He turned on leisurely wings, mildly curious to know what could be causing so much commotion and then, where the water of the lake glinted on the far horizon, his piercing eyes picked out the starlings and the crows mobbing the solitary magpie. Flexing his wings, the great kestrel sailed down the wind, aiming for the center of the battle, curious to know what was going on. As he grew closer, he realized that the magpie was Pica and that he was in real trouble. Like a stone, Falco dropped out of the sky, his eyes focusing on the center of the black crow's neck.

Pica and Mary were losing strength. The starlings continued to mob them on all sides and several crows swooped low, clawing and pecking. They constantly had to swoop and turn to avoid these attacks and every time Corvus gained a little on them, gathering more and more of the chain into his beak until the two birds were practically flying cheek to cheek.

"Well, Pica!" the black crow rasped, his voice harsh and mocking through his clenched beak, "This time *my* master wins, I think. . . ."

But at that moment, silent and deadly, the kestrel, Falco, fell on the crow's neck, killing him in an instant with a dreadful blow from his savage claw.

Corvus cried out once, a long, agonized croak of surprise and of death. As he did so the pendulum chain slipped from his beak. The sudden release of tension took Pica completely by surprise. He veered away, tilting dangerously in his flight and, gasping with the shock, he opened his own beak allowing the golden chain with its smooth nugget to fall like a glittering streamer toward the lake.

On the shore, William ran forward, crying out. He saw the kestrel strike the crow. He saw the crow fall, spiraling toward the water. He heard the croak of surprise from the magpie and, last of all, he saw the prize possession, the reason for the fight, his hope for the future, the golden pendulum of the Magician glitter and sparkle as it slipped beneath the surface of Goldenwater and disappeared into its depths.

# 18

# Meg Joins
# the Company

William was in despair. He was feeling anger
and frustration and misery all at the same time.
Worst of all was the terrible sense of failure. He
walked away along the shore, kicking stones, with
his hands in his pockets.

The birds were dispersing. The irritating chatter of the starlings was fading as they flew in a
pack, swerving and diving, toward the distant fir
forests. The few crows that were left wheeled
about, cawing fitfully, then, one by one, they disappeared back to where they had been when they
had each first heard Corvus summoning them to
the fight.

Falco, hovering on a warm thermal, was lifted
higher and higher into the blue sky. "Kee kee" he
called, to no one in particular, and the melan-
choly sound echoed and re-echoed across the valley before getting lost in the distant hills that only
he could see.

Exhausted and bleeding, Pica alighted on a flat rock that jutted out from the shore into the lake.

"Sorry about that," he whispered and, as he did so, Mary pulled herself toward the water and bathed the blood from a wound on her arm. She was too shaken to speak, too tired to want to do anything. The hair on the back of her head was matted where another wound was already forming into a scab. Her legs were scratched. There was a bruise throbbing on her forehead.

The magpie stood at a distance from her, eyeing her. Two of his tail feathers were sticking out in a lop-sided fashion, and there was blood dripping from under one wing. A tiny stab wound above one eye gleamed red against the midnight-black of his head feathers.

Pica laughed loudly.

"That was some fight!" he exclaimed. "Didn't do too badly, considering the numbers against us!" Then he stretched his wings and winced with pain. "We owe Falco, though! We were about done in when he arrived on the scene. Awkward that! I don't like owing. He and I aren't usually the best of friends, either. He will drop in and pinch my food after I've done all the hard work." He paused, looking round, a new thought occurring to him. "Speaking of food . . . Let's go and get a mouse or something. I feel quite hungry. Come on . . ."

"No!" Mary shuddered, fighting back a wave of

nausea as she remembered going hunting once, with Jasper. "You go, Pica. I don't very much like eating mice."

"You are all right," the bird said, in his harsh, cold voice.

"Yes. Yes," Mary replied. "I'm fine. I'll just . . . rest here . . ."

"No. I wasn't asking—I was telling you," Pica croaked. "You are all right, Mary. I like you. The Master's chosen well. I don't like many humans. We magpies don't. Your sort and my sort don't mix. But . . . I like you. If ever you're in a real fix—you shout for Pica . . ." and, flapping his wings, he flew away toward the beech woods.

"No, don't go now, Pica . . . please!" Mary called. "The pendulum. We must try to get it back."

"I don't swim," the bird squawked. "Ask Lutra—that's more his line."

Mary turned and scanned the flat surface of the lake. There was no sign of Lutra anywhere.

Alice was sitting with her back to the standing stone. The scratch on her hand had stopped bleeding, but one of the stab wounds on her arm that the crow had made with his beak was throbbing and sore. She sniffed and rubbed a hand across her tear-stained cheek. She hadn't realized she'd been crying. In front of her the lake stretched in a calm expanse, reflecting the blue sky and the distant trees. Spot was standing on the edge, lapping water, his tail between his legs. His throat was rough from all the barking, and his shoulder hurt where a hornet had stung him without his noticing. Turning his head to lick the wound, he saw Mary sitting on the rock farther round the shore.

"Mary!" he said, barking once, and he paddled through the water toward her.

"William!" Alice called. "There's Mary." She got up and walked slowly toward her sister.

William had gone in the opposite direction and when he turned and saw Mary she was some distance away from him. He had a picture of her sitting peacefully by the lake—a lazy, indolent scene. So typical of Mary to be just lying in the sun enjoying herself, he thought. It really made him angry. He couldn't believe that she was so totally unaware, so completely wrapped up in herself, that she wasn't sharing with him the awful thing that had just occurred.

He turned and started to run toward her.

"Where were you, Mary? What were you doing?" he yelled. "We needed you, Mary. Are you a part of all this or aren't you?" His anger was unstoppable. It made his voice shrill and ugly. As he drew closer to her he wanted to hit her. She looked so comfortable sitting on the rock, leaning on one arm, trailing her hand in the water. "This isn't a picnic we're on, you know," he bawled. "If you'd only been here to help us, none of this might have happened. . . ."

But then, as he reached the rock, Mary turned to look at him and he saw the blood, the wounds and scratches, her wild, disheveled hair and her bruised face. She wasn't sitting enjoying the sun, she was shaking and sobbing and big tears were running silently down her cheeks.

"What happened?" William mumbled, ashamed of his own behavior."

"She was flying with the black and white bird," Alice whispered, putting an arm round Mary and holding her.

"Pica," Spot said. "The Magician's magpie. She was with him all the time—right in the middle of the fight."

"Oh—Mary!" William sighed and, unable to look at her any longer, he squatted down, gazing out across the lake.

"Can't go home looking like this," he said, speaking to himself. "Phoebe'd have kittens. Besides——how are we going to explain all the mess?"

"We could say we'd been in a fight," Alice suggested.

"Who with?"

She shrugged.

"What will happen?" Mary asked, in a small voice.

"Happen?" William queried.

"Without the pendulum?" Mary sobbed, fighting back more tears.

"Don't know," William replied, in a strangely brusque voice. "We can't worry about that now. We ought to take you to a doctor, Mary."

"How?" his sister asked bitterly. "What could we say to him? That I've been attacked by a lot of birds? He'd think we'd gone mad."

"When I get hurt, I always go to Four Fields," Spot whined. "Meg knows how to help. Well, anyway, that's where I'm going," he said, walking away. "I got stung."

"Where?" William asked.

"On my shoulder."

"Only once?" William asked. "You were lucky, then!" and, as he spoke, he took off his shirt, revealing big angry red marks on his back.

"William!" Mary exclaimed. "They look awful. Do they hurt?"

"Of course they hurt," William snapped.

"You're being very brave," Alice said, studying the sting marks with enormous interest. "I'm sure I've heard of people being killed by being stung a lot of times."

"Thanks, Alice!" William exclaimed.

"She's right, though," Mary said. "They could be dangerous, you know."

"Come on, then" Spot barked impatiently, and he ran a few steps toward the beech woods and then looked back at them. "Meg will help," he told them.

Although the weather was so warm, Meg's kitchen was cool and gloomy. It had only a tiny window and outside a great tangle of ivy hung down, blotting out most of the light. The room was crammed with furniture, crockery, piles of old papers, books, rolls of string, empty tin cans, bottles and the accumulated mess of innumerable years. A hen was sitting on top of an old coat. A cat was asleep in a saucepan.

Meg had been dozing in the only comfortable seat in the room. This was a battered armchair that looked as if it had once been part of a three-piece suite. The springs had long ago collapsed and the stuffing was coming out through a hole in the back, but it had aged with its occupant and molded itself to Meg's shape, and it was here that she often dozed away the daylight hours when she wasn't looking after her few animals.

The children had called her name through the front door in vain. They thought perhaps that she was out. But Spot had pushed past them and led the way into the kitchen. And so, when she woke with a start from a dream that was immediately forgotten, she found three faces staring at her through the gloom.

"What's this?" she said, getting up quickly, as if she were embarrassed to have been discovered sleeping. "I didn't hear you."

"Sorry, Meg," William said. "We didn't mean to give you a shock. We called from the door. . . ."

"I was probably . . . miles away," Meg said, filling a kettle from a jug of water. "You'll have a cup of tea?" she asked, striking a match and lighting a primus stove. "I'm using this paraffin stove at the moment. Too hot to light the range. I told Phoebe she should get one. . . ." Then, in the middle of fussing about, clearing a space for them to sit and trying to find three mugs that weren't too chipped, she suddenly caught sight of the bruise on Mary's forehead. "Lord's sake, child! What's happened to your face?" she exclaimed and, peering closer, she saw the scratches and cuts on Mary's arms and legs and then the ugly gash on Alice's hand.

Meg pulled back, looking at the three children, frowning.

"You didn't come for a cup of tea, did you? What's been going on?"

"We . . . fell down a cliff," William sputtered.

"We got in a fight," Alice said at the same moment.

"And did these two events take place at the same time—or one after the other?" Meg asked quietly. "Come out in the light. I'd better take a look at you all," and, leading the way, she went out along the dark hall to the front door.

After Meg had inspected Mary and Alice's cuts, she looked at the stings on William's back.

"Oh, dear!" she said, tutting sympathetically. "These are not so good. I've got some cream that might help. Hornets, you say. Pretty rare, hornets. What makes you think that's what they were?"

William shrugged.

"I'm surprised you can tell a hornet from an ordinary wasp. And these scratches and cuts, Mary—how did you say you got them?"

Mary hung her head and was silent.

Meg looked quietly at each of the children in turn.

"Why don't you tell me what's really been going on? Just wait while I get my medicine chest," and she hurried back into the house, returning almost at once with a big leather Gladstone bag. "I keep everything in here. When I need something for one of the animals I can carry it to them. Now, let me see, William, turn round," and she dabbed cream on each of the sting marks. "You might have to go to the doctor, you know. So I'd get a good story together, if I were you!"

After Meg had finished treating William's back, she applied other lotions to Mary and Alice. First an antiseptic that stung painfully when it went into any open cuts and then creams and lints and elastoplast. She worked quickly and silently, and when she had finished, she dabbed Spot's shoulder with salt and water because he pleaded and whined until she asked what was wrong with him and Alice told her that he had also been stung.

"Get away with you, you great baby!" Meg said, stroking his ear. "You'll live, I expect."

Then, shutting up her medicine bag, she turned once more and looked at them.

"I was born in this valley, you know. I was once your age here. I know a lot that goes on. Now, are you going to tell me?"

William shook his head.

"We can't, Meg," he said.

"I've told you once before, William, told you all—there are things that go on here that can destroy you," Meg said in a quiet, urgent voice. "How many times must I warn you? How many times?"

"When you were younger, Meg," Mary asked, "did you see . . ." She shook her head, unable to finish the sentence.

"I saw nothing," Meg answered severely. "But I know what can be seen. And I know what can happen to people who get involved with these matters. Golden House. Golden Valley. Goldenwater. Gold. Gold. Gold. It destroyed my grandfather; ruined my father's life; and it's left me alone and lonely. All in the name of gold. I was once foolish enough to believe that there were stronger feelings than greed. Feelings that could overcome greed. I was wrong. . . ." She shook her head, as if trying to rid herself of an unhappy memory.

Mary stared at her thoughtfully.

"There was a man here, Meg. Someone you must know. He said you wanted to see him."

"A man?" Meg whispered. "What man?"

"Sir Henry Crawden," Mary answered.

Meg was silent for a long time—so long, in fact, that Mary thought she hadn't heard her.

"Sir Henry, Meg. He was in a wheelchair. He was with his son and that solicitor you went to see. They said you'd asked to see him. But he wouldn't come. Why Meg?"

Meg wasn't looking at them now, she was staring into the distance. Her voice, when she spoke, had a faraway tone.

"I wanted him to face me. I wanted him to tell me to my face that Goldenwater belongs to his family."

"But it does, doesn't it?" William asked her.

"If they say so. You can never argue with a Crawden. But there was a time when they didn't think so. Oh no. There was a time when plain Mr. Henry Crawden came knocking on my door— and why?" Her voice grew increasingly bitter as she spoke. She stared into the distance, shaking her head. "Why? Why did he come? Because his family wanted the lake—that was the only reason." She sighed. "They believed the land belonged to us. They sent him to get that land. He'd have married me for it. That's how much they wanted it. They've always wanted it. Always, through time. There'll be no peace here until they have it. Well, let it go, I say. My daddy said Henry didn't want me—only the land. He was right, of course. But, if I hadn't listened to him, Henry could have had both the land—and me. I think he'd have been glad of that. And I . . ." She shook her head again. "But my daddy said a Lewis could never marry a Crawden." She shrugged. "Well, there . . . Too late now, of course. But I just thought . . . if he came to see me, there could at least be some truth between us." She shook her head and brushed her hand down her skirt. "Let the Crawdens have the land . . ." she said emphatically.

"But, if they take the land, Meg, they'll destroy it," William explained.

"Good riddance to it! Let it go!"

"The badgers, Meg," Alice pleaded with her. "Your badgers. They'll put them on show. They're going to chop down the tree house. . . ."

"The badgers will survive," Meg said with a sob. "Besides, I won't be always here to look after them. Nature must adapt. You can't stop progress."

"Meg!" Alice cried, fighting back tears.

"You can't beat the Crawdens," the old woman said. "Believe me, I know."

"Meg," William said, trying to make his voice strong and firm, "just tell us one thing. Does the land belong to you really?"

"I don't know. No one knows now," Meg replied. "My grandad could have told you. He and old man Crawden made an agreement. They both signed a paper, each keeping a copy. But my grandad lost his. The Crawdens didn't know that at the time. Maybe they expected me to produce mine. Perhaps that's the real reason why I was written to by that solicitor. Of course, there's still the question of access. They need this bit of land—Four Fields. But there's more to it than that. Now—I think they know they've got me. Now I think whatever that agreement was is useless, because now, I think they know that they have the only copy. . . ."

"But—how could your grandfather lose something so important?" William exclaimed.

"Lost, stolen, or strayed. That's what he used to say," Meg replied quietly.

"And he never told anyone what the agreement was?"

"Honor among thieves, he used to say. Honor among thieves!"

"So there's no way we'll ever know what the Lewis family and the Crawden family agreed about the ownership of Goldenwater and the land around it?" William exclaimed. "I don't believe it. There has to be a way."

"Well, I dare say if you could go back in time you'd find out," Meg said, making light of the statement. "But there's no other way I can think of." Then she frowned and turned toward William. "Forget I said that!" she said severely.

"Forget all about Goldenwater! Please, William. Please, all of you. If you don't, it will destroy you as well."

"But just think, Meg," William said, speaking as if in a trance, "we might win—in which case this place would be safe forever—and Morden would be defeated."

"Morden?" Meg asked, in a horrified voice.

"I mean the Crawdens," William said hurriedly.

"Morden!" Meg sighed, "I haven't heard that name for a long time. You sound just like my grandfather."

"You have to help us, Meg. You're the only one who can. Please, Meg," William pleaded.

"When I needed help, you were there," Meg said quietly. "The badgers would tell me to help you. But I'm afraid for you."

"It's all right, really," Alice said brightly. "We have the best Magician on our side."

"Have you seen him?" Meg asked them, looking at each of them closely.

Their silence was all the affirmation that was required.

"My daddy spent his life regretting not seeing him—what is it you call him? The Magician? My grandfather called him the Magus, I think. As for me—I didn't really believe any of it."

"He's a good man, Meg," Mary said, putting an arm round the old woman and hugging her. "But he's old—and he's so afraid of what will happen to the valley if the Crawdens get their hands on it."

Meg nodded.

"He's right to be afraid. The Crawdens are pure greed. That's all that interests them. They're as rich as they can be—and yet they always want more."

"We must help the Magician, Meg. We must," William said, pressing the point.

"He's told you all this? This man from the past. I find it so hard to believe. If I could see him . . ."

Then she took a great gulp of air and breathed deeply.

"I'll do what I can to help," she said.

# 19

# Miss Prewett Comes to Lunch

Miss Prewett came to lunch on the following Sunday, bringing with her the book she had promised from the museum library.

The days between "The Battle Over Goldenwater" (as the event was now called by the children) and the Sunday were spent in a relatively low-key way. Phoebe was worried by William's stings and insisted on taking him into the town to see the doctor. The doctor seemed less concerned. He prescribed a stronger ointment to put on them and a course of antibiotics in case, as he said, any bugs were lurking.

Mary managed to keep most of her wounds a secret by wearing jeans and a long-sleeved shirt. But the bruise on her forehead and the angry, inflamed scratch on the back of Alice's hand were noticed by Phoebe and had to be explained away as climbing accidents.

The girls were anxious to get on with some-

thing—anything—that would further the task the
Magician had set them, but William was sullen
and depressed and didn't want to spend time with
them. On Saturday afternoon as Alice was coming
in through the front door to get a glass of lemon-
ade she discovered him emerging from the fireplace in the hall.

"You've been up to the room. You went without
us, William," she accused him.

But her brother simply shrugged and walked
toward the stairs.

"Go, if you want to," he said. "No one's stopping you. But it's a complete waste of time. He's
not there. I've tried every way I can think of to get
him—but it's no use." And, miserable and
dejected, he stumped up the stairs and out of her
sight.

That night Mary and Alice decided to tackle
him in earnest, and went to his room after he'd
gone to bed.

"I don't know what we're supposed to do," he
told them. "It's no use asking me."

"But you're the one who works things out,
William," Mary had protested.

"Yes—well, I don't now, do I? I've been told not
to, haven't I? I have to stop thinking, haven't I?"
He spat the questions at her in a petulant tone.

"You don't have to stop thinking altogether,"
Mary snapped. "You're so stupid sometimes."

"All right, Mary—you tell us," her brother

rounded on her. "If you're so clever—you tell us what to do."

There was a long silence broken only by Alice's sniffing, as she scratched her cheek, deep in thought.

"You mean, we're not going to try to help Mr. Tyler anymore?" she whispered. "Is that what you're saying?"

"Oh, Alice!" William hissed, bad-temperedly. "What are we supposed to do? I've tried everything. I've tried not thinking, thinking, willing the Magician to come, waiting in the secret room . . . Nothing happens. If only we hadn't lost the pendulum. If only . . ."

He looked so miserable now that Mary felt sorry for him and went and sat on the side of his bed.

"I suppose we could ask Lutra," she said. "He might find the pendulum."

"How? How do we get Lutra? I've tried."

"When?" Mary asked. She could feel herself getting angry again.

"Yesterday morning. Before you were both awake. . . ."

"You went up to the lake on your own?" Mary exploded crossly. "You left us behind?"

"I just wanted to see if I could find Lutra," William wailed.

"Well, of course, if you're going to go off doing things on your own, we haven't a hope," Mary said, flouncing toward the door impatiently.

"Oh, Mary, please!" William pleaded. "Don't lose your temper. I wouldn't have done anything serious without you. I just had to try. It was my fault that we lost the pendulum. I shouldn't have left it on top of the standing stone. I had to try to get it back."

"If we had it," Alice said, scratching her cheek, "what good would it do?"

"I don't know," William said, shrugging. "But the Magician said it was important."

"It could be anywhere on the bottom of the lake, couldn't it?" Mary observed thoughtfully.

"Or, worse still, it could have been sucked by the current through that opening in which case it could be miles away by now."

"How d'you mean?" Mary asked.

"You didn't go, of course," William remembered. "When Al and I went down with Lutra, we saw where the water exits from the lake. It gushes through a narrow opening and then . . . sort of disappears into caves, underground."

"But where does it go eventually?" Mary asked.

William shrugged.

"I don't know. If the pendulum has gone into the caves, it could be anywhere by now. We'll never find it. It's gone," William said, and he sighed and closed his eyes. "Go to bed! There's nothing we can do about it. We'll have to think of another way."

Later, as Alice was going to sleep, she remembered Blackwater Sluice and how frightened she had been when Lutra had taken her there and left her alone in the dark cave.

"I don't ever want to go there again," she thought and then she trembled, remembering how she had felt about the Dark and Dreadful Path. She hadn't wanted to go back there either, but circumstances had made it necessary. "Oh, no!" she thought, and she closed her eyes, willing herself to go to sleep.

Miss Prewett arrived at midday, driving a small, old-fashioned car, with pale blue paintwork and gleaming metal trimming.

"It's called Daisy," she called, tooting the horn. "And I love it to death!" Then, climbing out of the car, she closed the door carefully, and crossed round to the passenger side. From the seat she took a wicker basket and a square parcel and carried them with her into the house.

The basket contained a jar of crab apple jelly, a root of a plant and a box of chocolates.

"The jelly I made myself and it hasn't really set—but you can pour it over things. The plant is a rather spectacular double geranium from my garden and the chocolates are absolutely trustworthy—because I bought them in a shop!" Then, unwrapping the parcel, she produced the book that they had seen before, at Christmas.

On the title page, in fine handwriting, were the words:

"*The Alchemical Writings of Jonas Lewis, of The House in Golden Valley. Being completed this last day of the last year of the century, 31st December, 1899.*"

"Shall we look at it now?" Miss Prewett said eagerly.

"Well," Phoebe sounded a bit doubtful, "lunch is almost ready."

"Then we must wait," Miss Prewett declared cheerfully. "Mmmh!" she enthused. "What a wonderful smell! Roast lamb with rosemary?"

"No, I'm afraid not," Phoebe said hurriedly, noticing Alice shaking her head with a grim expression on her face. "We're vegetarians."

"All of you?" Miss Prewett demanded, sounding surprised.

"Well, we are when we're here," William explained.

"And I am now most of the time," Mary said.

"Mary is my true convert," Phoebe added.

"And what about you, my dear?" Miss Prewett asked, looking quizzically at Alice.

"Alice is still taking some persuading" Phoebe said with a smile. "But she's coming round, I think."

"Well, I think it's a jolly good idea," Miss Prewett beamed with pleasure. "Trouble is I'm too lazy to work it all out. Being on my own, I don't do much cooking. You'll usually find me with my head in a book and a dish of bangers and mash, I'm afraid."

"D'you like sausages?" Alice asked.

"My staple diet," Miss Prewett told her.

Alice wasn't sure what a staple diet was, but her opinion of Miss Prewett went up considerably.

They had lunch at a long table in the walled garden under a big apple tree. The table was covered with a white cloth and Phoebe had put tiny vases of wildflowers all down the center.

"It looks so pretty!" Miss Prewett exclaimed.

"We don't very often have guests," Phoebe explained shyly. "It was fun doing it."

"What about us?" Alice exclaimed. "We're guests."

"No, you're not, Al. You're family. And you can help with the serving," Jack told her. "It's a long way from here to the kitchen!"

The meal started with a cheese soufflé accompanied by a green pea sauce. This was followed by a dish of vegetable lasagna, that Phoebe carried steaming to the table, the smell rich with herbs and garlic. A green salad containing dandelion flowers fried in oil was served with this. For pudding there was a fresh raspberry cream with caramelized sugar on top. Phoebe called it Crême Brulée, which Mary said meant burnt cream. Alice had second helpings of everything and when there wasn't a space left for another morsel she leaned back in her chair and told Phoebe that she was without question the best cook in the world and that she was definitely giving up sausages for the rest of the day.

After they had finished eating, the children cleared the table while Jack made coffee then, sitting together in the cool shade with Stephanie sleeping in her pram and Spot curled up under the table, Miss Prewett opened Jonas Lewis's book.

"You will probably remember, from the last time you borrowed the book, that an awful lot of it is given over to charts and diagrams—all completely meaningless to me, I'm afraid," Miss Prewett explained, taking charge of turning the pages and sounding a little as though she was giving a lecture.

"Yes. D'you remember, darling?" Jack cut in, turning to Phoebe. "You were a whiz at translating the Latin!"

"God knows why," Phoebe said shyly. "I hardly did any Latin at school and what I did do, I was hopeless at." She looked over Miss Prewett's shoulder as the pages slowly turned, revealing drawings of suns and moons, flowers and fish, sheets covered with neat lists of letters and numbers. "The extraordinary thing is," Phoebe said, speaking half to herself, "I feel as though I've seen it all before. But I know I haven't. . . ."

"Look," Alice said, stopping Miss Prewett at one page. "That's a picture of your necklace, Phoebe." And Phoebe's hand went automatically to the little pendant of the sun and the moon with the twisting dragons between them that Jack had found in the house and given her for Christmas. There on the page in front of them was an identical colored drawing.

"And it's the same as the weathervane we found in the cellar," William added. "The one Dan and I fixed to the top of the dovecote." As he spoke they all looked toward the dovecote at the center of the garden and saw the weathervane at its top, with the silver disks below it that could spin in a breeze but which were motionless on this hot, still afternoon.

"Perhaps it's the crest of the original owner of the house," Miss Prewett suggested. "His name was Stephen Tyler and I believe he was highly thought of . . . though I can't find out much about him. Now, I mustn't get sidetracked. That's always been one of my failings. History gets under your skin. One tries to imagine how things used to be. This place, for instance. If only these walls could talk!" She looked round at the garden and the back of the house appearing over the brick wall. Then she threw up her hands. "There I go! Stick to the point, woman! Stick to the . . . I'll leave you the book to look at at your leisure. It really belongs here, after all."

"That would be great," Jack said. "I expect Meg would like to see it again. It was she and her mother who sold it, you know."

"Yes. It seems that the Lewis family have always been in straitened circumstances. Which brings us to a present crisis. By the way, two bits of news. I understand that the Forestry Commission have turned down an application for access across their land. Not that that means a lot, I'm afraid. Pressure can always be brought to bear on these government departments. And, of course, this scheme has the backing of our local MP, the ubiquitous Mrs. Sutcliffe. Ghastly woman. Always gives the impression that she knows better than anyone else. Heaven defend us from Members of Parliament! Funny breed! Now, where was I? What was I saying?"

"That you have two bits of news," Jack prompted her, kicking Alice to stop her staring openmouthed at Miss Prewett.

"What?" Alice said, jumping.

"Sorry! My foot slipped!" Jack said hurriedly.

"Close your mouth, Alice," Phoebe said, trying not to laugh. "You'll catch a fly. And don't stare!"

"Sorry," Alice said quietly. But really, she couldn't help it. She thought Miss Prewett one of the most peculiar people she'd ever met. She spoke so fast and used such weird words that being with her was like being with a foreign person.

"Two bits of news," Jack prompted. "You've told us about the Forestry Commission. . . ."

"Forestry commission?" Miss Prewett sounded totally mystified. "Have I? What did I say?"

"That they've refused access across their land to the lake."

"Oh! You've heard that, have you? I was going to tell you that."

"You just did," Jack murmured.

Miss Prewett threw up her hands and hooted with laughter.

" 'Age and its oft-time infirmities!' Don't get old, you children. It's ghastly. Sometimes I have a struggle to remember my own name! Now where was I? Think, woman! Concentrate. I've told you about the Commission. What was the other thing? Oh, yes. Miss Lewis." She beamed with pleasure. "It's so good when the old brain actually works. Now, I have a friend, Joan Benson. She works in Martin Marsh's office. Actually she's not a friend. But I know her. She's a very garrulous woman. Never stops talking. I can't get a word in edgeways sometimes. Imagine!"

All her audience were clearly finding it difficult to imagine anything of the sort, but for now they remained silent and politely attentive.

"Anyway, Joan Benson told me that Martin Marsh has received a letter from Miss Lewis turning down their offer to buy her out of her smallholding!"

"But that's wonderful news!" Jack exclaimed.

Suddenly their quiet conversation was disturbed by the noise of furious barking, and Spot shot out from under the table, snarling and yapping angrily.

"What's the matter with you, Spot?" Jack yelled. "Shut up!"

But Spot was too busy snuffling in the undergrowth on the other side of the path from where they were sitting to pay any attention to Jack's words.

"What's got into him?" Phoebe exclaimed, as Stephanie, disturbed by the noise, started to cry noisily. "Somebody stop that dog!" she shouted, picking Stephanie up out of her pram and rocking her soothingly.

"Spot! What's the matter with you?" Alice asked, running to the dog. Then she screamed and froze in her tracks.

"Now what's the matter with you, Alice?" Jack roared.

"There's a rat!" Alice wailed.

"What?" Phoebe cried. "Where?"

"There!" William shouted as, at the same moment, a big, gray rat shot from the cover of the bushes and ran fast up the garden path pursued by Spot, who was now barking hysterically.

The forest gate at the back of the garden was ajar and they all watched as the rat scooted out of sight, followed moments later by Spot. They heard the dog continuing to bark as he followed his quarry up the steep rise, beyond the wall, through the forest.

"Oh!" Phoebe grimaced. "Sorry! But I really hate rats!" and she cooed and cuddled Stephanie perhaps more for her own comfort than for the baby's.

During this entire distraction Miss Prewett had remained motionless and with her mouth open. Now that it had passed, she swallowed nervously and brushed some hair away from her forehead with her hand.

"Yes, sorry about that!" Jack said brightly. "Never mind. Panic over! Just one of the hazards of living in the country! Funny though. You don't usually see rats in the middle of summer—though they must be there, of course. Now"—he smiled reassuringly at Miss Prewett—"what were you saying?"

"Oh—dear Mr. . . . You can't expect me to remember? Not after all that excitement."

"Oh, yes!" Jack cried enthusiastically. "You'd just given us the good news that Meg Lewis isn't going to sell Four Fields to the crawly Crawdens!" And as he spoke they all returned to their seats.

Miss Prewett grimaced.

"I wouldn't be over the moon about that, if I were you. I'm afraid I think it only a temporary respite, Mr. . . ."

"You promised to call me Jack."

"Did I? How forward of me!"

"But if Meg says she won't sell," William insisted, "surely that's the end of the story?"

"Dear child," Miss Prewett scoffed. "They'll come back with a better offer. They'll get her in the end. Everyone has a price."

"Well, I'm sure Meg hasn't," William said, leaping to his friend's defense. "She loves it here—she's known the valley all her life."

"Well, we shall see—but it seems to me it would be far better to discover that none of the land actually belongs to the Crawden family," Miss Prewett insisted. "That would really cook their goose. You must agree with that?"

"Why are you so certain that it doesn't?" Jack asked.

"No, I'm not certain," Miss Prewett protested. "I didn't say that. But I am curious."

"But—why?"

"This book," she answered, tapping the book where it lay open on the table in front of her. "I just had this . . . vague memory at the back of my head . . . that I'd seen . . . something . . ."

"So—is there anything in the book that can help us?" Phoebe asked, sounding almost impatient. Miss Prewett's chatter was obviously beginning to irritate even her.

"Not exactly," Miss Prewett said, leafing through toward the end. "And yet . . . listen to this. It's from near the end of the book." She cleared her throat, adjusted her glasses, and started to read: " 'All is lost. The gold has reverted. Crawden has come to me. I think he knows what has taken place. He will take the house in payment. All is lost. I am finished. Fool's gold. Fool's gold.' " Miss Prewett took off her glasses and polished them. "It seems, though it's pretty hard to believe, that old Jonas Lewis thought he'd managed to make gold and with it he'd tried to pay off the debts he had incurred through gambling. I rather think he hadn't actually been gambling with Crawden—but he'd borrowed money from him. One of the ways the Crawdens made their money was through lending. At the end of the last century, there was a lot of poverty. A person with a private income could do very nicely. . . ."

"Miss Prewett, please!" Phoebe cried. "Just tell us what it says in the book."

"Sorry! Was I off again? Now, you'll remember the story. The house was at one time lived in by an alchemist—and this book, written by Lewis, is crammed with alchemical allusions. There's nothing all that unusual about that. I mean there are many books on alchemy. Some are still being written. But, of course, no one seriously believes that the alchemists could really make gold. And yet, here . . ." She stabbed her finger on the page in front of her. "Here is a man who claims that he has done just that—made gold! It's fascinating stuff."

"Well, if he did manage it," Jack said, speaking in a slightly mocking voice, "he didn't seem to do it very well! The stuff reverted. He says so there. If it was gold—it wasn't gold for long."

"Quite," Miss Prewett agreed. "But whatever had been going on, he lost the house because of it. Listen to this next page." She put her glasses back on and turned the page and started to read: " 'December 15th. We are to be out by the end of the year. Crawden will take the house. We have agreed on the land. Papers are to be signed. It is the best I can do. The Magus must not know. It will be good to be gone from this place.' "

Miss Prewett looked round at her audience.

"Now what do you suppose that means? 'We have agreed on the land. Papers are to be signed. It is the best I can do . . .' It sounds to me as though the land was being held in some sort of trust."

"But without the papers we can prove nothing!" Jack exclaimed. "Where are the papers?"

"I don't know," Miss Prewett answered thoughtfully. "Your solicitor told you that the house deeds had been lost in a fire. Is that right?"

"Yes."

"Mmmh," she mused thoughtfully, and she turned the page. "Listen! This is almost the last entry in the book." She started to read again.

" 'December 28th: I know what I must do.

This art must ever secret be,

The cause whereof is this, as ye may see;

If one evil man had thereof all his will,

All Christian peace he might easily spill,

And with his pride he might pull down

Rightful kings and princes of renown.

" 'The king comes forth from the fire and

rejoices. So be it. To the fire I will return all I have achieved.

" 'December 29th. Will Hardwick will help me with the stones. It must be done tomorrow. Crawden may find the secret room, but he must never find the laboratory. Or, if he does, in God's name I must see to it that it is empty' " Miss Prewett looked up again, her voice shaking. "What can it all mean? And then, finally, the poor man writes: 'Whoever reads this let him take heed. The Gold is not for use. The Magus watches. The Magus knows. The Magus owns us all. I am ruined. May the Lord God have mercy on my soul.' "

The silence that followed was broken by Phoebe shivering.

"Oh!" she exclaimed. "I didn't like that book the last time we had it in the house. I like it even less now."

"The laboratory," William said thoughtfully. "Where was the laboratory?"

"What does any of it mean?" Jack exclaimed exasperatedly. "It's so nonsensical!"

The three children avoided each other's eyes. They knew so much more than the adults. The book made sense to them because they knew that what Jonas Lewis had written had actually taken place.

"Fascinating stuff, though," Miss Prewett remarked, cheerfully, breaking the mood of tension that had descended on them all.

"Anyway," Jack continued glumly, "whatever it's all about, I can't see that it helps us in the slightest degree. Damn! I really thought we might find something. . . ."

"But we have, Mr. . . . we have. We know that there was some agreement between Crawden and Lewis over the land!" Miss Prewett cried.

"That doesn't help us," Jack exclaimed. "Not if we don't know what it was. Not if we can't prove it. In about five years' time, somebody will be sitting here in this garden with merry hell blasting forth from a funfair at the top of that cliff. But I'll tell you all one thing, it won't be me." And, getting up, he stamped away down the garden path and disappeared into the yard.

"Oh dear," Miss Prewett said mournfully. "I'm afraid Mr. . . . Jackson . . . is taking all this very much to heart. But you mustn't give up hope, you know. The battle isn't lost. Though I must admit I don't know where to turn for help."

# 20

# Thinking

Spot hadn't returned by suppertime. Alice stood at the forest gate, calling his name, until Phoebe came up the garden path and told her to come back to the house. Night was closing in over the forest and, after the heat of the day, a slight breeze was blowing.

"We'll leave the kitchen door open for him," Phoebe told her. "He's often gone off before. He'll be all right. He might have gone to see Meg. Come along, Alice. Don't worry anymore. . . ."

Reluctantly Alice walked with Phoebe back down the center path of the walled garden. As they were passing the dovecote, an owl hooted. Looking up, Alice saw him sitting on one of the top ledges. She hoped that it was Jasper, that he might have come with some news, but as she watched, the bird flapped its wings and disappeared, flying away over the roof of the house. A sharp barking sound made them both look over their shoulders, expectantly. Then Phoebe shook her head.

"Fox," she said.

Again Alice hesitated. She thought that it might be Cinnabar, coming in search of the children with some information. But once again she was disappointed for, moments later, they heard it barking farther away in the forest. Still she and Phoebe remained standing, listening to the night sounds; a late bird chattering, the breeze in the trees, the distant hooting of an owl.

"You would think a place like this would be safe forever," Phoebe said, putting an arm round Alice's shoulder.

"Is there really nothing we can do to stop them?" Alice asked her.

"I doubt it. In fact most people are actually in favor of the scheme. I suppose, in a way, I can understand it. There isn't a lot going on round here. The theme park idea would bring about a lot of building work. Then, once the place was opened, there'd be plenty of new jobs just staffing it and, of course, the visitors would bring in lots of extra capital. In a way it's true what was said at the meeting—going ahead with the scheme would bring a new lease of life to the area."

"So does it matter all that much if it goes ahead or not?" Alice asked her.

"It does to us," Phoebe replied. "But I'm sure

that's selfish on our part. So all we can do, if it comes to it, is cut our losses and sell up."

"Sell Golden House?" Alice asked, appalled at the thought.

"Yes. There isn't really any other alternative."

"Oh, Phoebe! You wouldn't?" Alice cried.

"We would. Jack and I have already talked about it. We moved here because we wanted peace and isolation. As soon as they start building up there—all that will go."

"But—you're going to turn this place into a hotel. Is that so very different?" Alice asked her.

As they were speaking, a big moon slowly rose above the forest trees, bathing the garden and the house beyond in silver light. The silence was profound.

"It wasn't going to be exactly a hotel," Phoebe explained. "More like . . . a place where people could come and stay; where they could enjoy good food and good company; where they could spend their days out in the countryside and their evenings quietly at home. A rest place; a retreat almost. Yes—that's it. A rest house—just like this place was originally. A place where people could come and forget, for a while, all the problems of life; where they could recharge their batteries, spiritually as well as physically; a place where they'd have the opportunity to experience all this." As she spoke she indicated the moonlit garden and the darkening woods. Then she sighed.

"But, you know, maybe it was a just a dream on our part. Jack and I aren't very businesslike! We'd probably have run out of money before we got as far as the official opening. One thing's certain, we can't afford to live here without doing something to earn our keep. Perhaps that solicitor was right. We should welcome the development and cash in on it. But we can't. It's not what we want to be part of . . . a money-making concern. So"—she shrugged—"we'll just have to sell up and go."

"Where?" Alice asked, shocked at the idea.

"I don't know—we haven't got as far as thinking that out yet."

Later that night Alice related this conversation to William and Mary as they all sat in the girls' room, whispering quietly.

"You know what'll happen," William said grimly. "The Crawdens will buy the place back. Then they'll have everything and Morden will have won."

"And the only way it can be stopped . . . is by us," Mary sighed.

"And we don't know how," William added.

"You know last time we were here," Alice said thoughtfully, "when I lost my temper with the Magician and he said there'd be no more magic? Is it like that now d'you think? Or is it different?"

"How d'you mean?" William asked, only half listening to her.

"Well—has he taken the magic away? Or is it

still there—but now it's up to us to . . . sort of find it?"

"I keep telling you—I can't! I've tried," William protested. "I can't get him to come."

"No, William. Not that. I don't mean that," Alice insisted. "Not trying to get the Magician to come and help us . . ."

"What are you saying, Alice?" Mary asked her.

"Well—what if things haven't gone wrong? What if they're going right?"

"That's not possible, Al," William sighed. "I mean it's obvious—we weren't meant to lose the pendulum, for instance . . ."

"But that's just it, William. You go on about losing the pendulum—but we don't know what it was for—or how it would help us. I bet it isn't all that important. If we could only work things out."

"But he kept telling us not to try to work things out!" William exclaimed.

"I don't care what he told us—he isn't here now," Alice responded with a sniff. "Go on, Will, do some brainwork! That's what you're good at."

William took a deep breath and thought for a few moments.

"We know," he said, "that in the Magician's time Morden is trying to gain power. We also know that after the Magician's death Morden will somehow take over this house. There's no question about any of that being changed, because it's history. The only hope the Magician has of trying to regain Golden House is to alter events after his death—in his future. So I think he has kept traveling through time in the hope of finding a way of getting Golden House and the valley back into his control. Or into his . . . plan; his scheme . . . whatever you call it."

"That's brilliant, William!" Mary said. "Only—if we fail him, like Jonas Lewis obviously failed him, what's to stop him going further into the future— I mean beyond our time, and trying to find someone else to help him? You know like . . . Steph's children, say . . . or even later still. Like in the middle of the twenty-first century?"

"He probably would try . . . his only problem is, he's an old man. Maybe . . . maybe he doesn't have a lot of time left."

"Why?" Alice asked.

"Maybe he's going to die soon," William said.

"Oh, Will! Don't say that," Alice whispered. "He isn't very old."

The children were silent for a moment.

"You know at Christmas, when Jack went to see Miss Prewett?" Mary said after a moment. "She gave him a list of all the people who've lived here. You remember, Will. You looked at it in the middle of the night—that's how you first discovered that Stephen Tyler lived here . . . before we met him."

"I remember, yes," William said, almost irritably.

"What was the next name on the list?"

"I can't remember—I don't think I even looked. I was so surprised to see *Tyler*. But we know it must be Morden, because we know that Morden comes to live here. Sir Henry told us that."

"But—if we knew what date Morden became the owner of Golden House," Mary continued, "then we'd also know when Stephen Tyler died— unless of course Morden just kicked him out."

"I don't see what you're getting at?" William asked.

"Well—if we only knew how long there is to go before the Magician's death, then we'd know how long we'd got . . . to change his future."

"Mmmh," William agreed thoughtfully. "Trouble is—we've never been told what the date is in the Magician's time when he travels to our time. . . ."

"Oh, stop it, both of you!" Alice exclaimed impatiently. "You're doing it again."

"Doing what?" William asked.

"Thinking about all the wrong things. Confusing everything. Besides, what are you saying? If the Magician still needs to go off and find somebody to help him way ahead in our future—then that must mean that we've failed him. Well, have we, William? Is that what you're saying?"

A long silence followed this outburst.

"D'you suppose it's all part of the alchemy?" William said at last.

"What's all part of it?" Mary asked.

"All this confusion," William replied.

"You're doing it again," Alice cried. "Keep to the point!"

"All right then, Alice," William snapped, dangerously close to losing his tempter. "If you're so clever, you do the thinking."

"All we have to do is find a way of stopping the Crawdens from building up at Goldenwater," Alice said, speaking slowly. "If we don't, we won't have completed our task. That's all we've got to do. We don't even have to know why we have to do it. I expect we'll understand . . . later. But that's all he's told us to do."

"All!" William groaned.

"So, how do we do it, Will?" Alice asked, as if she were challenging him.

"By traveling back in time ourselves," William answered spontaneously, almost before he had time to think of the answer, "and finding out what the agreement was that Jonas Lewis made with Crawden over the land."

Alive nodded and pulled a serious face.

"How do we do that?"

William thought for a moment.

"Find the laboratory," he said.

"Why?" Mary asked. "How will that help?"

"Because in his book Jonas says that he must hide the laboratory from Crawden. That means that the laboratory was somehow very important to him . . . and probably to the Magician. Don't forget Uncle Jack told us that alchemists were like early chemists. . . . Stephen Tyler, if he was a chemist, would have had a laboratory."

"Not the room at the top of the chimney?" Mary asked.

"That was his study," William replied. "His laboratory must have been somewhere else."

"Where?" Alice asked.

"Well, we've been all over the house with Uncle Jack," William said. "I suppose any of the rooms could have been used as one. . . . But, he mentions in the book someone coming to put stones down. . . . You know that blocked-up arch in the main cellar? The one Jack calls the crypt. D'you think that's anything to do with it?"

"Pretty obvious if it is," Mary said.

"Well . . ." William continued thoughtfully, "either it's a room that's been sealed off in some way. Or . . . it could be underground."

"If we found it," Alice said, "how would we go back in time?"

"Like I did, I suppose, when I saw Morden. In an animal. You see that's another thing we keep being told. Morden can't appear in our time— like the Magician does. He hasn't managed to do that yet. All he can do is . . . somehow . . . see our world by putting his mind into certain animals and birds."

"Like the crow," Mary said.

"And the rat," William agreed.

"You mean the rat at Christmas?" Alice asked with a shudder. "That was the worst."

"And the rat today," William said in a matter-of-fact voice.

"You mean . . . the rat Spot chased was a Morden rat?" Alice gasped.

"Probably," William answered. "I think he's probably got spies everywhere. Like the spider in the secret room that time. The one Jasper ate."

"That's something that puzzles me," Mary said. "When Jasper ate the spider . . . was he eating Morden? When Falco killed the crow at the Battle of Goldenwater—was he killing Morden?"

"No, I don't think so. It's more like . . . interference on a television screen. Morden wouldn't be able to see what was going on—or hear for that matter—when his spy was intercepted."

"But, when the Magician was in Bawson, at the badger bait, and that dog attacked . . . Well, the dog was attacking a badger—but the Magician has still got a bad arm from the attack."

William nodded.

"Maybe when you can actually time-travel—I mean really bring your body to the new time— maybe then the rules are different. Maybe then you sort of *are* occupying the other body. Before that you just know how the other body is feeling and see what the other body is seeing. . . ."

Alice scratched her cheek.

"That's how it was for me when I went in Spot after he'd been in a fight. I could feel all his cuts and bruises—but, I mean, I hadn't got cuts and bruises myself."

"But in that case," Mary said quietly, "how d'you explain me?"

"What d'you mean?" William asked, then his face registered a profound shock. "How do we explain you having all the wounds that the magpie suffered when he was being attacked over Goldenwater?"

"Exactly, William," Mary said, sounding almost frightened. "Why have I got all these scratches and bruises? I haven't started time-traveling. So how do you explain me?"

"How d'you know you haven't?" William said after a moment. "Maybe you were sort of time-traveling and you didn't know?"

"Oh, William!" Mary protested. "Things like that don't happen to me. I hardly have any magic. You and Alice have the magic."

William stared at her thoughtfully.

"All the same, I don't know why you've got the scratches," he said, as if he was agreeing with her.

"Please!" Alice whined. "You're off the subject again. Where do we go from here?"

"Sleep!" William said. "And in the morning— up to the lake."

"How will that help?"

"Because it's up there that I managed to see

back into the past—when I saw Morden. And it's there that Mary flew with the magpie. I think it's got something to do with that energy line the Magician spoke about. D'you remember? He told us that there are three energy lines up there. The dark path—that's The Dark and Dreadful Path; the light path—that's the bridlepath leading down from Four Fields; and then a secret, central line which he didn't give a name to. D'you remember when I was playing Ducks and Drakes? Those stones that came out of nowhere—and the way mine just disappeared into the air? I'm sure that happened at the crossing of that line. I think Morden was playing Ducks and Drakes in his time and my stones and his stones somehow . . . changed times." He shrugged and frowned. "It's a bit complicated and I haven't really worked it out yet. But I'm sure it was something like that."

"You are brilliant, William," Alice said, stifling a yawn. "I don't know what you're talking about most of the time."

"Then, when we went rowing with Stephen Tyler," William continued, warming to his subject, d'you remember how he stopped the boat very precisely? We were immediately across the same line then."

"But—what line? I never saw any line," Alice complained.

"Because it isn't there to see—unless you know what you're looking for. But we noticed it, Alice.

We all did. During the spring holiday, when we first went up to Goldenwater. You must remember. It runs through the middle of this house, through the yew tree, through the standing stone, straight up the middle of the lake and . . ." He clapped his hands excitedly. "Yes, of course, that tunnel behind the waterfall! That's on it as well. We should explore the tunnel. We'll take torches. We'll tell Phoebe we're going off for the day. She doesn't seem to mind now . . . I bet you that tunnel has something to do with the secret passage."

"What secret passage?" Alice whispered, her eyes wide with excitement.

"We were told that there's supposed to be a secret passage from the house all the way to the monastery that this house originally belonged to. Yes," William cried excitedly, "that's what we do next. We explore the tunnel behind the waterfall."

# 21

# Return of the Rats

So that was the plan. But when the following morning dawned and Spot still hadn't returned to the house Alice was so concerned about him that she persuaded the others to call in at Four Fields before they started anything else.

When they reached Goldenwater, William wanted to spend some time at the standing stone, and Mary was still hoping that they could attract Lutra to come to them.

"I mean Lutra must know every inch of the lake," she said. "I'm sure he could find the pendulum for us if it's still there."

But Alice was adamant.

"Please," she implored them. "Let's just go and see Meg first. Spot often goes there because he used to live there. I just have to know that he's all right, then I'll do anything you want."

"Well, you go on your own, Al," Mary said, crouching down by the water's edge and scanning the surface of the lake. But William shook his head and turned his back on the standing stone.

"I think for the time being we should stick together," he said grimly.

"Why, Will?" Mary asked, looking up at him.

"Because of what happened with that crow," he replied, looking round. "If Morden is really fighting now—his animals could be anywhere."

They approached Four Fields through the beech woods, reaching the gate in the hedge without following the main bridlepath. It was the route that they always took when visiting Meg after swimming and every step of the way was familiar to them.

As they were crossing the first meadow Mary noticed that the two cows and the six sheep were missing.

"I wonder where they are?" she said.

Alice was already climbing the second gate. Ahead of them now, in the corner of the next field, Meg's house, covered in creeper and looking more like an untidy bush than an actual dwelling, came into view. Everywhere was very silent. There was no sign of life.

William looked round, uneasily.

"It is very quiet," he whispered.

Even Alice, who had been so eager to arrive, hung back after climbing over the gate. They walked slowly toward the house in a tight little group.

"I feel as though I'm being watched all the time," Mary whispered.

"Maybe we should call Meg?" Alice said. But she was reluctant to do so herself and hoped one of the others might take up her suggestion.

They were almost at the door of the house before they discovered Meg's cows and her sheep. They were penned up on a small area of grass, surrounded by a fence of wire netting. They seemed quite peaceful. The cows were sitting down, chewing rhythmically, and the sheep were grazing around them.

Mary opened the front door. Two of the cats were fast asleep in the hall and one of Spot's brothers was stretched out on the floor. He sat up suddenly, as they entered, then wagged his tail and crawled toward them when he saw who had arrived.

"Hello? Meg?" William called. There was no answer. He pushed open the kitchen door.

The chaotic, cluttered room looked much as usual but Meg was not there. There was a strong smell that they couldn't at first recognize.

"Ugh! Paraffin!" Mary said. "That stove Meg uses really stinks."

"There's something wrong," William said, and he hurried back to the front door. "Meg? Meg?" he shouted. And then the girls saw him start to run across the field. "Meg?"

"He's seen something!" Mary shouted, and she also started to run in the same direction.

They found Meg lying on the ground beside the track that led to the Moor Road. She was unconscious, but she was breathing. There was a terrible gash on the side of her head and it looked as though she had fallen and stunned herself.

"What can we do?" Alice said.

"We must go for help," Mary said. She looked down the track. "It's miles from here to the town. The nearest farm is the Jenkinses'. We'd better go there. . . ."

The dog that had been shut in the house came running toward them, whining. He sniffed at Meg's face and licked her. Meg stirred and groaned.

"You stay with her," William said, starting to run down the track. "Did either of you bring any money?" he shouted.

But neither of them had.

"There's a phone box near the Jenkinses' farm. I'll get through to emergency. If only Cinnabar was here . . ." and then he stopped talking and saved his breath for the journey ahead.

Meg was half-conscious now. She seemed to be in great pain and kept groaning.

"Should we get some water?" Alice asked.

"I don't know," Mary said, sounding desperate with frustration because she didn't know what was the best thing to do.

"I'll go and get some water," Alice repeated, fighting back her own anxiety. She got up from kneeling beside Meg and hurried back toward the house to collect a mug.

"Bring a bowl and a towel as well, Al," Mary called. "Maybe we should bathe her face. Will you be able to manage? You'll have to get fresh water from the well."

"It's all right, I know!" Alice shouted, and she started to run, glad to be doing something useful.

Mary knelt beside Meg and held one of her hands. The old woman didn't respond at first, then Mary felt the grip on her hand tighten. She looked down at Meg's face and saw that her eyes were open.

"Rats!" the old woman whispered.

"What?" Mary said, leaning her ear close to the old woman's lips.

"A plague of rats," Meg whispered and, as she spoke, her hand started to tremble. "They were everywhere. The dogs chased them off." Then she became more agitated. "The animals . . ." she whispered.

"It's all right. They're all safe," Mary told her. "Where does it hurt, Meg?"

"Leg mostly," the old woman replied. "And the head . . ." Then she smiled. "I hurt everywhere to tell you the truth!"

"Don't talk," Mary said, gently mopping her brow with her hand. "William's gone to get help and Alice is bringing you some water."

\*　　\*　　\*

The smell of paraffin was terribly strong. Alice crossed the kitchen, squeezing round the cluttered furniture and reached the crowded dresser. She collected a china bowl, a mug and a large jug. Then she looked round for a towel. Seeing one hanging on a peg by the sink, she pushed her way across the room, tripping over a Wellington boot that was hidden under a pile of old papers and almost breaking the jug as she fell. As she was getting up again, she saw, in a corner beside the sink, an old blue can with a tap on the side. Paraffin was dripping from the tap onto the carpet beneath it. Alice tightened the tap and quickly washed her fingers in a bowl full of water in the sink. Then she grabbed the towel and ran toward the hall.

The rat watched her from the top of the dresser where he had climbed as he heard her enter the house. He waited until he was sure she had gone out of the front door, then he dropped down onto the ground and started to forage round the fireplace.

Once outside the house, Alice hurried to the well and filled her jug with water from the bucket.

William had almost reached the Moor Road when he heard a motor approaching. A moment later Spot appeared, limping up the road, with a Land-Rover following behind him.

"What's up, d'you know, William?" Mr. Jenkins,

the farmer, asked, leaning out of the Land-Rover. "Dog seemed in a great lather."

"It's Meg—there's been an accident. We'll need an ambulance, I think."

"Where is she?" Mr. Jenkins asked as William and Spot climbed into the Land-Rover.

"Just farther up the track," William said, gasping for breath.

"I've dreaded this happening," Mr. Jenkins said, crashing the gears and driving off at speed. "I'll just take a look at her, then I'll go for help. It'll be the end for her, I'm afraid. There's only so long an old woman can survive on her own. . . ."

Once Mr. Jenkins had seen Meg's state he got back into the Land-Rover.

"I don't like to move her myself," he explained. "You never know how much damage she might have done. Looks like a broken leg and a bit of a bash on the head—but I'm no doctor. You kids stay with her. I'll be back as soon as I can," he called through the window, as he drove off.

Spot lay down at the side of the track and licked his feet. Alice sat beside him and put a comforting hand on the back of his neck.

"What happened, Spot?" William said, as soon as the farmer had left.

"Meg said something about rats," Mary told them.

"Yes. There were rats. Hundreds of them," Spot said. "I don't know where Jasper was. That bird's never there when you need him. But, to be fair, we're all a bit lost at the moment. The Master isn't ever here," he grumbled, "and you lot don't seem to know what to do for the best."

"Just tell us what happened, Spot," William said, feeling the dog's reproof.

"Well, it started when that woman was telling you about that book she'd brought. I was having a nice sleep. One thing, when the Master isn't about, you have time for a nap! I didn't notice the rat for a bit. In fact the first thing I smelled, to be honest, was the assistant . . . and then one smell led to another. I chased it off, but it gave me a good run and I didn't manage to catch it, more's the pity. Then I got distracted by the scent of a rabbit and I didn't think much more about it, fool that I am! Because, of course, it'd heard all it needed to, hadn't it?"

"What d'you mean?" William asked.

"Well—that woman said she'd heard that Meg wasn't going to sell Four Fields. That's what this is all about. If Meg won't sell—then they'll need to get rid of her another way."

"Mr. Jenkins says she'll have to move now anyway," William said.

"I don't know about that," Spot said. "She can be a stubborn old woman!"

"Who are you talking to?" Meg whispered.

"Shhh! It's all right, Meg. Mr. Jenkins has been here. He's gone to get help."

"What a nuisance I'm being. The cows will need milking. . . ."

"Oh, fishcakes!" Alice murmured. "I hope we're not expected to do it. I can't get the hang of milking."

"It's all right," William told Meg. "Mr. Jenkins is coming straight back. He'll see to everything."

The rat found a box of matches on the mantelshelf. Gripping it in his teeth, he jumped down onto the draining board and from the draining board to the floor. Once there, it was an easy job pushing the box open. He'd watched humans do it a thousand times. Taking a match, delicately clenched between his big front teeth, he stood the box on its side, and ran the match across the rough surface.

A tiny spurt of flame crackled into life and then died.

The third match fell onto the paraffin-soaked carpet.

One of the cats came, shaking and terrified. Spot was immediately on his guard. He rose from the ground, the hair on the back of his neck bristling.

"What is it?" he yelped.

They saw the smoke as they were running across the field.

Mary stayed behind with Meg and so once again, she thought, she was missing all the adventure.

"Stay back!" William yelled, as yellow and red flames appeared through the ivy that covered a downstairs window.

"The cows and sheep, William!" Alice shouted.

They ran together and opened the makeshift gate in the wire corral. The cows were terrified and ran quickly away across the meadow. But the sheep were confused and went round and round in a circle.

"Blooming sheep!" Spot barked, and he snapped at their heels, making them move away from the house.

Then they stood, Alice and William shielding their faces with their hands to ward off the intense heat that issued from the burning building, and watched as all Meg Lewis's worldly possessions were destroyed by the fire.

"What's happening?" Meg muttered, twisting her hands, nervously.

"Shhh! It's all right. It's nothing," Mary told her, but, as she spoke, she saw a plume of smoke rising above the forest trees and she smelled the fire on the hot summer air.

Meg was taken into the emergency ward at the county hospital.

Mr. Jenkins rounded up the sheep and cattle and Meg's four hens and said he'd look after them.

The children collected together the dogs and, with each of them carrying a trembling, frightened cat, they returned to Golden House before lunchtime.

Phoebe was surprised to see them and Jack, when he heard what had happened, said he would drive in to the hospital that afternoon to see how Meg was.

When they were all sitting round the kitchen table, Phoebe suddenly said:

"It's almost too much of a coincidence, isn't it? The Crawdens have got all that they want now. I mean there isn't anywhere for Meg to live. She'll have to take their money now to buy a place." Then, surprisingly, she sobbed. "I can't bear to think of Four Fields destroyed. Where will she go, Jack?"

"I don't know," he said quietly. "She'll be devastated when she knows what's happened. Four Fields was her home."

"What about the badgers?" Alice said quietly. "She's got to be near her badgers."

"With the house burnt down, she'll not have much choice, will she?" Jack said. "She'll have to look for somewhere in the town, I suppose."

"But she'll hate it away from the badgers," Alice cried. "They're her family. She loves them better than humans. She said so."

"She can't live in a tent, Alice!" Jack said. "There is nowhere else."

Then Mary said quietly:

"Except here, of course. She'd still be near the badgers if she came and lived here at Golden House."

# 22

# The Place of Dreams

The following morning, soon after breakfast, the children went back up to the lake.

Meg's dogs had spent the night in the out-house across the yard from the kitchen door and the cats had slept in the hall some of the time, though they spent most of the night prowling round the house, and by the time Phoebe came down they had established their territory and were all fast asleep, curled up in front of the kitchen range.

Phoebe had been a bit reluctant to admit so many animals to the house and Jack was unrepentant in his resolve not to let any of the dogs sleep inside.

"One dog in a house is quite enough," he said, when Alice suggested that they could all sleep in her room if he was going to be mean about it.

Spot, however, seemed to agree with Jack and when one of his brothers tried to slip in through the kitchen door, while Phoebe was taking rubbish to the compost heap before going to bed, he had run barking and snarling at the poor creature, and driven him, squealing, into the night.

"Spot!" Alice had exclaimed. "I didn't think you'd be so beastly! They are your family, you know."

"They're outdoor dogs," he growled. "Besides, this is my place."

They had all gone in to see Meg in the hospital during the afternoon. But she was dazed and sleepy and they hadn't stayed long with her.

Since Mary's suggestion about her coming to live at Golden House no more had been said on the subject and the children didn't know whether the idea had been well received or not by Jack and Phoebe.

It was William who decided that they should go back to the original plan of exploring the tunnel. He'd slept very little and was up soon after dawn. He sat on Mary's bed, having woken both his sisters from deep sleep, and the three of them talked in low whispers.

"It's all our fault that's what's so awful," he said, referring to Meg's accident and the fire at the house. "We made her say she'd help us. That's probably why she wrote the letter to the solicitor saying she wasn't going to sell Four Fields. She did it for us. If she hadn't, none of this would have happened."

"But we didn't do it on purpose, William," Mary said, her voice still sleepy. It was a bit early in the morning for deep discussions.

"What'll we do, Will?" Alice asked. She was kneeling on the end of her bed from where she had a good view out of the window. The morning was bright and already warm. A soft breeze stirred the curtains and the sound of birdsong filtering in from the distant forest should have made her happy. But Alice sighed, feeling depressed when she remembered all that had happened on the day before. "We've as good as lost now, haven't we?"

"No, we have not," William replied firmly. "I'm not giving up. I'm more determined than ever to beat Morden. I've thought about nothing else all night. We're going to try to prove that land doesn't belong to the Crawdens. Miss Prewett was right—if we can only do that, then they'll go away and leave us alone."

"But then they won't need to buy Meg's land either," Mary said. "And now she needs the money more than ever. Maybe it'd be better if we let them go ahead. I mean—even if Meg comes and lives here—what will she live on? Jack can't keep her."

"Why can't he?" Alice asked. "I'm sure she won't be very expensive."

"He's hardly got enough money to keep himself and Phoebe and Stephanie," Mary said. "And Meg must be terribly poor—look at the state of the house she lived in. She didn't even own a proper armchair. Why must money always be so important? But it is. I can understand Jonas Lewis wanting to make some gold when he was broke. It's all right for the Magician. I bet he was really rich, living in a big house like this. But Jack's not—that's why he's taking so long to finish the house. And as for Meg—she's lost everything now, hasn't she?"

"She's only lost her house, Mary," William said. "And it wasn't much of a place. She's still got her animals. . . ."

"Wasn't much of a place?" Alice exclaimed. "I thought it was the best place in the whole world."

"And another thing, if she comes and lives here," Mary added, "what will happen to her cows and sheep? She can't keep those here. There isn't room."

"One thing at a time," William said. "First we've got to stop the Crawdens. Then we'll worry about everything else."

So, as soon as breakfast was finished, the children set off for Goldenwater. This time they carried backpacks containing a picnic, torches, and useful things like string, penknives, elastoplast and William's compass.

"You never know what we're going to need," William said.

Spot came with them, but he shooed the other dogs away and left them sitting in a row in the yard, greedily watching Dan and Arthur, the builders, who were in their van, eating breakfast sandwiches.

When they reached the lake, William didn't pause at the standing stone. He was in too much of a hurry to get to the tunnel behind the water-fall. He walked so fast that Alice had to run to keep up with him. Mary scanned the surface of the lake as they passed by, hoping for a sign of Lutra, but the only wildlife that they saw were some crows, wheeling in the air above the fir for-est on the far side of the lake and a race of star-lings, who sped across the sky like maniacs, chattering and laughing.

"Hateful birds," Mary murmured, and she hur-ried to catch up with William and Alice because she didn't want to be on her own.

Goldenspring flashed and sparkled in the sun-light. By the time they reached the ledge they were breathless and their hearts were pounding.

"It isn't a race, William!" Mary yelled, as she pulled herself up the steep slope and leaned against a boulder, breathing heavily.

But William was flushed and determined still. He only hesitated for a moment before he started to edge his way out toward the falls.

"Come on," he called. "The sooner we're out of sight the better," and, as he spoke he glanced up at the sky, where several crows were wheeling threateningly.

The dark closed round them almost at once. But they each had a torch and were able to see their way. The tunnel was no more than a narrow cleft through the rock, only wide enough for them to walk in single file. They came to the place where it broadened out. Here some daylight filtered in from an opening high up above.

"This is where the Magician had his meeting," William whispered. "The last time we saw him. I wonder why he chose here?" As he spoke, he shone his torch round the smooth rock walls that enclosed them.

"Is it a dead end?" Mary asked, disappointed. "I thought it was going to lead somewhere."

"So did I," William agreed. "Why did he choose this place to see us all?"

Spot whined quietly, sitting on the floor of the cave, looking up at William eagerly, as if trying to understand his words.

William walked slowly round the cave, shining his torch into every nook and cranny.

"This place is on a direct line with the standing stone and the yew tree, we know that," he said quietly.

"And the yew tree is in line with the dovecote and the windows in the secret room," Mary added.

"So we're on the hidden center line. Now, as we're talking, we're on it. What did he call it? An energy line . . ."

William walked slowly away from them, pointing his torch.

"What is this place?" he whispered. "What is it?"

"The place of dreams," a voice said and, a moment later, Stephen Tyler emerged from the dark shadows and stood in front of them, leaning on his silver staff, and carrying a lantern in which the yellow light of a candle flickered.

"Oh!" William sighed, relieved and overjoyed to see the Magician again. "I thought you were never going to come back."

"You had to think that, William. You had to get here on your own," the old man told him, talking gently.

"But where are we?" William asked.

"In reality—or in magic?" the Magician asked. "In reality this is a cave of great antiquity. In ancient times perhaps primitive people used it as a place of worship. See," and, as he spoke, he lifted his lantern to reveal vague lines on the smooth rock.

"It's a sort of horse," Alice gasped. "A drawing of a horse."

They crowded round, staring up at the rough simple drawing on the rock. As well as the horse, there was a hand print and another collection of lines that made no sense.

"A horse and a hand and—what?"

"Who will ever know?" Stephen Tyler asked.

"Someone, once, tried here to express what they had seen by drawing it. Think about it, William. The person who did this drawing—had never seen a drawing before. They were doing something entirely . . . utterly . . . new. How often do we do something original; something new? That's what you had to do, you Constant children. You had to think for yourselves. Usually we only think other people's thoughts. Our teacher, or our parent, or our Magician gives us ideas . . . and we make them our own. But in this work, this alchemy, sometimes it is necessary to be . . . unique. Why?"

He paused and the silence throbbed around them.

"Why is it necessary?" he repeated the question.

"Because we are unique," William replied. "There's no one quite like me. No one quite like Alice, or Mary . . . Or anyone else, come to that . . . Each person in the world is different. . . ."

The Magician nodded.

"However many millions of people are born—there are no two who are entirely the same. An unlimited number of variations on a theme. It is our uniqueness that is the gold in us; it is our striving to be the same that is the dross. You could only know that by being here in this place. This sacred place. Now, together, we must save this land of ours. Because it is also unique—there is nowhere quite like it. People don't find this cave by chance. The animals know it, the birds, the insects; the creatures of nature. They know it is here. And the person who drew these primitive pictures knew this place."

"But—is it really here?" Alice asked. "Or are we dreaming this?"

"Very good question," the Magician replied. "It is here—in reality—if you know where to look for it."

"I mean—could someone just . . . find it by mistake?" Alice asked.

"It might seem a mistake—but they wouldn't find it, if it wasn't right for them to do so."

"Does Morden know it's here?" Mary asked.

"Better question!" the Magician said, with a smile. "No—and if he did . . . say he followed you and came in here . . . it would be meaningless to him. It would be just a cave and these drawings would be merely scratches on the wall."

"Why?" William asked.

"Because he only sees what he expects to see and isn't prepared to believe the unknown."

The old man turned and raised his lantern again, dimly illuminating the racing horse galloping across the wall of the cave. As he did so, the children heard the sound of pounding hooves and a distant whinny.

"How can we stop Morden?" William asked.

"By not letting him matter," the old man said

with a sigh. "It's a hard discipline, but it is the only way. We give Morden too much attention. He thrives on that."

"But—that's what you told us to do. To stop him—or rather Charles Crawden—from taking this place and destroying it. I mean, I thought that was what our task is."

"Yes," Stephen Tyler replied. "And I want it even more than you children. But, if we don't get it—if my assistant wins and the whole of my creation comes tumbling to nothing—so be it. You have touched your uniqueness, that's far more important."

"I don't agree," William said. "I haven't come this far to let him win. He's destroyed Meg's house. . . ."

"You want revenge, William?" the Magician asked him, his voice ominously calm.

"No, not revenge. Justice. You said we should act justly. Well, I want that. But I don't want evil people to win all the time. If I act justly—then I want justice as well. For Meg's sake; for Jack and Phoebe and Stephanie; for the wild creatures who live here. I don't know." He shook his head irritably. "I don't want to fail, not now. I want to save Golden Valley."

"Is this what you all want?" the Magician asked. Mary and Alice nodded but couldn't bring themselves to speak.

"Then perhaps there is still hope," the

Magician said quietly. "But you must ask your-selves very seriously why you want this. If your reason is in any way selfish—then it could destroy you. Be very clear about this—act selfishly and you are lost—but act with a pure heart and you will save this valley. . . ."

"We're doing it because we must!" William exclaimed. "That's how it is for us. Maybe in your time it isn't so important. But it is today. Men like Charles Crawden are destroying our world. The rain forests are going; the whales and the dolphins are being killed; elephants are murdered for their ivory tusks; the earth is being poisoned; there's a hole in the ozone layer. These are things you don't know about, because you live in the past. But the reason for them all is greed—all our problems are brought about by greed. You've made me see that. Well, I can't sit back and let it happen here. I've got to try to stop it. It may not be the task you set us—but it's the task I've set myself."

"Go back to the lake" the Magician said. "Lutra will help you."

"Oh, no!" Alice wailed. "Not Blackwater Sluice."

"Go along, all of you," the Magician told them. "You have made your choice. My prayers will be with you. Be on guard all the time. Act for the common good; never for yourselves. That is all that is required of you."

# 23

# Journey Through the Underworld

Lutra was waiting for them. They saw his head appear above the surface of the water as they ran down a grassy bank onto the shingle shore.

"Yous a nuisance," Lutra called. "I was having a nice sleeps. What you want?"

William shrugged and squatted down, so that his head was almost on a level with the otter.

"Don't know," he said. "The Magician said you'd help us."

"So—what is it you wants?"

"To save Goldenwater," Alice said, flopping down beside William and picking up a pebble.

"Mmmh!" the otter hummed doubtfully. "Hows you going to do that?"

"With your help!" William said, with a grin. "We don't exactly know how, Lutra. I thought if we found the Magician's laboratory . . ."

"Is that all yous want?" the otter asked, sounding more cheerful. "That's easy! Yous all coming?"

"Oh!" Mary exclaimed.

"What?" William asked.

"It's happening," she whispered and, as she spoke, she dipped her head under the water and then resurfaced, shaking the moisture out of her whiskers. She saw William and Alice sitting on the shore and wondered where she was. Then she heard her brother whisper in her head:

"Ooops! Here we go!"

"Come on, Alice," Lutra called. "We's got to take yous all."

"Don't want to," Alice said, hanging back.

"Come on," Lutra wheedled. "It won't be so bad. Things is never so bad second time round."

Alice doubted his words but allowed herself to join the others. At once Lutra turned and, with a flick of his tail, he propelled himself toward the middle of the lake.

The water was calm and glassy-clear. They passed through a shoal of tiny gleaming fish who scattered and fled as the otter swam among them.

"Tiddlers!" Lutra snorted. "Yous must come on a trout hunt with us one day. Trouts is our favorite. Do yous like trouts?"

"Actually we do eat trout!" Mary exclaimed enthusiastically. It made a change to be traveling in an animal who ate the sort of food that she did. She decided that she was enjoying getting to know the otter. Then she remembered that Lutra's trout would be raw and so she decided not to encourage him. But it was pleasant swimming through the soft water, with the light of the sun bouncing off the water around them. The cold scarcely penetrated the otter's thick, waterproof fur and, although they were moving fast, there was very little exertion involved. "It's a bit like being on a boat, really," Mary thought, and she felt herself relaxing into the experience.

But then, when they reached the center of the lake, Lutra's voice changed to an urgent whisper.

"Are you ready?" he said.

And Mary's brief enjoyment came to an end as she heard Alice gasp and say:

"Oh, Lutra! Do we have to?"

"Yes," the otter replied. "It's the only way."

"What?" Mary whispered in their heads. "Where are we going now?" and only then, as Lutra, with another flick of his tail, dived for the depths, did Alice and William remember that Mary hadn't been through Blackwater Sluice before.

"Please tell me what's happening," she said, as the water surged past them and the light faded.

"Don't think!" Lutra hissed. "I's need to concentrate."

The pull of the current grew stronger. They could feel it dragging their otter-body along. The temperature was dropping and the cold was seeping into their veins. Suddenly, ahead of them, they dimly saw the rock wall of the lake. They were going too fast. Lutra thrust out his front legs and beat with his tail, trying to turn his body. The rock came closer and closer at a terrifying speed. They were going to be smashed against it. Something had gone wrong. Lutra couldn't turn his body. Using every bit of his strength, he flicked and flicked again with his back legs and his tail.

William concentrated on his legs. He tried to beat them in time to Lutra's rhythm.

"We're going to crash!" Alice screamed.

"What's happening?" Mary cried out.

"Blackwater Sluice!" Lutra hissed. "That's what's happening!" And then, when it was almost too late, the otter's body turned and, grazing along the rough outcrop of submerged rock, they were pulled along on the current toward the black hole of the sluice and, surging forward on the steel water, they shot through the narrow opening and were flung, dazed and panting, onto the floor of the cave.

Mary picked herself up. She felt terribly cold. For a moment she thought she was alone in the black dark. But then she heard Alice sniffing and William gasped.

"Bloody hell!" he exclaimed. William didn't often swear. When he did he usually had a good reason for it.

"Sorrys about that," Lutra said cheerfully, his voice coming out of the dark somewhere close by them, "Misjudged the direction. Bit tricksy getting through the sluice. Don't enjoys it much myself. And it's an awful long way round to get back to the lake. Can't go back up the sluice, the current's too strong. Right, come on yous lot."

"But how will this take us to the Magician's laboratory?" William asked.

"Waits and sees," Lutra hissed cheerfully.

The journey followed innumerable narrow passageways and dripping tunnels. Sometimes they were swimming in deep water, at other times they were crawling through gaps so narrow that they could feel the rough rock tearing at Lutra's body.

"What is this place?" Mary asked.

"The underworld," Lutra replied. "There's always an underworld, yous know."

Later they came to a series of tunnels that were high enough for the children to walk upright in.

"These is the mines," Lutra explained, trotting in front of them. "These is where men used to come and steal the rocks. Sometimes they stoles so much rock that the roof fell in. Once a man was trapped here. My Papa told me. He said his Papa helped the man to escape. I don't know if it's trues. Could be just another story."

They came to a place where they had to climb down a great cliff.

"S'all right," Lutra said. "I's not a good climber but there's water at the bottom," and, as he spoke, they felt themselves falling through the darkness and then they landed in more black water.

It seemed as though they were in some sort of river now, but of course it was too dark to see anything. However, the water was deep and there was a feeling of space around them.

"There's streams like this all over the underworld," Lutra told them. "They all ends up in the ocean. I's been to the ocean. It was big. All the water in the world stretches from us here. We're touching all over the world. And, yous listen to this bit. The water was here in before days and will be here in to come days. So this water stretches back into then and reaches forward into when. D'yous follow what I'm saying?"

"Not quite," William had to admit.

"There is no past and future, William," a familiar voice whispered in his head. "There is only now."

"Mr. Tyler?" William called out.

"I heard him as well," Mary thought.

"And me," Alice whispered.

"If there's only now," William thought. "Who says when now is?"

"Quite!" Lutra agreed. Then he said aloud, "We're nearly there."

"Where?" William asked, surprised.

"The Magician's laboratory," the otter replied. "That's where you wanted to go, wasn't it? Up there then," he added and, as he spoke, the children saw light filtering down a round stone funnel above their heads.

"It's like a chimney," Alice observed, as she lifted her arm up out of the river water. "There's a ladder up the side," she added.

"You go first, Will," Mary said.

William grabbed hold of the iron support that was fixed into the circular stone funnel. Alice was right. It was exactly like a chimney. Far up above he could see dim green light filtering down.

"Where are we, Lutra?" he asked.

But there was no reply.

"He's gone, I think," Alice said, pulling herself up out of the water as she followed William up the iron ladder, with Mary close behind her.

As they climbed steadily upward the light at the top became brighter. They could see the opening. It was covered with green, leafy branches.

"It's as though we're going up into a tree," William called.

"Like going up to the tree house," Mary observed.

"Like going up the steps up the chimney and going up the yew tree all at the same time," Alice said in a puzzled voice.

"Hey!" William gasped.

"What?" Alice asked.

"There's an opening here," William called down from just above her. "There's a way in," and, looking up, Alice saw William step sideways off the iron ladder and disappear into the wall of the funnel.

# 24

# The Magician's Laboratory

Beside the ladder, set into the wall, was a square opening, just big enough for a person to pass through.

Alice gripped the metal supports of the ladder with both her hands and reached across with her foot. Once she had a safe hold, it was easy to let go of the ladder and walk through the opening. As she did so, a spider's web brushed her cheek.

"William," she called in a whisper.

"Who's there?" an unfamiliar voice called.

"Here, Al," she heard William whisper and, looking in the direction of the sound, she saw a spider in the middle of the web.

"Oh, no! Please!" she thought. "Not a spider. I really hate spiders."

"Then that's because you don't know anything about us," the spider said in a thin voice. "We spiders are much maligned."

"Oh . . . !" Alice groaned. Then she only just

managed to climb up the web before a man pushed past her, coming from the dark interior of the room she had entered.

"Who's there?" he called again. Reaching the iron ladder and holding the support rail as he leaned out, looking up the round funnel to the leaf-covered opening at the top. "Will?" the man called. "Will? Is it you?"

Mary pressed herself against the wall of the funnel. The man's feet were on a level with her hands. If he looked down he couldn't fail to see her. But there was nowhere for her to hide. She remained motionless, gripping the iron rung of the ladder until it cut into her hands.

The man hesitated for a moment longer then, turning, he hurried back through the dark opening. Mary was unsure what to do. She had seen Alice disappear into the opening, following William. She had been on the point of reaching across and going in herself. But now she wasn't at all sure what would be the best thing to do. Who was this man?—she wondered—and what was he doing there? And, more important, where had William and Alice gone to?

"I'm here," a tiny voice whispered, and the spider, hanging on a thread of his own making appeared in front of her face.

"Is it safe?" Mary asked, as she climbed nimbly up the thread.

"Safe enough," William whispered and, swiveling her eight eyes, Mary saw the room and the roof and the floor and the lamplight and William hanging motionless in the center of his web, with Alice peeping out of a crevice in the stonework just beside him, all at the same time.

Mary spun a strand of thread and jumped across the opening. Then, finding a good position, close to the ceiling of the room, she settled herself and turned to watch.

The room they were in was like an underground cellar. The walls were made of stone and there was no window. The walls were lined with shelves and there was a big workbench in the center. On the shelves and on the bench and littered over the stone floor were vials and bottles, glass containers of every shape and size, pottery jars. A fire glowed in a small hearth. Lamps were alight. There were books and papers and diagrams scattered in heaps all over the floor.

A man, unfamiliar to any of them, was busily emptying the contents of the shelves and making a great pile on the floor between the fire and the table. He worked with frantic speed and seemed in a state of great agitation. The light in the room was so poor that they were unable to get a clear impression of him. He seemed tall and gaunt. He wore a dark-colored jacket and tight, narrow trousers. He darted round the room, throwing objects onto the pile. There was the sound of breaking glass and splintering wood as he broke and smashed and scattered everything that came into his reach.

Then he stopped, listening again, his head turned toward the opening in the wall.

"Mr. Lewis?" a distant voice called. "Mr. Lewis, are you there?"

The man hurried back to the opening, passing so close to William that he was able to see large beads of sweat on his forehead.

"I'm here, Will," he called, leaning out into the funnel.

Then stepping back into the room, he took a lantern off a hook and lifted it, surveying the scene of devastation that he had created.

Behind him, footsteps heralded the arrival of a young man. He was wearing thick woolen trousers, tied with string below the knees and an open-necked shirt.

"What's to do, Mr. Lewis?" the boy asked, then, seeing the mess in the room, he gasped. "What's happened?"

"You have not heard?" the man called Mr. Lewis asked him. "I would have thought it would have been the talk of the county. Mr. Crawden comes here to Golden House on the first of the month."

"I'm sorry, Mr. Lewis," the boy said, sounding genuinely upset. "Sorrier than I can say. I would not have the Crawdens living here for a year's pay."

"Well, Will," Mr. Lewis said, putting a hand on the boy's shoulder, "that's the way it will be."

"Where will you go, Mr. Lewis?"

"I keep the land. My wife and I and the babe will live up at the forester's cottage near Goldenwater."

"The land is yours?" Will asked.

"I have it in writing." As he spoke, Lewis crossed to the table and produced a thick book. "Here, I have the paper here, tucked into my journal."

Alice at once recognized the book. It was the one Miss Prewett had brought from the museum. Jonas Lewis's book.

"I can't read, Mr. Lewis, you know that."

Jonas Lewis held the paper close to the lamp and read aloud: " 'An agreement made between Jonas Lewis of Golden House . . .' Oh, you don't need to hear all that. 'All the estate of the said Golden House shall remain the property of the vendor and his family and descendants on the full and certain understanding that should he, or any member of his family or said descendants choose to sell the land, then, at such time, the purchaser, the above-named Edmund Arthur Crawden, his next of kin or his descendants shall have first refusal on the property for as long as the said Edmund Arthur Crawden, his next of kin or his descendants shall be the owners of Golden House. In the event of Edmund Arthur

Crawden, his next of kin or his descendants sell-
ing Golden House, he, his next of kin or his
descendants shall first offer the property to Jonas
Lewis, his next of kin or descendants . . .' That's
how it's divided, Will. Crawden has the house. I
have the estate. He gets the estate if I want to sell.
I get the house if he wants to sell." He laughed
bitterly. "Though what I could purchase it with is
a matter of some conjecture, as Edmund
Crawden very well knows. So there it is. I have
done the best I could. It's all legal. All signed and
sealed." As he spoke, he replaced the journal on
the workbench and threw the paper down beside
it.

"Then you've not lost everything, Mr. Lewis,"
the boy said.

"Everything, Will. I move out of this house
without a penny to my name."

"You have the land, Mr. Lewis," Will reminded
him.

"And no money to care for it. He's got me,
Will. I am punished."

Jonas Lewis walked slowly round the room
kicking over the rubble.

"What about the jars of chemicals, Mr. Lewis,"
Will asked, crossing to the shelves where rows of
bottles still stood.

"I have disposed of all the lethal toxics. There
is nothing dangerous left. At least I can leave a
tidy bench, Will."

"Tidy!" Will exclaimed, looking round at the piles of destruction.

"I have not done yet," Lewis said.

"Couldn't you make some money out of these things, Mr. Lewis? The quicksilver. That might raise a few shillings."

Lewis shook his head.

"I will not be making any more money out of any of this," he replied grimly. "My days of money-making are over!" and he smiled, bleakly, as if at some private joke. "No. Everything must stay. It does not belong to me."

"To Crawden? He owns all this as well?"

"No, not Crawden, Will. The house, more like. This all belongs to the house."

"Does Crawden know about this place?"

Jonas Lewis shook his head.

"Nor will he. I want a service of you, Will, for which I cannot pay."

"I've had payment enough from you in my time, Mr. Lewis."

"It will not be easy and it has to be done fast."

"I'll do what you asked. I'll shore up the opening for you, surely. I'll start now."

"You're a good man, Will," Jonas Lewis said.

"Tell me one thing, Mr. Lewis. All the experimenting—did it come to anything? Was it worth it?"

"No, Will. It came to nothing and it brought me nothing with it," Jonas replied with utter sadness.

"What was it that you were hoping for?" the boy asked. "I mean—what were you trying to make?"

"Something of myself," Jonas Lewis answered. "I was trying to better myself."

"Good Lord save us, Mr. Lewis. You were the master of Golden House. What more could you want?"

"There's always more, Will. That is the danger. Come, we must leave this place. How long will it take you to block the door? I'll help you."

Will Hardwick shrugged.

"Not long. But it'll be working under difficulties. I can do half the course from this side—then I'll have to climb out and complete the work on the well side. It won't be smooth with the wall. I'll have to leave myself a ledge to stand on. Then there's the stone to get down from the top and the mortar. . . ."

"Can you do it, Will?"

"Oh, yes, Mr. Lewis. That's my trade, isn't it?"

"And then you'll never speak of this place, Will. To anyone? For me?"

"How have I got a trade, Mr. Lewis, but thanks to you? Who looked after us when Dad died? You. I'll do it. I'll start at once."

"No, Will. Tomorrow. By then the fire will have died down."

"Fire?" Will asked, sounding surprised.

"I told you," Jonas Lewis replied. "I will leave a tidy bench." And, as he spoke, he picked up one of the lanterns and threw it at the pile of refuse he had made between the fire and the table.

The oil from the lamp seeped out, as the glass lantern smashed against the stone floor. The flame from the lamp ignited the oil and with a hollow roar the papers and books started to burn.

"Out, Will! Quick now," Jonas Lewis said, pushing the boy toward the door. "There are chemicals here that will make a merry blaze."

"But, sir, won't the fire bring the whole place down?" Will had to shout to be heard above the increasing sound of the fire.

"I think not, Will. I think the Magus chose his laboratory well. These solid stone walls will withstand a holocaust. Out boy, out! The heat is intolerable."

Jonas pushed Will before him toward the opening. The flames were leaping through the great mound of papers and wood. The fire was well constructed and, as it grew in strength so it gathered into its blazing heart large pieces of wood and bigger, heavy leather-bound tomes.

"Goodbye, scene of my despair!" Jonas Lewis said, from the door. Then he was just about to step out of the opening, when he saw his journal lying on the table.

"My journal!" he cried and, covering his mouth and nose with his arm, he beat his way back into the raging, smoke-filled room, and grabbed the book up off the table. Then, coughing and spluttering, he made a dash for the opening and disappeared.

"Will!" Mary screamed. "The document! The paper he was reading from. He's left it on the table."

"Come on," said the spider, "this place is getting too hot for my liking."

"No! Wait!" William cried and, as he did so, he fell onto his feet on the stone floor.

The smoke was filling the room and now several small explosions indicated that some of the chemical jars were bursting, filling the air with noxious fumes. William was gasping and coughing. His eyes were running and the heat from the fire was singeing the hairs on his head.

"Will!" Alice screamed, trying to reach him.

"Go back, Alice!" he shouted. "You and Mary get out. I've got to try . . ."

Flames were leaping across the floor, following a trail of oil, between him and the table. Covering his face with his arm he jumped across this river of fire and grabbed the paper from the bench where Jonas had thrown it. Then, turning, he saw that between him and the opening the ground had turned into a raging inferno as the flames devoured everything combustible within their reach.

"William!" Mary screamed, her voice coming from the funnel on the other side of the flames.

"Help me!" William wailed, panic seizing at him and making his legs weak and his spirit waver.

"Take care, William!" a voice in his head whispered. "If you act with a motive—you must look after yourself."

"I'm not doing it for myself!" William cried.

"Well—do this for yourself, boy, all the same," the voice insisted. "Get out of here, William, NOW!"

And, as he heard this urgent command, William ran as fast as he could, straight through the middle of the flames toward the opening.

He arrived, coughing and spluttering, at the iron ladder. Stuffing the folded paper into the belt of his jeans, he started to climb as fast as he could. Below him he could see smoke and tongues of flame issuing out of the opening. The funnel was acting exactly like a chimney, drawing the fire upward.

William pulled himself up the ladder, rung after rung, until he felt a fresh breeze blowing on his face. Looking up, he saw the branches of a huge bush blocking his way. He reached the top of the ladder, and forced his way through the clutter of branches over the side of a low wall. Then, squirming and turning, he pushed his way through the bush and with a final effort fell out of a jungle of leaves and twigs onto a side path at the corner of the walled, kitchen garden of Golden House.

Mary and Alice were waiting for him, clinging together desperately. Their faces were covered with soot and grime and there were tears on their cheeks.

"Oh, Will," Mary said, running and putting her arms round him. "I thought . . ." and she couldn't speak anymore for the tears.

"What are you three up to?" a voice said, and turning, they saw Dan, the young builder, standing by the yard gate.

"Nothing. We've just been playing," William said, quickly.

"Playing?" Dan said. "You want to be careful playing in that corner, you know. There's an old well behind that bush. I've told Jack about it. It needs boarding over or a metal cover putting on it. Dangerous things, wells," and he went off, into the yard.

"Are you all right?" Mary asked William, as soon as he'd gone.

He nodded and wiped his grimy hands on his jeans. One hand brushed a thick sheaf of papers sticking out of his belt. He pulled them out, remembering.

"What is it?" Mary asked.

"The missing document," William said, looking at the large copperplate writing on the first page. "It's the Bill of Sale drawn up between Jonas Lewis and Edmund Crawden."

"Oh, Will!" Alice whispered. "Does that mean we've won? Have we saved Golden Valley?"

"We have the proof now that the land belongs

not to the Crawdens but to Meg—yes, maybe we've won," William replied, but his voice sounded doubtful.

"Let's tell them at once!" Mary cried.

But William shook his head, looking at the paper in his hand with a puzzled expression.

"No, we must wait," he said.

"Why?" the girls cried in unison, their impatience showing.

"I'm not sure," he replied. "We must get it right this time. We mustn't make Jonas Lewis's mistake. . . ." and he walked away from them, deep in thought, stuffing the document back into his jeans.

# 25

# "The Matter
Is Finally Closed"

On a soft summer evening, two weeks later, the
children returned to Four Fields. They climbed
the steep hillside behind Golden House and,
skirting the badger sett, they passed the yew tree
and the standing stone, reaching the shore of the
lake as the sun was beginning to set in a haze of
golden light over the hills behind Goldenspring.
Birds were singing in the boughs of the forest
trees and the surface of the lake reflected the
milk-blue sky like a discarded mirror.

William had been strangely morose and
unforthcoming since the events in the Magician's
laboratory, which had infuriated the girls, who
were anxious to tell Jack that they had found the
missing document and that therefore they could
save Goldenwater from the Crawdens.

"It really proves that the land doesn't belong to
the Crawdens!" Mary exclaimed excitedly after
they'd all studied it closely.

But William had continued to be deeply troubled and wouldn't talk about the subject. For the next few days he had carefully avoided any further discussions. This hadn't been too difficult, because the children had been busy helping to prepare a room for Meg, for her to use when she came out of hospital. But now, as they were walking toward Four Fields, he knew the time had come when he couldn't put it off any longer.

They were to meet Jack and Phoebe, who were driving there, taking Meg with them. It was the first time Meg had been back since the day of her accident and it had been her suggestion that they should all go together. She had been discharged from hospital the week before and had agreed reluctantly to stay at Golden House.

"But only temporarily," she'd added shyly, when Phoebe had invited her. "I mustn't be a nuisance to anyone."

So Meg was installed at the front of the house in the Tudor part of the building, in the room that they had prepared for her. Her cats had moved in with her and the dogs slept outside her window and, in a matter of days, the place had started to take on the cluttered appearance of the kitchen at Four Fields.

During all this time the children had waited in vain for the return of the Magician. Jasper told them that the old man had not been well, but that he would know precisely all that had taken place and he'd come when it was necessary.

"That's the way it is with the Master," he told them. "He comes when you least expect him and rarely when you want him!"

Now, as they walked slowly along the shore of the lake, William explained why he longed to see Stephen Tyler more than he had ever done before.

"I don't know what to do," he told them.

"About what?" Mary asked.

"Jack says the planning permission comes up for discussion before the council next week. If we're going to stop the Crawdens pushing through their plan—we have to do it now."

"But we can stop them, William," Alice insisted. "Show them the legal paper thing."

"I daren't," William whispered.

"Why?" Mary cried.

"Two reasons," William said, taking a stone and flinging it out across the surface of the lake.

"What reasons?" Mary insisted.

"Well, first," William said, pushing a lock of hair away from his forehead as he spoke, "the Magician always said we weren't allowed to change history. I think that's why he kept looking into the future. I suppose it's all right to influence events before they've taken place. But, if you change something in the past . . . then it makes a nonsense of everything that follows after it. Like say . . . if somebody in the past had died, but we decided it would be better for some reason to keep them alive a bit longer, so we warned them of what was going to happen and saved their lives . . . then all the events that followed afterward—still in our past—couldn't work. Because everything would be different. The person would be alive . . . instead of dead. History would have been changed. We can't do that. We can influence the future, we can't change the past."

"But it's only some pieces of paper, William!" Alice protested impatiently. "We could have found them anywhere."

"But we didn't, Alice. We know they were burnt in that fire . . . or rather, they should have been burnt," and, as he spoke, he produced the folded pages from inside his shirt, where he'd put them for safekeeping before they set out. "I suppose, in a way," he said, looking at them thoughtfully, "I've already changed history. I should have let them burn."

"But you didn't—so I think you should use them," Alice said quickly.

"No, Alice!" William's voice was racked with fear. "That's how it starts!"

"What? What starts?"

"Using the magic for our own ends."

"But that's what we were told to do," Mary pointed out.

"Never," William said, shaking his head. "We were never told to use the magic. That's how Jonas Lewis ended up making gold. Don't you see? He wanted to be free of his debts. He wanted the gold for his own use. We want to prevent Crawden from building his Theme Park here. Well, doesn't that mean we want the magic for our own use as well?"

"But we were told to save the valley."

"Yes," William nodded. "But somehow we have to do it ourselves. All the magic should do is help us, ourselves, on our own, to achieve our ends. So that we do the saving—and don't just leave it to magic. Otherwise we could just sit back and . . . whenever we wanted something changed . . . we'd work a spell, like what happens in fairy stories. But it isn't like that—or it shouldn't be. In fact it mustn't be."

Mary nodded.

"We can use the knowledge, though, can't we?"

"How?" William asked.

Mary shrugged.

"I don't know. But, I mean, we can't pretend we don't know what's in the Bill of Sale. We can't pretend that we didn't see what happened in the laboratory. It may have been by magic that we know these things—but we can't pretend now that it never happened. What I'm trying to say is—we've seen certain things only because the magic led us to them."

"Yes. I agree with that," William said reluctantly.

"So," Mary insisted, "you agree that the magic can be allowed to help us to know things?"

"To influence us, yes, of course," William said with a nod. "But then it's up to us what we do with the knowledge. I just wish I could see what we're supposed to do with this!" And he held out the Bill of Sale document toward the girls.

"Couldn't we . . . by mistake . . . happen to drop it somewhere where someone would be sure to find it?" Alice asked hopefully. "Preferably someone like Uncle Jack, say?"

"It should have been burnt in that fire," William insisted doggedly. "That's what really happened—until we came along and, with the help of magic, saved it." He sighed. "We've done what he warned us not to. We've changed events. We've altered history. No, not we—me. I did it. I was so determined to prove the Crawdens wrong. It's my fault."

"But, you're not doing it for yourself."

"I am, Mary. I want us to win—no matter how we do it."

"You mean, it's all been a waste?" Alice asked. "You mean we can't use the truth—just because we got it by magic?"

"Maybe not that exactly," William said. "We can't produce this document . . . but we could . . . let them know that we know what it contains."

"Why would that be any different?" Mary asked.

"You see—they have a copy of this," William said, holding up the folded paper in his hand. "And they are banking on the fact that Meg Lewis doesn't possess the one that her grandfather, Jonas Lewis originally had. And, of course, they're right. But—if we somehow . . . made them think that Meg *did* have a copy . . ."

"But, if she had a copy, surely she'd just produce it?" Mary said.

"Which she can, if we just give it to her," Alice agreed.

"Only really it was burnt," Mary said quietly. "What are you going to do, Will?"

"Well, I can't do anything without both of you agreeing. But I think . . ." as she spoke he produced a box of matches from his pocket, "it has to be burnt."

They were silent for a moment, then first Mary and then Alice solemnly nodded their heads.

"Should we try and learn the words by heart first?" Alice suggested eagerly.

"I don't need to. I don't think I'll ever forget the words," William said.

They went to the flat rock, jutting out into the water, where they often in the past had picnicked, and William crouched down, facing the lake.

"Are we sure?" he said quietly.

"Go on, Will," Mary told him.

"We won't ever save Goldenwater now," Alice said mournfully. "We can't possibly."

"We might," William said, sounding far from confident. "But, if we do, we must do it ourselves," and he struck a match and set fire to the corner of the document. Mary and Alice knelt on either side of him, watching as the flame grew in strength, reducing the paper to thick gray ash.

"I hope we're doing the right thing," Mary said.

"Too late now, anyway," Alice observed, watching as the last of the flames licked up toward William's finger and thumb.

"We're doing what we believe to be the right thing," he said. "Maybe that's all anyone can hope for." Then he dropped the corner of the paper he was holding and the flame flickered and burned itself out.

A gentle breeze was blowing. It gathered up the gray ash from the rock and wafted it away over Goldenwater until it disappeared from their sight.

"We'd better go," William said, rising. "We'll be late for the others."

Mary and Alice also rose and Alice turned to walk with William toward Four Fields. But Mary hesitated. The beams of the setting sun were staining the surface of the water a rich, honey-gold. The ripples sparkled in the evening light. But what had caught Mary's attention was the glitter of another gold, a sharper, brighter, more brilliant light, that flashed beneath the surface of the lake, right there at her feet.

"William! Alice!" she shouted excitedly.

Her brother and sister turned back, enquiringly.

"What, Mare?" William asked. He still sounded subdued. It had been hard for him, burning the only proof they needed to defeat Morden's plan.

"Look!" Mary exclaimed. And, as she spoke, she knelt down on the edge of the rock and put her hand into the lake. Then rising, she held out in front of her the golden chain with the smooth nugget hanging from it that they had last seen falling into the lake at the Battle of Goldenwater.

"The Magician's pendulum!" she said in amazement.

"But—how did it get there?" Alice asked. "When it fell you and the crow were miles out over the lake, Mary."

"Don't let's ask how," William said. "Let's just be glad we've got it."

"Oh, Will! D'you think it's a sign from him?" Mary pleaded. "D'you think he's telling us that we did the right thing burning the document?"

"I don't know," William said with a sigh. "I don't know anything. You keep it, Mary. . . ."

"No," she said, shaking her head. "You, Will. This is your story really."

"Why d'you say that?" William asked. "It's all of us."

"But you've worked things out, Will. I mean really worked things out. You keep it—at least until it's all over."

"All right," William said, taking the pendulum on its golden chain from Mary and putting it in his pocket. "But it isn't mine. I'm just looking after it."

When they reached Four Fields the evening was filled with birdsong. Rooks were cawing noisily and a blackbird, perched on a gate post, was singing his heart out to the approaching night.

Jack was pushing Meg in a wheelchair round the ruin of the cottage and Phoebe was standing under the apple tree in what had been the garden, holding Stephanie in her arms.

"Is Meg all right?" Mary asked, following Spot as he raced across the meadow.

"As right as she can be," Phoebe told her. "She was so insistent on us all coming here tonight—so she must want to be here."

Spot, meanwhile, continued to race across the field, passing Phoebe and going in the direction of the forest track where they could just glimpse Jack's Land-Rover by the gate. He was barking in an agitated way and his hackles were up.

"What's wrong with Spot?" Jack asked, emerging from the blackened front door of the cottage, pushing Meg in front of him.

"Someone coming, I think," William said, as the sound of a car was heard driving toward them. They all walked a few paces toward the track and then stood in a group waiting to see who it was who was approaching, so late in the day.

The car that drew up beside the Land-Rover was large and opulent. Out of the driving seat climbed Charles Crawden. He went to the boot, from which he produced a folded wheelchair. Martin Marsh emerged from the passenger seat and then, as the group in the meadow continued to watch, the two men, helped Sir Henry Crawden out of the back of the car and settled him in the chair.

This whole procedure took place without a word being spoken. It was so silent and slow that it was almost like watching a dream.

William put his hand into his jeans pocket and gripped the pendulum without knowing quite why he did so other than because of an acute feeling of nervous anticipation.

Sir Henry, once settled, stared from one to another of the group standing in front of him. Finally his eyes came to rest on Meg, who was sitting upright in her wheelchair, her hands clasped on her lap, her head held high.

"Miss Lewis, we have come as you instructed," Martin Marsh began, then he was interrupted by Jack, who turned to Meg with surprise.

"You instructed him, Meg?"

"I wrote to Mr. Marsh, yes. Your young builder posted the letter for me. I felt we had to have a meeting, all of us. I thought that here would be the most suitable place."

"We were sorry about your accident, Miss Lewis. And very distressed about what has happened to your house," Mr. Marsh continued.

"Thank you, but it could have been worse," Meg answered him. "After all, I could have been in the house when the fire started."

"My clients wish you to know that they are willing to meet your higher figure for the purchase of this property. . . ."

"Higher figure?" Jack said. "You've made a deal with them, Meg?"

"It seems that I have," Meg replied, looking at Jack with clear eyes.

"Without telling us?" Jack asked her, not disguising the hurt he felt.

"I couldn't tell you, Mr. Green. You have all been kind to me . . . so kind. But I can't live on charity and the offer that these gentlemen are making will allow me some independence. I will find a place to live. . . ." She looked slowly round at the long shadows and the gathering dusk. "But not near here. I would rather remember this place as it's always been."

"We will draw up the necessary papers then," Martin Marsh continued.

"Your hand on it, Mr. Crawden," Meg said, proffering her hand and forcing Charles Crawden to walk across the grass toward her.

He shook the hand with a stiff awkwardness and then retreated to his father's side as though he felt more comfortable in the company of his own kind. All the time Sir Henry remained silent, sitting and staring at Meg.

"You should have warned us, Meg," Phoebe said bitterly. Stephanie was whimpering and Phoebe rocked her gently as she spoke. "I was really hoping that you'd stay with us at Golden House, at least for as long as we're there. I was looking forward to having another woman around the place. You could even have baby-sat, once in a while. Jack and I never go out. . . ."

Meg looked at her.

"I don't belong there, dearie. Much as I'd like to," she said. "It doesn't feel right my being there. . . ."

"But it is," William said, surprising himself with the sound of his own voice. "The place should have been yours. Or rather you should have been asked if you wanted to buy it back from the Crawdens before they sold it to anyone else."

"What are you talking about, William?" Jack said. "We bought the house in good faith. . . ."

But the reaction of Martin Marsh and Charles Crawden was so remarkable that Jack was silenced. They both swung round, looking at William. The color of Martin Marsh's face had gone chalk-white and Charles Crawden raised his hands as though warding off a physical attack.

"Where have you got this nonsense from?" he demanded.

"Am I not right in thinking that a Bill of Sale was drawn up between Meg's grandfather and Sir Henry's uncle, Edmund Crawden?" William replied, gripping the pendulum in his pocket for dear life.

"Bill of Sale?" Martin Marsh gasped. "What Bill of Sale? You have no copy of such a document. If you have then you must show it to us. . . ."

There was a long, electric silence as the two men tried to outstare William. Mary and Alice closed in on either side of their brother. The three of them stared back at the men.

"You want me to tell you precisely what is in the document?" William asked. "How the house went to you Crawdens and how Jonas Lewis retained the estate . . ."

"We must have further private consultation," Martin Marsh blustered.

"You have seen a copy of this document?" Charles Crawden gasped.

"Wasn't it agreed that all the land should remain the property of the Lewis family?" William insisted, ignoring the question and trying not to let his voice tremble.

"This is all highly irregular!" Martin Marsh stormed.

"You will have to prove all this in a court of law," Charles Crawden said savagely. "Produce this document, prepare your case! Even if it exists, which I deny—you will never make it stick. This land is ours. We have always used it. It is ours by common consent. Ours by adoption. I will do with it as I like."

"No, Charles," Sir Henry said quietly, his eyes still on Meg. "If the land hereabouts could possibly be proved to belong to the Crawden family— then it would still belong to me. . . . I am, after all, still the head of this family."

"We have drawn up papers, Sir Henry," Martin Marsh interrupted him shrilly. "You have agreed to relinquish your rights. You said you would allow your son to administer the estate."

"You may have such papers, Mr. Marsh. But I have not, as yet, signed them," Sir Henry rejoined irritably, "as you very well know. Nor, incidentally, did I shake my hands on the deal—as my son has done with Miss Lewis. It seems to me that you have a sale on your Four Fields, Miss Lewis. I'm sure my son would not go back on his word as a gentleman, certainly not when he gave it in front of so many witnesses. As for the rest of the estate, it is obvious that the boy knows what he is talking about. I have no intention of dragging the family name through sordid litigation in a court case that we would certainly lose for if any court of law found in favor of the Crawdens, then it would prove forever that the law is an ass."

"Father!" Charles Crawden exclaimed.

"Shut up, Charles! You've been outmaneuvered by this child. At least have the grace to lose with a certain amount of dignity."

"Father," Charles Crawden pleaded. "All our plans depend on this land."

"Find another place for your funfair, Charles. The Goldenvale is not suitable. Now let this be an end to it; to it all. I will have this matter finished, as it should have been finished many years ago. Golden House and the valley have all but destroyed our family as it destroyed the Lewis family. Now it must end. There will be no building up here. Not while I am alive and before I am very much older, I will see the estate returned to its rightful owner."

"Father, you are ruining me!" Charles Crawden cried.

"You are ruining yourself, my dear boy," his father said, speaking gently. "We have a copy of the Bill of Sale, Charles. We know what they're talking about. You gambled that the Lewis family no longer had their copy in their possession. You lost the gamble. Do let it go now, Charles. Please, just . . . let it go."

"So your family really did know all along, Henry," Meg said quietly. "It was true what my father told me. You never came to pay court to me—it was only my property that you sought."

"No, Meg," the old man said in a tragic voice. "It was you I came to see. But you would never believe it. And in the end you turned me away. It has been a long life, Meg Lewis. A long life without you."

The old couple stared at each other across the gathering gloom, each in their wheelchair, surrounded by their memories.

"Miss Lewis," Sir Henry said at last, speaking very formally, "you will hear from my solicitor. Not this cheapskate, but the family's usual firm. Any claims that the Crawden family may have harbored in the past for the Goldenvale estate will be formally relinquished. . . ." Then he gestured with an impatient wave of his hand. "Take me home, Charles. The matter is finally closed."

# 26

# Mary Sees
# the Next Step

There was great jubilation at Golden House on the night after the meeting with the Crawdens and Martin Marsh at Four Fields. Jack was particularly impressed with the way William had handled the affair.

"How did you know what that Bill of Sale would contain?" he cried as he pulled the cork on a bottle of wine and filled glasses for Meg and Phoebe.

"Yes, Will," Phoebe said. "How could you possibly guess?"

William felt himself blushing and, searching for an answer, he dug his hands deep into his jeans pockets. His fist closed round the Magician's pendulum and once again he felt some comfort from holding it tightly.

"Of course," Jack said suddenly, "we knew there was some sort of document in existence from Jonas Lewis's book—and Meg, you said that your father knew of one. I suppose a calculated guess would have come up with what you said, William. But I must say I'm very impressed!"

"Actually, I didn't say very much really, you know. They did most of the talking themselves."

"That's right," Jack said, remembering. "Brilliant, William! Maybe you should go into the law. You have a perfect legal mind! Say as little as possible and let the other party hang himself with his own words!"

"Well, Meg," Phoebe said. "So now you're the landowner round here!"

"Yes, dearie," Meg said quietly. "A landowner without a house!"

"I wish you'd think about staying on here," Phoebe said. "We really have so much room and—even if we ever get to the point where we open the hotel, there would always be a place for you."

"It's odd being here. . . ." Meg said, looking round at the kitchen.

"Don't rush her, Phoebe," Jack said gently. "Just know that we would love to have you, Meg."

"Thank you, dear," Meg said.

"And you would be near the badgers," Alice said quickly.

"It's up a steep hill, though," Meg said with a smile. "I'll have to get on my feet again if I'm to see them each night. No more sitting about in a wheelchair. I've got exercises that I'm supposed to be doing. . . ."

And mercifully the conversation moved away from William and he was spared the ordeal of having to answer any more questions until the children went up to their rooms. Then his sisters started to interrogate him.

"I thought we weren't supposed to say anything about the legal papers?" Alice challenged him as soon as they were on their own. "I thought that was the whole point of burning them and everything."

"So did I, Al," William replied. "Don't be cross with me. I was as surprised as you were. I was terrified that someone would ask a question that I couldn't truthfully answer without blowing the whole thing."

"But no one did," Mary said thoughtfully. "It was perfect. They did what Jack said just now . . . they condemned themselves—because they thought you knew more than you were prepared to say."

"I'm not sure about that," William admitted. "When I saw that vile man . . ."

"Which one, Will?" Alice asked eagerly. "I think they're both vile."

"Martin Marsh is the one I really detest. He's slimy, like a slug," William said.

"Ugh!" Alice grimaced. "Oh, I do hope the Magician hasn't got a tame slug. I don't think I'd like that!"

And once again their thoughts returned to Stephen Tyler.

"I wonder how Jasper knew he was ill," William said.

"D'you suppose it's still his bad arm from the dogbite that's bothering him?" Mary asked.

"I don't know," William said, then he looked rather ashamed and turned his face away.

"What William? What's the matter?" Mary asked.

"It's just something . . . silly really. You know when Phoebe took me to the doctor after the Battle over Goldenwater—when I had all those hornet stings! Well, he gave me a course of antibiotics."

"Yes?" Mary said.

"Well, I didn't take them. I saved them."

"What for?"

"Mr. Tyler," William said quietly. "I thought maybe they'd help him get over the dogbite—if there was any infection."

"But that's wonderful, William!" Alice exclaimed. "We'll be able to help him get better. . . ." Then she sniffed loudly and scratched her cheek.

They were silent for a while, each deep in their own thoughts.

"Oh, boobs!" Alice exclaimed.

"Is that a new swear word?" William asked.

"Bosoms and boobs!" Alice replied haughtily.

Then they all became silent again.

"We can't give him those pills, can we?" Mary said, sadly. "We can't help him to get better . . .

because we'd be changing things. Like you said, William. That's it, isn't it?"

"I'm not sure," William said. "I think it'd be all right to help him. I mean, if we found him starving, we could give him some food. . . ."

"But antibiotics?" Mary argued. "They hadn't been invented then."

"Well, anyway," William said with a sigh, "there's not much point talking about it—if he doesn't come to see us." As he spoke he took the pendulum out of his pocket and held it out in front of him. They all stared at it thoughtfully.

"We must keep it safe," Alice said.

"Somewhere here, I thought," William said.

"But where?" Alice said, looking round.

"I don't know," William said with a shrug.

"We'll give it to Spot," Alice said. "He'll guard it for us. Don't you think that'd be best, Mary?"

But Mary hadn't been listening. Her mind was on other matters. Realizing that the other two were looking at her she turned to them and said, in a matter-of-fact voice:

"If the Magician won't come to us, we'll just have to go to him, won't we?"

"What?" Alice exclaimed. "But how?" She was both excited and scared by the idea.

"I don't know how," Mary said with a shrug, dismissing the idea as though it were a minor detail. "We'll have to work out how. We've come this far. We've seen through animals. . . ."

"We've already been back into the past," William said, tingles of excitement running down his back.

"But that was sort of by chance, wasn't it?" Mary said. "He helped us. But—if he's ill, he might not be able to help us. . . ."

"So we'll have to do it on our own," William finished her thought and the full enormity of what they were proposing made him tremble.

"It must be possible," Mary said, speaking gravely. "For Mr. Tyler's sake . . ."

"You mean . . . go back to his time?" Alice asked, wanting to be quite sure what they were talking about.

"Why not?" Mary whispered.

"But when?" William said.

Mary shrugged.

"It's going to take time, and there's not much of this holiday left."

"The next time we come is half term. That's not long either," William said thoughtfully.

"Maybe it'll be easier than we think," Alice said, staring at the pendulum, dangling from William's hand.

"Well, at least we can try," Mary said.

And that's how the idea was first born.

# About the Author

WILLIAM CORLETT, after being educated at Fettes College in Edinburgh, trained as an actor at the Royal Academy of Dramatic Art, in London. He soon started writing plays for the theater, including *The Gentle Avalanche* and *Return Ticket,* which were performed in London. Many television plays followed, including the award-winning series *Barriers,* for which he received the Writers' Guild Award for Best Children's Writer and a Gold Award at the New York International Film and Television Festival. His script for the children's series *The Paper Lads* won him another Writer's Guild Award for Best Children's Writer.

Between 1978 and 1988, William wrote a number of novels for young adults, including *The Gate of Eden, The Land Beyond, Return to the Gate, The Dark Side of the Moon, Bloxworth Blue,* and *The Secret Line.* He also co-wrote *The Question Series,* which is a series of six books about world religions. His adaptation of the Jill Paton Walsh novel *Torch* was filmed by Edinburgh Films during 1990 and earned him another nomination for the Writer's Guild Children's Writer of the Year Award. In addition, his adaptation of the Elizabeth Goudge novel *The Little White Horse* was shown on BBC in 1994 and won a Silver Award at the New York International Film and TV Festival. William went on to write the highly acclaimed and best-selling *Magician's House Quartet,* originally published by The Bodley Head, which recently became a major BBC television series. It won the Emmy Award for the Best International Children's Television Series in 2000.